A Lover's Promise

CONRAD CHRONICLES
BOOK THREE

C.K. MACKENZIE

This is a work of fiction. Names, characters, places, and incidents are either the product of the author's imagination or are used fictitiously, and any resemblance to actual persons living or dead, business establishments, events, or locales, is entirely coincidental.

A Lover's Promise Kaya and Paul Book 3

Conrad Chronicles Book 3

COPYRIGHT © 2023 by Emelia Publishers LLC and C.K. Mackenzie

All rights reserved. No part of this book may be used or reproduced in any manner whatsoever without written permission of the author except in the case of brief quotations embodied in critical articles or reviews.

Contact Information: ckmackenzieauthor@gmail.com

Cover Art by Graziana Masneri

Publishing History

First Edition, 2023

Paperback ISBN 979-8-9850526-6-4

Published in the United States of America

Thank you to all who continue to join me in this journey!

San Grigori, Italy

"It's so quiet here," Kaya Conrad said to no one in particular.

No one stood beside her in the small cottage, barricaded against the harsh winter storm. The shutters occasionally rattled against the windows, sending the entire structure shivering, as if it, too, froze in the cold. The mountain wind sneaked through the gap under the door and slithered around her ankles. In the kitchen, which was blocked off only by a long wooden table, a wood fire burned brightly.

It did nothing to warm her.

She closed her eyes and let the constant wind soothe her. "I never thought a snowstorm would be so...calming. Cold, yes, but calming."

She looked over her shoulder to where she expected her husband to stand, but the room remained empty. Paul lay in the darkened bedroom, sick in bed, still recovering from the last weeks' events. Kaya rubbed her hands, but they were numb, more due to all that had happened in this small village than the current snowstorm howling outside.

Six months ago, when Kaya watched her grandfather sign the marriage contract, she had not expected that she'd be standing alone in a tiny mountain village in the middle of a snowstorm. New adventures? She craved those. She didn't even mind the snow; this was her first true experience with it.

"Paul, this was not how I envisioned our life together."

"Nor I," came the rasping answer from behind her.

She whirled from her position by the table and stared in surprise. "You look awful," she blurted out before she could stop the words.

Paul snorted and wobbled. "I feel awful." He shuffled to the table and sat in one of the sturdy chairs.

Rounding the table, she tilted his head to look at him. He didn't feel warm and, though pale still, didn't look as if he were about to be sick. Nonetheless, Kaya eyed him warily. "How's your stomach?"

He grinned and took her hand, holding it between his warm ones. That touch did more to steady her than anything had since they'd arrived in San Grigori.

"I think the worst is over, sweetheart." He pressed a kiss to her fingertips. "There's nothing left in my stomach."

"True," she allowed. She forced her feet to stay at a safe distance. Just in case. "There's bread left, if you wish."

Paul looked to the shelf where a half loaf sat from earlier, but he shook his head. "Not just yet."

Kaya ran her fingers through his hair, her nails scraping his scalp. Paul sighed into her touch, and the lines around his mouth eased. He might not have felt nauseous anymore, but he was still in pain. A pain she did not understand and had no idea how to ease.

The door blew open, startling her enough to reach for her khanjar. Paul immediately released her hands, letting her take the lead in defending them. She felt him brace and heard him mutter something about finding a safer place.

Before the intruder could step into the room, Kaya rounded the table and stood at the door, ready for an attack.

"Marta." Kaya breathed again, annoyed at herself for suspecting anyone else.

"I bring food." Marta spoke in Calabrian. Of course she did, but it took Kaya more than a moment to realize what she'd said. Kaya and Paul had been speaking in English. "And fresh blankets." Marta eyed the dagger as Kaya sheathed it but said nothing of its presence.

"*Grazie.*" Kaya took the thick wool blankets and hesitated. Rather than setting them on the bed, she placed them at the end of the table. Paul huffed out a laugh, and she met his gaze. He knew she didn't want to return to the small bedroom and the stench of sickness that still lingered.

She shook a blanket and draped it over his shoulders. He remained quiet, and his shaking didn't diminish with the added warmth. Kaya knew it wasn't the cold—at least, not only the cold—that made him shake.

"How is he?" Marta whispered, avoiding Paul's gaze.

He flinched and looked at the fire. Kaya moved to where Marta stood by the door and took the food tray she'd carried from the village inn. "Better," Kaya said. It was a partial lie, they all knew.

But she didn't know. That was the problem. She didn't know how to handle any of this. The sickness, the shakes. The absolute loss of control. His and hers—Kaya felt as if she, too, had spiraled out of control, as if she were as caught up in the haboob of Paul's drinking as he was.

Without a word, Paul stood and retreated to the bedroom. Marta didn't watch him, but Kaya caught his eye. He offered a small, sad smile, and she nodded.

Returning to the table, where Marta looked so uncertain, Kaya asked, "How long will this last?"

"What?" Marta backed toward the doorway, afraid of being in her own home. Kaya didn't blame her. "Will what last?"

"His shaking. His sickness."

"I've never known any man to stop drinking." Marta

frowned, and Kaya wondered about her husband. About all the men in the village. "They all drink."

"Oh." At a loss as to what to say to that, Kaya looked to the dark bedroom.

She wished there were a door between the rooms, but the stone archway was the only separation between the main room and the single bedroom.

He'd said something about the drink as they traveled *al-ṣaḥrāʾ al-kubrā* from Cairo to Damietta. Or had it been after, in Sicily? It didn't matter. Kaya remembered him talking about his walk from Bombay to Cairo, through the Sinai. The lack of wine. The shaking and cramps and sickness.

He hadn't gone into detail, and even if he had, she doubted she'd have understood. She still didn't understand now. Her insular life had not prepared her for a woman who did not wish to stay in her own home and a husband sick from too much drink.

It terrified her. This not knowing. This uncertainty. She didn't know how to help Paul. How to ease his shaking or what to say now that he was awake. She also had no idea what to say to Marta, a woman whose friendship Kaya had come to treasure.

Marta stood near the long kitchen table, watching the flickering fire. She had not bothered to take off her cloak or gloves.

She looked as lost as Kaya felt.

"Marta?" Kaya asked, slowing her approach.

Marta startled and pushed the tray along the table toward Kaya. She struggled to smile, her fingers retreating to her skirts. She did not, however, move from her spot, seemingly frozen by the cutting table.

"Mutton." Marta let out a sound that vaguely resembled a laugh. "Olivia was very specific. She didn't want you upset."

Kaya took the tray and smiled at the woman. Her first friend. "*Grazie.* And please, thank Olivia, too."

Grasping at the faint threads of polite conversation, Kaya gestured to the scarred wooden table and chairs. "Would you like to sit and join me?"

Marta stiffened. "No." Her gaze swung wildly around the house. Her house. From the bedroom to the unused kitchen and the small alcove whose candles had long since burned out.

Kaya hastily set the tray on the table and took Marta's hands. She had no idea what to do or say, no experience with any of this. Not friendship or the obvious unease with which Marta now stood in her own home.

"Marta." Kaya repeated her name until the other woman looked at her. "Marta. Yes. Look at me, Marta. Good. Yes."

Eventually, Marta's breathing slowed, and the wild, frightened look in her dark eyes lessened. She didn't look around the house again but kept her gaze on Kaya's.

"I have to get back to Olivia."

Kaya let her friend have the lie. Olivia was the most self-sufficient child Kaya knew—that she knew only two children, both amazingly resilient, mattered little. Marta needed her daughter. That, Kaya understood.

"I'll come to the inn tomorrow," Kaya promised as she opened the door.

"No." Marta shook her head, her eyes wide and scared. "No, best not. It's not safe."

As Marta rushed out, Azizi trotted up. The half wolf, half dog didn't spare a glance at Marta, who ignored her as well. Kaya watched her friend disappear into the storm and wondered what strength Marta had to continually make the trip from the inn to this cottage she hated.

"Oh, there you are!"

Azizi yipped in excited greeting and butted her large, dark head against Kaya's outstretched hand. Kaya ushered her new pet inside and closed the door against the swirling snow. The room instantly quieted. "Did you have a good hunt?"

Azizi shook herself, spraying cold droplets all over. Startled, Kaya laughed. The dog's antics presented a welcome break from the heaviness settling into the house. And the village.

"Yes, good Azizi." Kaya rested her hand on the dog's large

head and scratched behind her ears. Azizi let out a contented sound that made Kaya want to pet her forever. The dog stretched into her hand, almost like a snuggle. There was something so soothing about petting an animal. Kaya had not realized that before finding Azizi, who was still a pup, and her dying mother in that mountain cave.

"Go lie by the fire," Kaya said as she eyed the tray of food Marta had brought. It was not high enough for Azizi *not* to reach.

Kaya had learned quickly not to leave food out where the dog could reach it, and Azizi was large enough to reach most shelves. Paul had laughed at Kaya's speechless shock when the dog had looked her straight in the eye and taken bread off a tray. It only took once, he said. He was not wrong.

"I'm sorry," Paul said as he exited the bedroom.

"For Azizi's perpetual hunger?" Kaya tried to smile as she sat at the table and warily watched Azizi follow her, ever hopeful.

Ignoring the dog, Kaya ate a bite of the heavy stew. It didn't carry the spices she was used to. No cumin or pepper or saffron; however, the onion and garlic flavored the beans and warmed her insides.

"No." There was a small snap in Paul's voice as he sat beside her. But he sighed and shook his head. "For a lot of things."

"Not everything is your fault," Kaya whispered. "You did not know Appleby would be here."

"Perhaps not." Paul broke off a small piece of bread and stared at it. "I didn't even know he was still alive."

"You spoke of making amends." She ate another bite of stew. "Perhaps this is a step. A way forward."

"By miraculously appearing in a small village in the middle of the Apennine Mountains, which my *old friend*"—his sarcasm on those two words was heavier than her stew—"just so happened to be threatening?"

Kaya opened her mouth. Then she closed it without a sound and tilted her head. "Yes."

Paul snorted and ate the bread. He grimaced but swallowed.

Then he lifted a cup of juice but didn't take a sip. He just stared at the contents for a long, long time. Finally, he sighed.

"You know me too well, Kaya. It's terrifying."

"I know," she quietly agreed.

Paul watched her for a silent moment. The firelight danced over his face, casting his eyes in shadows. Kaya wanted to reach out and touch him, pull his body to her, feel his warmth and strength against hers.

Neither moved. The strange, awkward distance between them reminded her of the early days of their marriage, when she knew nothing about him other than he hadn't stolen her jewels and left her for dead in the desert.

Finally, Paul stood, unsteady on his feet. He pressed his fingers into the table so hard they turned white, but he eventually straightened.

"I'm sorry," he mumbled. Meeting her concerned gaze, he shook his head. "I'm—" He broke off and swallowed hard. His fingers brushed lightly over her cheek, and his eyes, a lovely blue-green, softened.

"I know," she repeated.

He nodded and retreated to the bedroom. He walked on shaky legs, but before Kaya could stand to help, the darkness of the room swallowed him.

Kaya sat at the table and stared at the fire, blinking back sudden tears. She missed Cairo and her home there, despite the prisonlike quality of her life. She missed her grandfather and Derya. Even the shisha smoke of her unseen neighbors.

Derya died in the food riots the day before Kaya met Paul. And Gidd, well, he'd married her to Paul without so much as a pause. Then, with a kiss to her forehead and a nod of encouragement, he'd escorted her out of the only place she'd ever seen.

She missed them with a fierceness that ached, that stole her breath and brought tears to her eyes.

Blinking rapidly to stem those tears, Kaya fought to control her breathing. Grief choked her in a way it hadn't since those first married days. Only six months had passed, but today, sitting in this small cottage, so isolated and utterly alone, it felt like six years.

She hastily set aside the stew, not at all certain the food would settle in her stomach.

"You would've liked Cairo, I think," she told Azizi, who continued to look at her with such hopeful eyes Kaya almost laughed. She swallowed tears instead. "Though I'm certain Derya would never have let you inside the house. Not even for protection."

Patting Azizi's head, Kaya stood and set the unfinished stew high on the cupboard shelf. She had no idea if Azizi could still reach it, but she wouldn't put it past the dog to try.

Azizi, sensing no meal for her, snorted and wandered to the fire. She settled in front of it and quickly began to snore. Jealous of her dog, Kaya rubbed her eyes. It had been a series of long, hard days. She only knew whether it was morning or evening from Marta's food deliveries. Her own sleep had come in quick snatches that did little to help her rest.

Instead, she'd been plagued by nightmares. Terrible, bloody, what-if images of Paul dead in the snow, his blood staining the crisp white a horrifying crimson.

No sound emerged from the bedroom. Silence enveloped the house, heavy and thick, a stifling reminder that Kaya was very much alone in this house. In this world. She grasped for the calm of just an hour ago, but it slipped through her fingers.

Marta refused to stay in her own home. Not that Kaya blamed her after what she'd endured these last months. The horrid abuse, the cruel violation at the hands of Harry Appleby. The kidnapping of half her village to make ready the opium balls for sale throughout the country.

The illegitimate child she now carried.

Paul was suffering the aftereffects of too much drink. Rubbing her eyes, Kaya settled in the chair and watched the fire. It still did nothing to warm her.

She petted Azizi, lost in thought. What happened now?

When would Paul wake? What would she say to him when he did? Had anything changed between them, or did it only feel that way because he'd been in and out of consciousness for days and days now?

"When he does wake, will things go back to how they were?" she said aloud, as if the dog could understand her. Perhaps she could. "I doubt that. It is not as it was before, when I didn't understand what he meant by 'the drink.'"

She still didn't understand. Not completely. The craving he had for it, the constant need. Wine was better than opium, she supposed. But then, she had such little experience with that, too.

She'd seen the aftereffects of opium. When they'd first landed on the mainland in Villa San Giovanni, they'd befriended a family who'd lost a son to the opium dens. It seemed so long ago, but, now that Kaya thought about it, it was only perhaps a month past.

Time moved so strangely when events happened all at once.

A month or so ago, she and Paul had pulled Marco from the filthy, horrific floor of an opium den. They had not stayed to see if he recovered.

"Maybe I'll write Antionette Spanò." Did it help hearing her voice? Yes. Better than the suffocating silence. "See how Marco is faring." Kaya frowned at Azizi, who continued to watch her with half-closed eyes. "I do not know how to write in Calabrian. Perhaps Marta can help."

Azizi yawned, and Kaya smiled. Siting with the dog in the silence of the cottage did, indeed, soothe her. "Would you like to learn Egyptian? Instead of speaking to you in English or Calabrian, I shall teach you Egyptian."

Her gaze drifted to the bedroom and Paul. In their six months together, she had taught him much of her language—not that they'd traveled anywhere near another Arabic-speaking country, but it comforted her knowing she could speak to him in her native tongue.

Azizi licked her hand. Kaya laughed and met her dog's gaze.

Determined, she switched to Egyptian Arabic. "Though I suppose there are wonderful things in life, too, yes? I would not have met you if we hadn't walked into this village." Kaya gazed at the door, shut firmly between her and the winter storm. "Nor Marta, nor Olivia. I have lived such a sheltered life," she whispered. "I was unprepared for...well, life."

The wonderful highs and the crushing lows. The good she shared with Paul, and even this. Him once more sleeping in the other room, and her here with Azizi.

No, she had no idea how to help Paul; she didn't even know if she could. Perhaps he needed to walk through this haboob himself.

She grabbed one of the blankets from the table and slid to the floor beside Azizi. The dog stretched and scooted closer to Kaya, as if sensing she needed comfort and warmth.

"Life is much more difficult than I imagined, Azizi." She looked down at the dog's large brown eyes, so alert as they watched her. Azizi lifted her head onto Kaya's lap. "I had no idea how caring for others would affect me."

Azizi made that contented noise in the back of her throat but didn't move. Kaya ran her fingers through the dog's coarse hair again and again. Yes, petting a dog was highly soothing.

"I never want to see him go through this again," she whispered into the dog's fur. "However, I have a feeling that is not how this works."

Kaya's eyes slipped closed, and she was far too exhausted to keep them open. "I hope we make it through this."

Two

Kaya jerked awake, her heart hammering in her chest, her breath too fast to calm its racing.

She hadn't slept long. Though she'd fallen into a deep sleep, it had not been dreamless. Images of the men she'd fought in that cave crowded her mind, pushed against her as if they meant to suffocate her.

Her frantic search for Paul in the blinding snowstorm. The smothering terror, even now gripping her, that she wouldn't be able to find him in the winding mountain pass. Or that she'd be too late. Derya and Gidd were also there, standing to the side, judging her—for not finding Paul, for leaving him in the wilds of the Apennine Mountains.

"I'm here." Paul's quiet voice, rough with his recent sickness, jerked her attention back. "It's just me. Breathe, Kaya."

His fingers were warm on her wrist as they stroked her skin, tentatively taking her fingers. Her heart slowed, and the dream faded, though it didn't completely disappear.

"I can't believe you snuck up on me," she said. The laugh stuck in her throat, and she coughed, struggling to ground herself here in the present.

Paul grinned. "There's a first time for everything." Azizi

huffed and stretched her long body, only to curl back into her tight ball and go back to sleep. "Then again," Paul continued, one hand holding hers, one on Azizi's back, "this is probably the last time I manage such a feat."

That brought a genuine smile to her lips. "No doubt."

He laughed with her, and for a wonderful moment, Kaya thought the terrible, awkward tension between them had broken. But then the laughter faded, and she and Paul continued to sit in front of the fire in a house haunted by its own past.

The silence pushed around her, heavy, oppressive, a weight against her chest she could not shift. No sounds echoed from outside. No shouts of neighbors or even the call of wild animals. The snow covered everything in a silent blanket.

"I take it you didn't sleep well," he said in that same quiet, raspy voice.

"I dreamed you died in the snow, and I couldn't find you."

He only nodded. "I dream that a lot."

Without another word, he turned and stoked the fire, bringing it back from the embers. Kaya took a moment to stretch before rising from the floor where she'd slept. It wasn't the least comfortable place she'd slept these last months, but she did miss her bed. She turned for the small basin and washed her hands and face with melted snow and small portion of pomegranate root she'd brought from Cairo.

Then she pulled the tray from the upper shelf, ate the last of the bread and stew, and wondered what came next.

There it was. For the first time in her life, Kaya had nothing to do. There was no one to tell her to study or train. No new wonderous experiences to be had. They were trapped in this cabin in the snow. She had already brought in more wood for the fire, a task she had not expected to enjoy. Even in a snowstorm.

Azizi had accompanied her. Kaya didn't think she needed protection, but apparently the dog did. She didn't mind; it was nice having a companion. Even if Azizi didn't talk back.

"What happens now?" she asked, offering Paul the last bit of bread.

He took it and ate, though she could tell by his grimace his stomach didn't agree. "Now, as in now that we are trapped by the snow? Or now as in what happens between us?"

Yes, all of that. "Now, as in how are we supposed to occupy ourselves for the rest of the day?"

Paul offered a silent chuckle and shook his head, an aborted movement that ended with him resting his forehead in unsteady hands. "Not used to being idle, eh? No, that doesn't surprise me. What did you do all day in Cairo?"

She frowned into the bucket of water, then she poured the remaining contents into a cup and opened the door for more snow. The cold wind knocked into her, stealing her breath. This wasn't the Egyptian desert. The sky was still dark, and she had no sense of time.

To think she'd been utterly fascinated with her first snowstorm. The beautiful swirl of white. The way it blanketed everything in such crispness that every sound seemed both muffled and amplified. It fascinated her.

"Study, train." She hastily scooped the bucket through the heavy snow and slammed the door closed. "Practice my forms. Read tactics and history, study my languages." She set the bucket by the revived fire. "You?"

She watched him as he hunched over the table. Her heart flipped at the sight of her strong, determined Paul, now so uncertain and unsteady. Leaning against the table beside him, Kaya rested her hand on the nape of his neck and leaned down to kiss the top of his head.

"The army keeps you busy." His voice sounded muffled and distant. She felt him take a deep breath and straighten, and when he looked at her his gaze was steady and focused. "Probably very similar to your days. Enough down time, but lots of drills and marching. Formation practice."

"However did you manage to find so much trouble amid all your drills?"

Paul laughed. It was the first strong, real laugh she'd heard from him in far, far too long. Since before arriving in San Grigori. "Where there's a will, my dear Kaya, there's a soldier determined to find trouble."

Kaya smiled and shook her head. "Clearly I have much to learn from you about degenerate behavior."

He smiled again, looking stronger and much less pale than even a few minutes ago. "I'm not sure whether I should share all my secrets and corrupt you, or keep them to myself."

Paul's hands settled on her hips and tugged her before him. Her heart soared, and yes, *yes*, this had to be a positive step forward.

Resting her hands on his shoulders, she grinned down at him. "Oh, share, definitely." She pressed her lips to his forehead. "I've had enough rigidity."

He laughed, and the sound warmed her heart. This was not the end of them as she'd feared. They were stronger than this, even after so few months together. Kaya ran her fingers through his hair and watched his eyes close in contentment.

"The couple that shares together, eh?" He shook his head, a slight movement, but his eyes remained clear.

Kaya watched him for an explanation. "I do not understand. Is that not the point of being married? To share a life together?"

"I'd think so, but you have to understand, Kaya"—his smirk widened—"this is my first marriage."

She snorted. "Your last, too. I've decided to keep you, and I'm not sharing."

Paul's hands tightened on her hips, and he turned serious. "I'm never letting you go. I don't believe I can. *Ya rouhi*, is that not what you said?"

"Yes." Kaya swallowed the lump in her throat. "My soul."

In the silence that followed, with the wind beating against the house, Kaya realized what kept her here. Not the snow, despite its depth.

It was Paul. She would not leave him.

"Lie by the fire," she whispered, cupping his cheeks. He leaned into her touch, his eyelashes fluttering against her palm, his breath even. "You need to rest, and I need to...do something."

"We'll work on you relaxing." But Paul stood and did as she bade, moving slowly around the table to the fire. He bunched one of his blankets into a ball and leaned against the stone of the fireplace.

"We can," Kaya agreed, feeling strangely free. "However, I'm uncertain how long that might last."

"Us working on it? Or you relaxing?" He shook his head and closed his eyes. "I'll work on us..." He trailed off, the exhaustion of the last weeks catching up with him.

Kaya watched Paul for several moments, a soft smile on her face and a lightness in her heart. This might not have been how she'd envisioned their life together, but at least they were together. Azizi opened one eye, lifted her head to look at Kaya, then shuffled closer to Paul. Or perhaps the fire.

"I'm sure Marta has a cleaning brush." Kaya spoke to both her husband and her dog, though neither answered. Still, she had no wish to sleep again—not after the unsettled dreams—and she had nothing to read. "And soap, perhaps."

It only took a moment to locate the cupboard that held a cleaning brush, a jug of vinegar, and a worn wooden bucket separate from the one she used for bathing water. She filled this second bucket with snow, then set it before the fire and marched into the bedroom.

Kaya didn't look around the dark, musty room. She just quickly scooped up the blankets from the bed and set them on the kitchen table to warm. Then she pulled the trunk at the foot of the bed into the main room, where she eyed it as if opening it might release the ghosts of this house.

A torn chemise. A pair of trousers and suspenders. Several

pairs of wool socks in various stages of wear. Hidden deep in the trunk, she found a beautiful green ribbon that had been folded carefully and tucked into a corner.

"I'll burn the chemise," Kaya said to Paul.

He hummed in agreement but didn't fully wake. Somehow, that made her smile, one that only widened when Azizi echoed Paul's sound of agreement.

"I don't know what happened to the fabric, but I'm sure Appleby touched it." She stood from the trunk with the chemise. The hem was frayed and the sleeves worn. That mattered little with the rend from neckline halfway down.

Loath as she was to burn such fine material, anything that odious man had touched deserved to be incinerated. She couldn't very well expect Marta to do it.

Tossing the chemise onto the floor, she returned to the clothing.

"I doubt you'll fit into these trousers." She shook them out and held them up to judge. "No, definitely too short for you. They must've belonged to Marta's husband."

Kaya held them to the firelight and looked closer. They were patched at the knees, but they still looked sturdy. She'd spent considerable time in this house, but she had not seen anything else that might've belonged to Marta's husband.

Had Appleby destroyed everything? Had Marta and her nameless, faceless husband not had many possessions to begin with? Had they been forced to sell everything? Or had Marta burned everything when he died?

"Do you know anything about her husband?" Paul asked, the words slow but clear. He must've shaken himself from his doze.

"No," Kaya admitted. "Nothing. Only that he's dead." She paused and added, "Or that Marta considers him to be."

"Hm."

Part of Kaya didn't wish to disturb him. Didn't want to wake him from whatever sleep he managed. And part of her wanted the company, even if Paul didn't answer her. However, a small, secret part of her, the part that raged at him, the part that simmered in anger and betrayal, wanted to throw things.

If only to relieve the anger and uncertainty still within her.

No matter how often she reminded herself that Paul had done what he did to help Marta, as Kaya had asked, a part of her refused to be mollified. It simmered beneath the surface, her anger, and she honestly had no idea how to calm it.

Kaya pressed her fingers to her eyes. She took a deep breath, hoping to still her thoughts. The smoke from the wood fire tickled her nose, a strange scent she was unused to. Cairo had precious little wood, let alone wood to spare for burning. But the fire heated the room, eased her earlier chill.

"One step at a time," she said aloud. "Gidd taught me that."

Paul stirred again. He met her gaze, though she didn't know how alert he was. Still, she kept speaking, as if that might mitigate her anger, even as she wanted to race toward their future, leave this cabin, the village, and the people behind. "He used to say, 'The next step cannot be completed until you master the first one, my child.'"

"Always knew he was a wily old codger," Paul muttered. "Didn't take him for a philosopher." He snorted. "Should have."

"Perhaps," Kaya agreed and returned to her cleaning.

Her thoughts, however, whirled like the snow outside, jumping from Gidd and Derya to Paul and the months they'd shared. She shied from the present and did her best to focus on wiping the past from this house. Time passed. Paul dozed again, the fire burned low, and Kaya kept working. Though exhaustion bade her sleep, she couldn't bring herself to find any comfort in that.

A sound at the door startled her from her thoughts, the darkness she spiraled down into and didn't understand. When she opened the door, Azizi suddenly by her side, Kaya was only a little surprised to see Oliva.

"*Buon pomeriggio!*" Oliva smiled. She did not, however, step foot into the house. She didn't look anywhere but directly at Kaya.

With her heart breaking for the child, Kaya stepped into the swirling snow. Shivering, she patted Azizi on the head and smiled at Olivia.

"Come to play with Azizi?"

"Yes," Olivia said, shier now. Quieter.

"I do not own her, and I am certain she is happy to see you as well." Kaya smiled and nodded, stepping back into the house. "Don't wander into the woods, though. Stay in the clearing."

Olivia nodded and raced after Azizi. The sun struggled to peek through the clouds, and with the high mountaintops, no light bounced off the snow. However, both child and dog seemed to see each other well enough, and they laughed and yipped as they raced over the clearing.

She didn't close the door. Not yet. Watching Azizi and Olivia chase each other and jump in the snow, Kaya leaned against the doorframe and let the innocence of the scene wash over her.

"I do not understand owning an animal," she said to Paul, though he probably couldn't hear her. "But it makes me happy to see Olivia and Azizi together."

With one last wistful smile, she closed the door and returned to her cleaning. She piled the unwanted clothing by the door, hoping it would stop the wind slipping through the gap. Shaking out her own soiled, gown, she draped it over a corner of the kitchen table, careful to fold the bloodstain out of view.

She'd borrowed a dress from Marta after the fight in the opium cave. It was too short at the hem and too loose around the bodice, but Kaya was nonetheless grateful to be rid of her own bloodied gown.

"It must be near dusk," Kaya said, still speaking more to herself than Paul. "Marta should be here shortly."

"Marta?" Paul roused himself and blinked at her. "I'll leave then." He shook his head, as if shaking the sleep from his mind. "Go back to the bedroom."

"I—" She didn't want him to. She liked that he sat with her out here, clearly making progress in his health. But eventually, Kaya nodded. "It's probably for the best."

Paul stood and disappeared into the bedroom. Kaya wanted to call out and tell him not to disappear from the house, from their life. But she swallowed those words, unsure what else she might say if she started.

"This is lonelier than Cairo," she whispered to Paul's back.

"Kaya?" Marta called as she opened the door. Frowning, she asked, "Are you well?" She looked around the empty room. "I thought I heard you speaking to someone."

Before the door closed behind Marta, Kaya heard Olivia's laugh, a joyous, carefree sound that tugged at her heart. Azizi's answering bark made her smile.

"I—" Kaya cut herself off, uneasy about sharing so much of her past with Marta. "I was remembering," she finally admitted as Marta set the tray on the table. "The woman who raised me died the day before I married Paul." Her gaze drifted toward the bedroom, but she heard no sound. "I was forced to leave my grandfather. My only family."

"I'm sorry." Marta sounded so sincere; those simple words brought tears to Kaya's eyes. She crossed the room, as silent as the grave, and took Kaya's hand, squeezing it.

The lump in her throat returned, and she met Marta's soft brown gaze. Nodding, Kaya squeezed Marta's hand in return and felt lighter than she had since before she and Paul literally stumbled into this village. She was not as weighed down, as if a yoke held her in place.

"Thank you." She meant it and tried to smile. "I'm not the only one to experience grief and loss." She cleared her throat and nodded at the covered tray Marta carried. "Will you join me for the meal?"

"I...no." Marta shook her head and backed toward the door.

"Marta." Kaya hastily grabbed for the woman's hands. "He's dead. He can't hurt you. Not ever again."

A bitter laugh welled from deep within Marta and spilled over. "He'll continue to hurt me for the rest of my life."

Kaya resisted looking at Marta's belly, which was carefully hidden by her dress. She didn't have an answer to that, so she simply guided her friend to the table.

"Derya, she was my mother's—lady's maid." Kaya stopped from using the Turkish term at the last minute. The Ottomans were not welcome in Calabria. "My mother died in childbirth; it was a long walk through the desert."

Marta slowly met her gaze but didn't comment. Kaya uncovered the tray and set one of the bowls of stew and a cup of juice before Marta, hoping she'd eat.

"I never knew my mother or father. Derya raised me in my grandfather's house."

"What happened to your father?"

"He was killed protecting my mother. Theirs was a clandestine marriage—no one approved. My mother was set to marry another."

Was that another lie? Derya had told her the story of her parents, their secret affair and marriage. She never said how they met, only that they loved each other.

"She escaped?" A note of wistfulness crept into Marta's voice.

"Yes. She found my grandfather, but it was a hard journey." Kaya cleared her throat against the pain of losing those she loved. The lies they may or may not have told her. She didn't know what truly happened, if what she believed was real or not.

"You?" she asked instead. Marta's wistful tone had not escaped her. "What of you?"

"Me?" Marta laughed bitterly. "I've lived here my whole life. I'll die here."

That hadn't been what Kaya meant. Or perhaps it had been. "I spent my life locked in the house," she admitted quietly. "Unable to leave. I could not even see the street or speak to neighbors."

"How did *you* escape?" Marta leaned forward, her eyes bright, eager. "Did you walk out? Simply...leave?" She waved a hand, as if packing her few possessions and stepping out of the house was as easy as that.

Perhaps it was.

"I was contracted to marry Paul."

Would she have left otherwise? Kaya didn't know. With Derya dead, would she have simply stepped out that front door, a move that had been previously barred to her? Would she have disappeared into the city? The thought both tempted and terrified her.

"Ah. Yes." Marta sat back, bitterness once more creeping into her voice. "Marriage."

"What of your husband?" Kaya asked carefully.

"Died in the *terremoto*." Marta shrugged and sighed. "Before —well, before they arrived."

Kaya let Marta have her silence. She was trembling again, looking as if she wanted to flee the house. She didn't know what had changed, but Marta suddenly sat straighter and met Kaya's gaze.

"I'm sorry."

Marta nodded. She opened her mouth as if to say something, yet also looked as if she could not. Finally, she whispered, "I am not sorry."

This, Kaya understood. Not having a say. In the months since leaving Cairo with Paul, she had come to know how lucky they were to care for each other. Love each other. "Growing up with stories of my mother's love for my father, how she defied her parents to marry him, I did not believe in anything else."

"They were lucky." Marta sighed. "But you did not know Paul before your marriage?"

"No."

Marta grinned. "Then you are lucky as well, Kaya. That man will walk through hell for you. Kill for you."

Three

"Yes." Silent and still, Kaya half turned to look into the bedroom. Paul *would* walk through hell for her, she knew it, and yet that rage choked her again. Why? Kaya had no answers, even as she knew she'd continue to fight for him.

"Yes." She looked back at Marta.

"Alonzo would not have walked through hell for me." The words must've slipped out, because Marta looked horrified.

"It's all right." Kaya leaned over and took her hands. "I promise to keep your secrets."

Marta stared at her. Kaya didn't say a word, merely waited, holding her hand. Was this what friends did? She honestly had no idea, but it felt right, sitting in the warm silence, letting the storm spend its temper outside while they shared secrets inside.

Did Marta realize she was Kaya's first friend? How did one confess such a secret? She had many secrets—too many for her to comfortably share, even with Marta. A lifetime of secrets kept locked away.

Outside, the wind continued to beat against the shutters. It occasionally brought in the happy cries of Olivia and Azizi, slipping joy through a house that had seen so little of it. The fire cracked and sparked, and still Kaya held Marta's hand.

"There are not many families here," Marta began softly. "I had thought to run away with one of the traveling performers, but—" She shook her head, her lips curling up in longing. She sighed, and her face softened. "You will like them. The performers, they tell stories and sing songs, put on shows from across the land."

Kaya felt herself smile, entranced by Marta's description of these musicians. She leaned back, satisfied that Marta remained in the present. "I've never seen performers; I should like to." Kaya wished to ask more about them, but she had a keen ear for deflection. She had practiced it often, as a way to hide her hurt when denied by Derya or Gidd. "You wished to join them?"

Marta met her gaze. "I did not wish to marry Alonzo," she said flatly. "He was a lazy, ignorant layabout who wanted control of the inn. When Olivia was born, he wanted to leave her in the mountains to die. He wanted a boy. I am not sorry he died in the *terremoto*."

Marta looked stricken, like she was about to be sick. "May God forgive me." She quickly crossed herself, but her face paled further, and her hands shook. "But I am not sorry he died."

Kaya wasn't either—not if he'd wanted to leave a newborn Olivia in the woods—but she held her tongue. "It's hard," she said haltingly. "Hard to admit how we feel when it's not how others think we should feel."

She frowned, not certain she made any sense. Was she speaking of Marta, or herself? Would Paul understand if she told him about her secret rage? Even—especially—if it was directed at him?

"I have to go," Marta whispered, tears clogging her words.

"You don't—" Kaya stopped and nodded. "Come back later. You can tell me more of these performers."

Eyes wide, Marta merely nodded and fled through the door, as if Kaya might condemn her for not mourning the loss of her husband. But Kaya was hardly in a position to condemn anyone for wanting their own life.

For a long minute, Kaya stared at the closed door. She didn't hear anything from the bedroom and wondered if Paul had fallen asleep. She stepped toward the room, then stopped. If he was awake, she didn't want to speak with him.

And not only with him. Kaya didn't want to speak with anyone, and she had no answer as to why. She only knew she needed the silence, even if she didn't want to be alone with her own thoughts. Out of sorts, she roamed the bare room and stared at the religious shrine in the corner, lost in memories of her own longing.

Sitting before it, she closed her eyes and let her mind wander. All those hopes and dreams she'd once envisioned as her future. Her constant need to escape being trapped in her Cairo home.

The door burst open, and once more Kaya found herself ready with her dagger. Marta stood there, carrying a pair of bowls. How long had she been lost in thought?

"I brought *tè al tarassaco*." Marta cleared her throat, and her shoulders relaxed as she held out a small bowl of steaming liquid. "It is for Signore Paul. To help with his pain."

"Thank you." Kaya sniffed the tea, but it didn't smell familiar. "What is in this?"

"It is a flower that grows in summer. We also make salad with it." Marta held up another bowl containing several cuttings of greenery. "This is the last. Mama, she says it helps ease the pain of drinking. Makes men feel themselves again."

"Thank you," Kaya said again and set the bowl aside. She didn't want to disturb Paul now, not when he slept.

"Are you joining me for supper?" Kaya asked. She took down the bowls Marta had brought earlier from the cupboard Azizi couldn't reach. "I should like to hear more about these traveling performers."

"*Sì, sì.*" Marta cleared her throat again, her eyes wandering to the niche in the wall and the objects there. "I brought lemon and salt." She hesitated again. "For cleaning."

She set each item on the table by the tea but didn't explain further. Lemon, Kaya understood. Salt? She had no idea how that was used for cleaning.

Kaya sat and ignored the other items, determined to focus on Marta and learn more about the traveling storytellers. "These entertainers, do they know the old stories?"

"Oh, yes!" Marta suddenly grew animated, sitting forward and grinning. "They know so many. Comedies and tragedies; they can make you cry even while you laugh. There are acrobats, too. And the songs! *Madrigali Cantanti* is..." She sighed. "Those singers are...there is nothing else like it."

It welled within Kaya, a feeling she knew far too intimately. Excitement. Anticipation. Worry had drained her, and exhaustion had begged her to sleep, but disquiet kept her awake and moving.

Now, sitting here listening to Marta talk about traveling performers and singers, it all came back. She had seen acrobats in Sicily, amazing feats of walking across thin ropes and soaring through the air, jumping from person to person. Kaya didn't know what *Madrigali Cantanti* was, but that, too, sounded fantastical.

"I should very much like to see them." The joy at discovering something so new and wonderful burst through her.

"You will love them," Marta promised. "And I shall ensure Giovanni shows you the most wonderful routines."

Grinning, Kaya tilted her head. There was something in Marta's voice, but she didn't know what that tone was. "Who is Giovanni? He is one of the performers?"

Marta blushed. Stunned, Kaya stared at her and tried to think what she'd said to warrant such a reaction. She ate a spoonful of stew and schooled her features to look interested—but not too interested.

"He is, yes." Marta's voice dropped. "He owns the troupe.

They travel here every year after Easter. We are their first stop once the mountain pass clears."

"When is Easter?" Kaya asked, breaking off a chunk of bread.

"Oh, six weeks or so, I believe." Marta looked into her bowl, but her smile did not leave her face.

Six weeks sounded like an eternity.

Kaya opened her mouth to make an excuse as to why they probably couldn't stay, but then she saw Marta's cheeks. That faint blush from earlier had returned, and her smile hadn't diminished. Something tugged at Kaya's memory.

"Is Giovanni the reason you wished to join the troupe?"

Marta's cheeks flushed darker. "Yes," she admitted in barely a whisper.

Intrigued, Kaya broke off another piece of bread and chewed slowly. She suddenly knew where the beautifully preserved green ribbon had come from. "Why did you not?"

"Papa...he promised me to Alonzo." Marta shook her head. "He wouldn't listen to my pleas. Alonzo had a large herd of sheep; he was very well off."

"Understandable." Kaya knew nothing about sheep. Then again, she knew nothing about traveling acrobats, either. But she did understand stability. "He wanted you to be secure. But you were not happy?"

"No." Marta snorted and drained her cup. She angrily tore into the bread, shredding it into her bowl. "Alonzo's father was good. Worked hard. Increased his flock. Alonzo did not. He and his brothers drank and gambled."

A chill ran down Kaya's spine, and her gaze involuntarily slipped to the bedroom. Suddenly, she saw not the life Marta had been forced to live, but a life *Kaya* could've been forced to live.

"Did he hurt you?" she whispered.

Fingers stilling, eyes closed, Marta nodded, just a fraction of a movement. "Not like Appleby. Appleby, he was cruel. Angry. Vicious. Alonzo, he was drunk. Always. Pretended to be kind so everyone saw only one side of him."

Kaya's chill returned, and she reached across the table to rest her hand on Marta's. "It is all right not to mourn such a man," she said into the silence.

"God will punish me," Marta spat. A tear ran down her face. She jerked back from Kaya's touch, balling her hands in front of her. "I dishonor my husband."

"Your husband dishonored you. He did not take care of you or keep you safe." Kaya straightened, her fingers pressed into the wooden table. "He will not meet you in paradise—in heaven."

"Perhaps." Marta shook her head. "But I cannot stay here."

Before Kaya could ask what she planned, Marta pushed back the chair, which crashed to the floor. "I should leave." She sniffed and wiped her cheeks. "I should leave."

For the second time that afternoon, Kaya watched Marta race out the door. She took a step to follow her but stopped. Would she want Marta to follow her after such a revelation? No. No, she would not.

"Far different," she said to the open doorway. "Paul would never hurt me. But this." She closed the door. "This is what might have happened."

"Don't blame yourself."

Kaya jerked and whirled to stare at him with wide eyes. He wanted to laugh, as this was the second time he'd startled her, but he didn't want to change the subject. This was about Marta, not about him sneaking up on his wife.

"I can't blame anyone for wanting their own life," she whispered. But she looked troubled, as if their presence had caused Marta harm.

Perhaps it had; Paul knew his being here certainly didn't help. He shuffled to the door and whistled for Azizi. Kaya looked lost standing in the middle of the small cottage, and he wanted to take her into his arms and hold her.

The dog took her time sniffing through the trampled snow from where she and Olivia had played.

"Come on," he called. "Inside."

Azizi trotted through the door and promptly shook herself off. Paul closed his eyes as cold snow droplets flung around the place. Then, meeting Kaya's stunned gaze, he chuckled.

"Go on," he told Azizi. "Lie by the fire."

Kaya moved toward the chairs by the table and sat down, looking bewildered. Paul couldn't tell if it was because of Azizi or Marta, or if everything was catching up to her. Probably a combination of all three.

As he pulled a chair beside her, Paul tried not to wince at his own weakness. He knew he ought to eat more than the meager bites of bread he'd managed, but his insides cramped like the devil, and he had no desire to be sick. Again.

"Her husband died in the earthquake," Kaya said without preamble. "How much did you hear?"

His fingers tightened around hers, and he brought their joined hands to his cheek. The feel of her touch on his skin settled deep inside him. He hadn't realized how much he needed her touch, how he'd missed it, especially in these uncertain times.

"Not much; I didn't want to eavesdrop. She's wary enough around me. No need to frighten her."

The guilt of what Appleby did to this village—specifically to Marta—churned in his gut every moment. The responsibility he bore for involving Kaya made him want to run far from her, leave her in peace despite needing so badly to be near her.

Instead, he asked, "How is Marta? How is she really?"

"She is uncomfortable in her own home. Olivia does not like it in here, either." Frowning, she combed her fingers through his hair, and he tried very hard not to purr like a cat against her touch. "I fear her husband was not kind to either of them."

"Too many aren't." He hummed in contentment, unable to keep the sound to himself. "Don't stop."

He felt her smile though his eyes were closed. Her breath of amusement brushed over him as she continued to run her fingers through his hair, letting both of them relax at the soothing touch. "Did you know she carries Appleby's child?"

Paul stiffened. Pushing up, he peered at her in sickened shock. "What?"

"Yes," she whispered, looking sick herself.

She steadied his shoulders, but Paul barely felt it. Beneath her touch, his skin trembled with anger. Rage over what that man had done to Marta. What the entire village had allowed him to do. All so they could save themselves.

"The sacrificial lamb," he spat, his stomach churning in disgust. He gasped and swallowed hastily, but it was no use. Kaya jumped back away from him.

Just in time, too.

Hunched over the chair, Paul squeezed his eyes shut. "I want to kill him again."

He looked up at Kaya as she moved to the far end of the kitchen. She'd tied a *fazzoletto* around the lower half of her face and returned with the candles, a bucket, and some rags.

"No, Azizi," Kaya ordered.

The dog settled beside Paul, who petted her in an attempt to keep them both out of the way. "Are you keeping Kaya company? Hm?" he asked, more to distract himself from the blinding rage that scorched through him than in any real hope of her answering.

But Azizi yipped as if she understood. Perhaps she did, more than Paul gave her credit for.

"Dogs are not for company," Kaya reminded him, carefully holding the rags as far from her body as possible.

Paul stood on shaky legs and opened the door. Kaya nodded her thanks and dropped the rags outside. Then she slammed the door closed with more force than he thought the wind warranted, untied her *fazzoletto,* and rinsed her hands. "They're for protection."

"They're for both," he reminded her, but his voice sounded

weaker now. He accepted the cup of juice Kaya offered and hoped it stayed down. "I'm glad you have her."

"Me too," Kaya admitted, and the tautness in her shoulders relaxed.

"Tell me more about Marta." He stopped and cleared his throat. "What is she going to do with the child?"

"I do not know," Kaya admitted, rounding the table again. "Come, sit on the pallet."

He did as she bade, glad he didn't have to sit in the chair when he could barely remain conscious. She carried a bowl of lukewarm tea and held it out for him to take. "I don't think I can keep anything down," he said.

"Marta said it's for the drink." Kaya sat in the chair and waited. "It helps with the pains."

"Kaya, my stomach—"

"Drink it," she snapped, that tense anger back in her words, her posture. "Just—please. She said it helps."

"I'll try anything," he muttered, eyeing his wife carefully. Paul didn't blame her for her irritation, her resentment, but he wished she'd talk to him about it. "I'm sorry." He held out his hand for the bowl, and his hands shook.

"It's all right." Wrapping her hands over his, she met his gaze. "I'm here."

"Do you want to be?" Paul asked before dutifully drinking the tea.

"What do you mean?" Kaya asked, but he could tell she already knew.

He finished the tea and snorted. "This is disgusting."

"It's an herb that grows here," she said, but he heard the deflection in her tone. "It is also good for salad."

"Did Marta have any ginger?" He handed the bowl back and watched her.

Kaya looked away and set the bowl on the floor. Azizi sniffed at it. Apparently deciding it wasn't worth even a last lick, she curled up next to him on the pallet.

"I'll ask when she brings breakfast."

"Kaya." Paul grabbed her hand and held it tenderly. He didn't shake when he touched her; his grip was solid and real. "Do you want to stay here?"

"Without you, you mean," she said flatly.

"Yes."

"Why do you keep trying to leave me?"

Her hands jerked in his, but he held them tight. He wasn't— he couldn't. And yet perhaps she had a point.

"I don't." He frowned. "It's only—" He sighed but didn't release her. "I want you to be safe. And you haven't been safe with me since we left Damietta."

"I disagree," she spat, her anger boiling over. "But you seem intent on leaving me. I admit, I wanted that. Before. When I hadn't realized what our life could be like. When I wanted to experience things on my own."

"Because you never had." He said it calmly, but the fury with which she glared at him should've ignited him into flames on the spot. "And now?"

"Now I—I don't know." Jaw clenched, she curled her hands into tight fists. "Now I know I love you. I want to see you well. I want..." She trailed off. "I don't know."

His lips quirked. "Fair enough. I don't know either." He scrubbed a hand down his face. "I need a bath."

She let out a weak chuckle.

"I love you beyond reason, Kaya. If you want to stay here, we can make a life for us. If you want to continue on, north or west, we can do that, too. Whatever you want."

"What do you want?"

Paul shrugged. "Never thought about it before. Wine, good food, no memories of the past."

"That isn't a want."

"No," he admitted. "That was running. See how far that got me?" he added with a grimace. "Straight back to where I was before I met you."

"And now?" She tentatively reached for his hand. Azizi let out a faint snort, and Kaya smiled at the sound. "What do you want now?"

"I want you to look at me without uncertainty."

"I don't understand so much of this," she admitted. "It scared me, the way you were...after."

"Me too." He tightened his hand around hers. "I can't promise it'll never happen again."

"That scares me, too."

The silence stretched between them, and Paul wondered what she was thinking. He couldn't tell. Her shoulders had relaxed, but her mouth remained tight with tension, and her words were halting, uncertain.

"Do you want to lie down?"

That was all he'd done for days. Paul had lost all track of time, but he knew it'd been longer than he suspected. "Lie with me," he coaxed.

Kaya smiled, and they settled onto their makeshift pallet, the blankets cocooning them in a warmth that had little to do with the fire.

"Does anyone else know?"

She paused, stiffening in his arms. "Know? About Marta? I— no, I do not think so. She seemed anxious about how the village would respond. I don't know if she told Olivia or Caroline."

Caroline, Marta's mother, was a forceful, angry woman. Paul doubted she'd react well to the news her daughter carried the illegitimate child of a man who'd intimidated the village.

"The village won't be the same," Paul said. In the flickering firelight, Kaya looked wan and fragile. So very tired from tending to him, doing what she could to help Marta. "It might take a generation or two before they trust anyone again. Anyone outside their own." He closed his eyes and tightened his arms around his wife. "If then." With his lips brushing the nape of her neck, he said, "Perhaps we could send Marta and Olivia to Antoinette and Roberto in Villa San Giovanni. Give them a better life."

"I don't know," Kaya began, hesitant, "if Marta has ever had a choice."

"Talk with her," Paul urged. His stomach cramped again, but he rode out the pain, hoping Kaya didn't realize it. He hated to worry her.

Kaya reached up and ran her fingers through his hair. He kept his eyes open despite the soothing comfort of her touch. She smiled and seemed loathe to disturb this peace.

"You captivated me from our first meeting," he finally admitted. "You were not at all what I was expecting, and you—I couldn't look away. That sway hasn't lessened in the intervening months, Kaya." He caught her hand and kissed the back of her fingers. "It's only grown stronger. I can't imagine you not being in my life."

"I can't imagine you not being in my life, either," she confessed. Azizi whined, and Kaya reached over to scratch the dog's ears. "You too, Azizi. Don't worry. You belong, too."

Paul chuckled and wondered if he dared another sip of juice. Not just yet—not when they spoke so openly and honestly.

"I doubt we could've stayed," she finally said. "In Cairo, I mean. There was so little food. Riots, lack of money. The economy was collapsing, and the Ottomans were again exerting power over the country. No, we couldn't have stayed. It would've been madness."

"Madder than crossing the desert and then the entire island of Sicily?" Paul asked, even as sleep tugged at him.

She laughed. "Perhaps not." She rolled to face him and kissed his forehead. "But I wouldn't trade these last months with you for all the food in Cairo."

Paul laughed and grabbed for her hand. When he brushed his lips against the inside of her wrist, he felt more than heard her suck in a breath. "I wouldn't trade you for anything, my wife."

"Nor I you, *ya rouhi*," she whispered.

Four

Paul ignored the shaking of his hands. He ignored the foul taste of the *tarassaco* tea, even if it was the only thing he managed to keep down. He ignored Azizi's snoring beside him by the fire. His attention was focused on Kaya, who was painstakingly writing a letter to the Spanò family in hopes they might take in Marta, Olivia, and the unborn child.

And Bravo, the donkey. Bravo, who only liked Olivia and didn't let any adult near him.

Paul didn't blame the animal for that.

"What are you doing with this dress?" he asked, finishing the last of the seams.

The jewels they'd carried from Cairo spilled over the floor, glittering in the firelight. The Egyptian *piastre* and *akçe* they hadn't spent in Damietta also watched him. For a bizarre moment, Paul felt as if the coins were judging him, and he heard Tahir's voice demanding to know whether he'd done a good job of protecting Kaya.

Paul ignored that, too.

He shook his head and wondered if the drink—or lack thereof —had addled his brain.

"We should keep the fabric," Kaya said, blinking up at him.

She stretched, stood from the table, and rolled her neck from side to side. "We haven't the time to make Olivia anything from it, but the fabric itself is still valuable."

"I'll try to scrub the blood out." He frowned at it. "Not sure what removes blood, to be honest. I'll try the vinegar first."

He gathered their jewels and gold from the floor and set them on the table. Paul didn't know what made him pocket the Egyptian coins. But he slipped them inside the waistcoat that tried very hard to keep him warm, tucking them safely out of Kaya's view.

"How's the letter?" He nodded to the paper.

He hated this feeling, their awkward standing, his being unsure as he spoke with his own wife. Paul tried to remember a time when they'd spoken to each other so awkwardly. Maybe he didn't expect it to feel as if they'd known each other for years, but at least they could do without these stilted scraps of conversation.

It made the skin between his shoulder blades itch.

"I've never written the language, so I hope Antionette understands." Kaya frowned and looked down at the letter, as if Antionette Spanò would magically answer her.

Paul nudged her hand away from the scrap of paper that Marta had generously provided. He didn't think he'd ever seen her so nervous. Stricken by that, he urged her up and guided her to their makeshift pallet by the fire. Wrapping an arm about her shoulders, he leaned against the stones and grasped for words that would soothe her.

"I don't know," he admitted. He wanted to bite off his tongue. Not the comforting words of wisdom he'd hoped for. "I know you're nervous about sending them south, but Marta agreed it's for the best."

From what Paul had inferred from the conversation, Marta would rather travel to complete strangers in Calabria than travel with him. Marta refused to leave her country, and neither he nor Kaya wanted to stay here. He knew it pained Kaya, but it was Marta's choice, and they both respected that.

Kaya pulled back and eyed him. "Sneaking out with the snow blocking our path?"

"Not ideal," he agreed and shrugged. "I don't have a better idea, much as I've tried. Leaving before the snow melts leaves a trail for anyone to follow, but once we move south and west, down the mountains, it'll be harder for anyone to find us."

Their plan was to leave as a group and head west over the mountains to Palmi, on the Tyrrhenian Sea. There, Marta, Olivia, and Bravo would continue south to Villa San Giovanni, and he and Kaya—and Azizi—would head north.

"How do you feel about taking a boat?" Paul asked, completely unsure what her reaction would be.

Kaya shuddered despite their closeness to the fire. "I do not like that idea at all." She sighed, and he knew she was seriously debating the merits of boat travel versus walking.

"It'll be faster to Rome and the Papal States." Personally, Paul didn't want to be there, either, but at least it was better than Calabria—too many memories. "We can walk anywhere in the country from there."

"With me seasick and you still recovering from your illness?" She shook her head and reached out for his hand. "What a pair we make."

Paul snorted. "I'll find a boat that hugs the coast," he promised. "And hopefully we can have a nice leisurely walk from Rome to wherever we plan."

"We *plan*?" Kaya pulled back and eyed him. Her lips quirked, and his rose in answering amusement. "I have not known us to *plan*, Paul. How very bold of you."

Laughing, he kissed her cheek and tugged her to him. He maneuvered so they both lay on the pallet, pillowed by the bedroll and facing each other beneath a blanket. The fire burned hot at his back, casting away the constant chill that had settled in his bones.

"By plan, I didn't mean a well-thought-out strategy." He

brushed a few stray strands of hair off her forehead. "More a generalized direction northward."

"Yes," she said quietly, her eyes dark and serious. "North is a fine plan."

"Would you—" Paul stopped and tried to reword his thought, but it hammered insistently. "Do you want to write a letter to Tahir?"

Kaya jerked, but her steady gaze showed him she'd already thought of that. "Yes, I do," she admitted. "However, I doubt *that* is a good plan."

He tried to smile, but the heaviness in her voice stopped his weak attempt. "I know, sweetheart."

Paul gathered her into his arms, pulling her head to his chest. It still hurt to breathe, and every muscle felt weak and neglected. He'd need more than the tea Marta brought, but food held little appeal to him.

How had he managed to walk through the Sinai to Cairo? Not that he remembered that walk, but he'd somehow survived it.

"In my heart, he still lives." Kaya spoke into Paul's vest, her fingers curling tight in the worn wool fabric. "The famine has not touched him. He still commands respect and authority, and the Ottomans cannot take that from him."

Kissing the top of her head, Paul held her tighter. He understood what she meant, even if he'd never cared for another as she did her grandfather. In the whole world, in his whole life, the only person he'd ever loved was Kaya.

And he honestly didn't know what he'd do if he lost her.

"Marta," Kaya breathed as the other woman pushed open the door.

"I can't stay long." She looked over her shoulder, her long hair wild in the winter wind. The tray she carried shook in her hands. "Mama dislikes that I spend so much time here."

The sun had barely risen over the mountaintops, casting weak fingers of light across the forest. Beside Kaya, Azizi stirred.

"*Aibqaa muta'ahiban*," she ordered the dog. "Stand ready" was one of the few commands Azizi willingly obeyed.

"Does she suspect?" Kaya asked as Azizi slipped past them and paced outside. She pulled Marta into the cottage and closed the door. "Where's Olivia?"

"She's in the kitchens." Marta looked at the door as if she suspected Caroline, or perhaps the entire village, ready to storm it.

"Sit by the fire." Kaya took the tray and brought it into the bedroom, where Paul waited. He'd taken to staying there when Marta came. It was easier on her, knowing he was there without being confronted by his actual presence.

"We should leave tonight," Paul said as he took the tray and placed it on the bed. "If she's this paranoid, she'll give something away, and all will be lost."

Nodding, her fingers brushing the khanjar at her waist, Kaya pressed her lips to his in a quick acknowledgement.

Marta paced around the open room, her gaze always on the door. Her fingers twisted together, and her breath came too fast. Paul was right—they needed to move now, before Caroline or anyone else realized what they'd planned.

Kaya and Paul had spent the previous week readying for their departure. Though he hadn't said as much, Kaya knew Paul feared retribution from the villagers once the weather cleared— they'd been hostile before they'd disrupted the opium wagon. Neither he nor Kaya had left the cottage because Paul didn't trust their goodwill.

Apparently, he'd been right in that.

"Marta." Kaya stepped before her and grabbed her hands. "We'll leave tonight. Is Olivia ready?"

Marta offered a jerky nod, though her gaze slid from Kaya's to the door. "She's sad, but she understands."

Kaya feared the child understood more than either of them

realized, and she worried for her future. Marta watched the door again, and Kaya shifted to block her view.

"Marta," she snapped. "We will protect you. Understood?"

Marta didn't answer right away, her gaze still darting from Kaya to the door and back again. "So you have said." Marta glanced at the khanjar at Kaya's hip. "But what happens after we leave here? Will I be free?"

"You—" Kaya had no idea. But she didn't think so, not as long as Marta held onto the past.

"No." Paul's voice made both women jump. "Leaving here will not make you free, I'm afraid."

He'd stepped into the main room, just visible by the firelight. He made no move toward them but held Marta's gaze. In the uncertain light, he looked stronger than he had when they'd concocted this plan, but Kaya still worried about his health. They had to walk so far over rough mountains in thick snow. Marta was heavily pregnant. Desperation moved them forward despite the odds.

"When I was in Bombay, I had a friend, Basu." Paul shook his head, watching Marta. "He taught me about his holy book. In it, there's a saying. I'm not sure how accurate it is—Basu was a great one for spouting holy verses and breaking them in the next breath."

His lips curved into a smile, and Kaya's heart eased. He didn't speak of Basu often, a handful of times at most. This was the first time she'd seen him smile over his friend.

"He said that life is taking the beauty along with the ugly. Nothing is permanent just as the waves of the sea against the shore are not." Paul blew out a breath. "I may have crossed my metaphors there. Anyway, all that may be true, but I've learned that if you carry your past with you, all you'll have is that past. You'll have nothing else."

"How do I forget all that has happened when I carry his child?" Marta's voice cracked, and Kaya led her to the table, urging her to sit. "I can't leave the past behind."

"I don't know," Kaya admitted, kneeling in front of her. "But starting anew is not a bad idea."

She swallowed and looked to Paul. She had such limited knowledge of the world outside her Cairo home. However, she didn't want to push him to share anything he didn't wish to.

"When we met," Kaya said, turning her attention back to Marta, "I thought he was going to murder me in the desert."

Marta jerked; her eyes went wide. "What?"

"What?" Paul asked then chuckled. "Of course you did."

"I did not know you!" Kaya turned back to Marta. "He broke into the house intending to steal from us!"

"He did?" Marta's eyes widened again, and she looked from Kaya to Paul. She leaned forward, and her voice dropped. "I see the way he looks at you. How you look at him. There is no suspicion in your marriage."

"Trust is not always a signed agreement between two people. It is earned, and only through action—not words." Kaya smiled softly, remembering how Gidd used to say that to her. "My grandfather used to tell me that."

"I shall miss you, Kaya Hartley." A tear broke free of Marta's control, and she angrily swiped her cheek. "You are a woman I consider a friend."

Kaya's throat closed with Marta's admission. She smiled, her own eyes suspiciously blurry with emotion. Squeezing her hands, she leaned in and hugged the other woman. "And I, you."

"Conrad." Paul's apologetic voice came from closer than Kaya realized. "It's Kaya Conrad." He sighed and raised his eyes skyward. "We, ah, had to change our names in Egypt."

Kaya swallowed a chuckle. What Paul meant was they'd forged new papers in Damietta. Anyone following them would be looking for a Sergeant Paul Hartley of the East India Company, not Mr. Paul Conrad, gentleman.

"You—but..." Marta trailed off, confused. "As you wish."

"Conrad is what the Spanós will know us by." Paul looked embarrassed but shrugged it off. "So there's no confusion."

"So they don't think you're lying," Kaya added, probably far too bluntly, but this was important. She'd forgotten about the Hartley/Conrad problem. She'd forgotten a lot of things in the last weeks. "We are Kaya and Paul Conrad."

Marta nodded but didn't look as if she completely understood. Kaya pushed that aside for later. They still had weeks, possibly months, depending on the snow and their walking pace. They could remind her again. She and Olivia both.

"Now." Kaya stood and pulled Marta up with her. "You have all you need?"

"*Sì, sì.* We are both ready, Olivia and I." Marta's lips twitched. "I think Bravo is less ready, but Olivia is happy he joins us."

Kaya smiled and led Marta to the door. "Once you return with the evening meal, we'll leave. Eat what you can; pack the rest."

"I'll send Olivia with the food we have saved." Marta opened the door, looking far less afraid but no more ready for tonight. "Thank you," she whispered. "Thank you."

Before Kaya could clear her throat enough to speak, Marta disappeared. "Come inside, Azizi." Closing the door behind the obedient dog, she turned to Paul. "She's terrified."

He nodded, closing the distance between them. "With good reason. If anyone suspects she carries Appleby's child, she'll be shunned. Possibly stoned—I don't know if they still do that, but this village is hurting and angry. They'll take that out on whomever they can. You, me, Marta. Olivia." He shook his head. "Keep Azizi close until we leave. No sense stirring the pot."

"How much longer before sunset?" Kaya looked to the windows, whose shutters were locked tight against the cold.

"Too long." Paul turned for their bedroll. "Come on, let's pack up now. No sense waiting until it's too late."

"How do we know when it's too late?" Kaya asked, setting the bread aside and scooping a bite of stew.

"You know when we run for our lives." He sighed and accepted the bowl she held out. It was the *tarassaco* tea, which he'd forced down daily along with his bowl of stew. "You'll know it's too late when they're literally screaming for your blood."

Curious, she eyed him. "And you know this from experience?"

"Too much." He drank the tea in one swallow and grimaced. "This is still disgusting. But it works." Setting the bowl on the table, he grimaced again. "We'll leave gold for Caroline?"

Kaya nodded, though she hated to leave anything for Caroline. "She is a mean woman who does not understand what her daughter did for the village. But yes. It is only right we pay her for the food." Kaya frowned. "And whatever Appleby drank. I'm certain he never paid for his wine."

"I'm certain you're correct." Paul began packing their bedroll and blankets.

"Is this a bad idea?" she asked, staring at his movements without registering them. "Leaving as we are?"

"I don't know." He tightened one of the straps and grunted at the force. "Probably, but I don't see another option. We can't let Marta bear the brunt of the village's anger." He sighed and straightened, setting the pack on the table. "And once they come for her, they'll come for us. Right now, I'm not strong enough to protect you."

Kaya offered a slight grin and met his worried gaze. "I can protect us both."

"So you can, my beautiful, terrifying wife." He drew her to him and kissed her softly. "But I prefer knowing you're safe. So we'll leave. And hope the snow isn't too difficult to navigate."

"Then north. Rome, yes? I suppose we should try the boat." She grimaced but nodded. It was, by far, the better and faster option to see them as far from here as possible. "At least see how far we can manage."

Paul kissed her again, his arms tightening around her. "You'll be all right. It's not far, and from there, we can travel wherever you wish."

Five

It'd been a long, cold trek from San Grigori. The snow had hampered their journey far more than Paul anticipated. Neither Marta nor Olivia was prepared for such a trip, though Bravo had proved his worth ten times over. Stubborn donkey that he was, he carried an exhausted Marta for more than half the journey down the Apennines.

Once relatively free of the snow, they'd purchased a cart, which had carried both of them the rest of the way. Marta, who had eventually come to accept if not enjoy Paul's company, had regaled them with stories she'd learned from the performers who visited the village yearly.

Unfortunately, their time together had come to an end. Paul had spent yesterday securing passage on a vessel sailing north, to Rome and beyond, and he'd mapped out the best way for Marta to guide Bravo to Villa San Giovanni.

They wanted her settled before she gave birth.

Now they stood on the beach, the rising sun barely lighting the morning, delaying their goodbyes. Paul couldn't blame Kaya and Marta. They'd grown so close, and he knew his wife treasured Marta's friendship.

"Are you sure you're ready?" Paul asked. He studied Olivia sparring on the deserted beach as the sun inexorably climbed over the horizon. Marta watched Olivia practicing her forms from her nearby rocky resting place.

"I am." Kaya paused, and he turned from his scrutiny and studied her.

"Are you?" He squinted at her disbelievingly in the predawn light.

"No," she admitted on a long sigh. "I'll miss them. They— I've grown to care for them." She tilted her head. "Olivia, keep your arm raised!"

"I'll miss them, too," Paul admitted. "It's been an interesting few weeks, traveling with them."

Not unpleasant, but it lacked the intimacy he and Kaya had shared on their journey. Still, he'd come to appreciate the slower pace. In Egypt, he'd pushed them to escape the secrets he ran from. He hadn't realized Kaya carried her own as well. In Sicily, they'd tried to enjoy themselves but found suspicious villagers everywhere they turned. In Calabria, well—the past did have a way of finding them.

"Do you think they're ready?" Kaya slipped her hand into his.

It wasn't the hesitant gesture he'd come to expect and loathe. Rather, it was a natural one. Paul lifted her hand and kissed it.

"No, but I think if we wait any longer, it'll just be harder on all of us." He sighed and shrugged—he was doing that a lot lately. "It's not a long walk to Villa San Giovanni. Two, maybe three days, depending on Bravo's stubbornness. You sent a letter to Antionette already." They'd done so the moment they reached the coast. "Marta has a second letter of introduction."

"And if Marta's family tries to find her?"

He snorted. "They won't. I have a feeling the stone we left as payment was enough to cover the loss of two workers, as well as any expenses." Paul shook his head and searched for the words to explain most families—most families in his experience, which, granted, wasn't all that much.

Kaya turned to face him. In the warmth of the rising sun, her gaze was dark and sad. The sea breeze washed over them, and in the distance, he heard the calls of fishermen. The town would be waking now, and it was an ideal time to blend in, to part ways.

"You think the jewel was enough to—to barter for their lives?" Kaya looked shocked but sounded disgusted. Resigned. "I do not understand." She sighed and held his hand tighter. "I would say that Gidd would never have done such a thing, but the farther we get from Cairo, the more uncertain I am about that."

"I'm positive Tahir would never have sold you." Paul shook his head and turned to whistle for Azizi. "He could have at any point before writing to me. And he did not."

"True."

Kaya said nothing else. Paul wondered if her not wanting to write Tahir had more to do with her memories of the past or her fear that Tahir could not respond. That the Ottomans or the famine or time had finally caught up with him.

"Go on, into the shade. I'll gather them." Paul nodded to where they'd camped last eve, in the shadow of a rocky outcrop along the beach, well away from nosy people and wild animals.

"We have enough fish from yesterday to last the morning meal," Kaya said. She turned just as the sun breached the horizon.

Paul watched her disappear into the shadows, then he crossed to where Marta and Olivia spoke.

"Olivia, no." Marta breathed heavily and laid a hand on her belly. "I don't think Bravo will like that."

"What do you think, Signore Paul?" Olivia asked, her eyes wide as she turned from her mother. "About arming Bravo."

Paul blinked. "With a knife?" He snorted. "I don't think he can carry one."

"Of course not," Olivia sighed. "I mean with armor. Like in battle."

He wanted to ask what she knew about armor and battle, but Olivia looked so serious, he swallowed his question. The girl knew more about the world than any of them liked to admit. No doubt

Kaya's stories about great Egyptian battles had inspired Olivia's idea. "I think it might be difficult finding armor for a donkey."

Olivia looked dejected for a heartbeat. Then she raised her chin. Paul opened his mouth, not entirely sure what he was supposed to say. He settled on, "It might be possible. Why don't you speak with Kaya about it? I'm sure she has ideas."

Olivia nodded and ran off.

"I don't like encouraging her," Marta sighed, watching her daughter run to Kaya.

For a fraction of a second, Paul was stunned to realize he could see his daughter running to her mother. Their child, his and Kaya's, as she ran off to talk about armor and tactics. It terrified him. It also filled him with a longing he couldn't name.

"But I don't like her being helpless even more." Marta's voice brought him back to the present, and he blinked down at her.

Marta didn't look at him. She seldom did so, but at least they spoke now. Rarely alone, true, but Paul didn't mind. He knew he reminded Marta of Appleby. Though Paul had tried to stay away, it'd been difficult while the four of them traveled.

"I'm not sure there's a good answer to that," Paul admitted as he watched Olivia hover at the rock. "Kaya and I both want you to be safe. This is the only way we know how to help."

"You've given us a second chance." She looked at him quickly. "I'll never be able to repay you."

"I owe you far more," Paul whispered.

"I won't miss you," she admitted. "But I will miss Kaya. She is a friend I didn't ever expect to have, and it makes me sick that we must part ways." She stopped and glared at him. "You don't deserve her."

"I know. But I'll die for her." The words were a vow, searing along his skin as if burning that promise into him. He meant it. Kaya was his life, and whatever he needed to do to see to her safety, he'd do.

Marta nodded and started for their small camp. "Olivia, she's a much better traveler than I."

Olivia also wasn't about to give birth, but Paul didn't say that. Instead, he offered his arm to a clearly exhausted Marta. She looked at him and slowly reached for it, hesitatingly accepting the offer of help. Paul didn't comment, just silently led Marta back to their camp, such as it was. The sun warmed the day despite the early hour, and Paul enjoyed the silence of their short walk. The sound of the sea against the shore, the birds overhead, the wind—it was far more soothing than he wanted to admit.

"You're leaving today?" Marta asked just out of Olivia's earshot.

"Yes." Paul swallowed. "You'll be safe with the Spanòs."

"I'm not worried about that." Marta gave a rueful laugh. "I'm not worried too much," she admitted.

"It's—we only want you and Olivia safe."

She nodded as Kaya exited the shadows listening to Olivia's excited ideas about armor for Bravo. "I want a better life for my child." Marta rested her hand on her belly and met his gaze. "I want her to have a happier life than I had."

"I don't know how to guarantee that," Paul admitted. His gaze drifted to Kaya, and he wondered what their children might look like. Act. How they might fare in this world. "But if anyone can fight for it, Marta, it's you and Olivia."

She nodded and walked to Kaya and Olivia. Paul let them say their goodbyes as Azizi bounded up to him, panting and wet. Bravo eyed the dog warily, but over the last weeks, they'd formed a strange kind of...not trust. More like tolerance.

"Where have you been?" He eyed the dog, who shook out her fur with what could only be described as a grin. "All right. Go say your goodbyes. We're leaving."

Kaya stood on the deck of *The Santa Hyacintha* as they sailed up the coast. Azizi lay at her feet, nearly on her boots, as if she knew

Kaya's sorrow. She couldn't see Marta or Olivia, of course. They'd left shortly after breakfast.

"I don't like saying goodbye," she whispered around a tight throat.

She swiped at her cheeks and struggled for control. She turned to look at her husband in the midday sun and hoped he heard her. She didn't want to repeat anything, afraid her precarious hold on her emotions would shatter.

"I know." He took her hand and raised it to his lips, brushing a soft kiss over her gloved knuckles. "I'm sorry."

She swallowed hard several times before managing an abortive shake of her head. "What do you have to be sorry over?"

Her last words were lost in the wind, but she couldn't find the strength to repeat them. Her fingers tightened around his, and she hoped he understood.

"I'm sorry you had to leave them. I'm sorry they had to leave their home." Paul sighed and tugged her closer. She appreciated his warm touch, though it threatened her control. "But I'm not sorry you met them." His lips pressed against her temple. "And no, I don't think I'm sorry they had to start fresh. I think it might be the best thing for them."

"Even Bravo?" Kaya asked, trying to lighten the mood. She wasn't sure she managed.

"Especially that stubborn donkey." Paul laughed and hugged her close. "What did you hand Marta before they left?"

"The ribbon." Kaya smiled at the memory, pleased she could bring her friend some semblance of happiness. "I found it in the trunk. It was wrapped in a piece of cloth; it was the only item there that looked even remotely taken care of."

"She seemed pleased to have it. Why did she not take it when we left?"

Kaya shook her head. "I don't know. I think she might've forgotten about it. I had only a vague idea of what it might mean to her, but I was right. It's from Giovanni, the traveling performer. The one who taught her the stories she told us on our journey."

"Ah, her first love?" Paul chuckled. "I'm sorry she won't get to see him again."

"She said it was for the best." Kaya frowned. "She didn't want to admit to him what happened."

"I don't blame her." He paused and asked quietly, "How are you feeling? On the ship, I mean."

Kaya wasn't certain the packet boat could be called a ship, but she hadn't bothered to learn much about the differences between sailing vessels. However, the wind blew refreshingly around them, caressing her face and staving off any sickness. *The Santa Hyacintha* did, indeed, hug the coast, though her stomach didn't appreciate that.

"It's early," she said. "I enjoyed that first night on *The Cyprus Rose*."

"I don't think we'll be longer than a day and a half," Paul said. Azizi huffed. "Don't you get sick, too," he warned.

Kaya laughed, but it ended on a choked sob. Clearing her throat, she squeezed her eyes closed. "We don't seem to be as far from shore as we were."

She wanted a change in subject. At least when she left Cairo, she had a new adventure awaiting her. That hadn't made it any easier to grieve, but the excitement of new days in new places kept her moving.

"Would you like to go to our cabin?" Paul whispered against her cheek. "For a little privacy?" She looked at him askance, but he merely chuckled.

It wasn't that the privacy of their cabin wasn't welcome, but that she didn't know how her stomach might take to a close, confined space. Instead, Kaya rested her head on Paul's shoulder.

"Let's stay here for a while longer," she whispered.

"And enjoy the view?" Paul nodded, holding her close.

This was what she wanted, Kaya realized. The closeness of his body. Not necessarily in an intimate sense, though she did miss sex between them. More the closeness and comfort of holding him and being held.

"Once in Rome, what do you plan?" she asked.

"We can stay. We did promise Olivia we'd write, so we can send a letter from there." He held her tighter. "But I think it's not the place for us."

"No?" She pulled back and looked at him, curious. "Too many people?"

"We do seem to be better when we're alone." Paul glanced at Azizi. "And I'm not sure how she'll handle crowds."

"All right," Kaya said easily.

"Ah, Signore Conrad."

She turned to the stout man with the jovial face who was walking toward them. Captain De Luca smiled at them, hands clasped behind his back as he easily navigated the ship's deck. Kaya's stomach turned, and she hastily swallowed. Closing her eyes didn't help, and she turned quickly to look back at the horizon.

"Captain," Paul greeted the man. But she heard the note of concern, and he hadn't released his hold on her. "We're grateful you've added us to the manifest."

"Aye, aye, never hurts to carry passengers." He laughed. "More profitable than the mail!" He stopped beside Paul. "You travel to Rome?"

"Yes, it's a stop on our way north."

"We can take you to Genoa if you want. We travel the coast, up and back, several times a month."

"Thank you," Kaya managed. The mere thought of being on this boat longer than a day made her fingers tighten around the deck rail. "But we're interested in seeing Rome."

"Bah." The captain shook his head, and she peered at him curiously. "Thieves, nothing but thieves."

Kaya frowned at him, not sure what he meant by that assertive yet vague statement. "You suggest Genoa instead?"

De Luca shrugged. "I suggest buying your own ship and sailing the world." He looked out at the Tyrrhenian Sea, and Kaya thought she detected a wistful note in his voice. "But there are thieves out there, too."

"I'm afraid that is inevitable," Kaya admitted. She tried not to think about a life at sea. She'd never survive. "People always try to take what is not theirs."

"*Sì, sì.*" De Luca nodded. He eyed her khanjar, and when Kaya caught him, he shrugged. "You know about this, yes?"

"Too well," Paul said and tugged her elbow. "Azizi, come."

He guided her away from the captain. Kaya didn't need to watch De Luca to know he studied them. Paul waited as she descended the stairs belowdecks first, then helped Azizi, who most definitely did not like the stairs.

"I'm not sure I like Captain De Luca," she admitted as they entered their cabin, such as it was. She barely fit, let alone Paul. Kaya had no idea how Azizi did as well. "He seems...too curious," she settled on.

Opening the small porthole, Kaya tried to feel the breeze, but the open window did nothing to ease the stuffiness in the room. She carefully sat on the bed and took inventory of her stomach as Paul sat beside her.

"Which is why we'll be disembarking in Rome and heading east." He pressed a kiss to her jaw and urged her to lie down. "How are you feeling?"

With his body pressed to hers and his mouth teasing along her throat? Kaya shivered and wrapped her arms around him. "Don't stop."

Tangling her fingers in his hair, she sighed into his touch. She pressed her mouth against his and kissed him slowly, enjoying the taste of him, the way his mouth met hers in a slow dance.

"I've missed you," she whispered against his lips.

Kaya held him tighter and wondered if he knew she'd missed him not only while they traveled with Marta and Olivia, but while they stayed in the cottage. She didn't know how to tell him all that, afraid if she brought it up, they'd find themselves back at the beginning, uncertain and undefined.

"I won't leave you again," he promised, slipping his hand down her leg to gather her skirts. "I don't ever want to leave you again."

Paul's fingers grazed up her leg, teasing the top of her stocking. She arched against him, a silent plea for more. Her fingers curled into his shoulders, and all her breath left her. He pressed his hand between her legs, and she shuddered again, his name a moan she couldn't stop.

Her body thrummed with desire, with the nearly insatiable need to feel him within her, to move together.

"Paul," she gasped as his fingers teased her sex. "Paul, please," she begged aloud even as her hips moved into his touch.

He slid two fingers inside her, and Kaya gasped. Head thrown back, her body stilled for a heartbeat.

"That's it, sweetheart," Paul said against her throat as he kissed along her shoulder. He moved his fingers in a slow, steady rhythm as the heel of his hand pressed hard to her clit. "Let go, Kaya; let me see you undone. I want to undress you. Taste you."

His fingers moved faster, the heel of his hand pressing harder, and she felt her orgasm tightening, pushing her toward that peak. With each gasp of breath, desperate and panting, she spoke his name in a constant chant, and her fingers tightened in his hair.

Paul curled his fingers within her, thrusting faster, and Kaya's nails raked the back of his scalp, then tugged his hair, bringing him closer to her. With his teeth grazing her skin, his scent wrapped around her, she lost control.

She cried out as she came, arching into his touch. Paul's fingers slowed within her, his other hand stroking her cheek as she whimpered and gasped for breath. Groaning, he pulled from her, kissing the corner of her mouth as she blinked open her eyes. He tilted her chin and met her gaze, kissing her softly.

"I love you, Kaya. No matter what."

"Paul," she breathed, trying to orient herself after the bliss of her orgasm.

He kissed her lips again, a soft, tender touch. "For you, I'll do anything."

San Marino, Papal States

EARLY MAY, 1785

"Give us your coin, or your woman dies."

Paul stared impassively at the brigands standing between them and their ideal view. The three men, armed with naught more than knives and anger, brandished their weapons like a Maypole ribbon.

The beautiful, warm spring day shone down on them, the wind threatening both his hat and his patience. He had planned to spend the day with his wife, enjoying the view of the Adriatic Sea from high atop the Apennine Mountains.

Enjoying the view while holding Kaya as they picnicked on the overlook had sounded wonderful.

Now he calculated how best to disarm the three men, who looked more apt to scream at them than stab them. Azizi had disappeared over the next hill, into the trees of Monte Titano, and didn't seem inclined to return anytime soon.

"So much for our guard dog." Paul whistled for her.

Kaya laughed. "She's a curious creature and likes exploring."

He resisted a sigh. "Should I feel something more than annoyance about this latest robbery attempt?"

Paul eyed the trio and couldn't bring up more than that emotion. They held their knives like they planned to stab dinner, not unsuspecting travelers. One stiff breeze from the sea might knock their knives and them off the cliff. It bothered him, this ineptitude.

"This is the third attempt this week," he grumbled.

"Perhaps we should have taken the boat," Kaya allowed. "The trip from Palmi to Rome seemed smooth enough. And Captain De Luca did warn us."

Paul glanced at her, his lips quirking at her comment. Kaya merely smiled, a real smile, which she'd shown more and more of these last months. It wasn't the taut, strained smile from their time in San Grigori.

"Still an option," he offered. "And one that looks better all the time."

One of the men shifted, but Paul didn't look at him. The three men seemed to have stilled, uncertain when their prey didn't behave as they thought prey ought. And where had Azizi wandered off to?

Kaya met his gaze, her hands loose at her sides. "Perhaps." She looked doubtful, however. "I had not realized the Papal States were so besieged by brigands."

"Give us your coin," one of the men snapped.

He moved forward, confident in his anger and the weak blade he called a knife. In a country where most men carried knives, Paul expected better. Skill, at the very least, or perhaps he was simply biased in his and Kaya's own skill. Paul met the bandit's gaze, confident. Everything in him strained to protect her, even as he knew she could protect herself. Especially from this trio.

"You've interrupted an outing with my wife," Paul growled. "'Tis a beautiful day, and we've a picnic planned. Run along, and we'll forget we ever saw you. You can even keep your knives."

The man stopped, seemingly stunned at Paul's answer. Then he laughed, an ugly sort of guffaw that curled Paul's lip. In the near distance, he heard Azizi's sharp bark.

"I'm going to gut you and then enjoy your pretty wife."

"You'll do no such thing," Kaya snapped.

Paul didn't have to look at her to know she now held her khanjar, the beautifully carved knife her grandfather had given her. Nearly eight months of marriage, and he was still jealous of that knife. One day, they'd have to find a blacksmith and have one made.

"Sorry, sweetheart." Paul spoke in English and spared her a glance. "That one is mine."

"*Kama chaa.*" She shrugged and waved him on.

The man lunged. Paul, annoyed by the entire encounter, easily sidestepped and knocked the knife from his hand. He caught the offending blade with his left hand and punched the man with his right. Staggering backward, holding his nose, the man's brown eyes widened comically.

As rough as these men looked, they also looked hungry. They stood here because they needed money to buy food, or wine, and they were desperate enough to attack them on this mountain pass.

None of it compared to Paul's lifetime of fighting.

Through the blood and pain, the man mumbled, "I'm going to gut you and watch you bleed out slowly."

"Not likely." Paul held up the knife. "I have your only weapon."

From the corner of his eye, Paul caught the other two men move in unison, They ignored Kaya completely. She stepped between them and brandished her khanjar, and with quick, graceful movements, she sliced the back of both men's hands before they even realized she was a threat.

It was her favorite move when it came to bandits, injuring them just enough that they were no longer a threat, but never enough to truly harm them. Their knives clattered to the ground. Paul loved watching her fight, even in something as basic as scaring off clumsy would-be thieves.

The man with the broken nose lunged at him, a bungling attempt that made Paul scowl.

They couldn't always scare off brigands with a quick slice to their hands. Paul suspected these boys were far more frightened than he and Kaya were. Or perhaps just desperate. The wealth on the peninsula was vast and outlandish, and the poverty was soul-crushing.

Just then, Azizi bounded over the hill as if she always listened to the first summons. But she seemed more interested in sniffing the fallen knives than anything, and barely spared a glance at the trio of bleeding men.

"Good girl," Kaya said in Egyptian, scratching the dog behind her ears. "You keep the men at bay. *Aibqaa muta'ahiban.*"

Azizi sat guard and growled. The two men with bleeding hands, who hadn't moved since Kaya disarmed them, now stumbled back in shock. Clearly, they had expected easy prey—a defenseless couple walking a deserted path along the mountainside, with no guards or footmen.

"You can run off now," Paul told the man with the bloody nose. "Or we can continue this." He flipped the ill-weighted knife and wondered where the man had found it. Or maybe he made it. "You won't win."

Scowling, the man jerked his head and disappeared over the hill Azizi had just come from, into the trees littered along the mountainside.

"Clearly not how they expected their afternoon to go." Paul watched the remaining two fumble about, as if hoping to recover their knives, before they ran off in the same direction. "Not how I expected to spend mine, either." He took a step toward Kaya but stopped before he could reach for her. "You're unharmed?"

"I am." She smiled. Not the smile from before, but not the strained one, either. Progress. But for every step forward, they fell two back. "All is not lost." Kaya eyed the knives on the rocky ground with disdain. "I find it difficult to believe those knives scared anyone." She met his gaze. "Or those men. They looked quite uncertain in their attempt to rob us, and they were half-starved. If they'd asked politely, I would've shared our meal."

"Perhaps that was their first attempt." Paul bent and scooped up the knives. Plain, short things with dull blades. That surprised him, but he couldn't figure out why. Dull blades were hardly uncommon, but if one were planning a crime with only a knife, it should be a decent weapon.

"Then again," Kaya continued. She picked up their basket, which sat perfectly untouched between them. "These three were better than the gang we met outside Rome."

"True," Paul agreed darkly.

A day after stepping off the boat in Rome, the Tiber glistening around them, the weather warm despite the early spring, they'd been beset in the center of the city by a larger, more organized band of criminals. Ten men had surrounded them and demanded their coin and their dog.

Azizi had not liked that. She planted herself in front of the stocky leader, growling and snarling enough to make even the most fearsome man pause. When those men threatened her dog, Kaya attacked. Paul tried not to make that muddy, messy alleyway fight into any sort of omen.

But now, weeks later, it still weighed on him. Not the robberies, per se, though those were annoyingly frequent, but the heavy, aching fear that he'd irreparably damaged their relationship. That choking, soiled knowledge that the man he thought he'd left in Bombay lurked just beneath the surface. He regretted showing Kaya the man he had been before meeting her.

"We're not far from the summit," he said and took the basket from Kaya. He paused, uncertain. "Or did you want to turn back?"

"After all this? Definitely not." She smiled, petting Azizi's large head and turning on the path. "As much as I enjoy the views, all these brigands are..." She waved a hand and turned to face him. "Worrisome."

Paul snorted and took her hand, a gesture as natural as breathing. She didn't flinch from his touch, and something in him relaxed. Every time he reached for her, he feared she'd pull back, recoil in horror and disgust. She hadn't, but the fear gnawed at him. "Worrisome? That's what you call four threats in a week? Worrisome?"

"Is there a better word? Annoying? Exasperating?" She shook her head, and her headscarf flittered in the wind as they crested the final hill. "Oh, this is beautiful."

She stopped and closed her eyes, letting the mountain wind blow around her as if she were naught more than a statue. Still and stunning, a slight smile on her face, hand still in his, Kaya stole his breath.

Paul wanted to always see this serene contentment about her.

Silently setting the basket on the ground, Paul stepped behind her and wrapped his arms around her waist. He rested his chin on her shoulder and took in the view. As stunning as the view of the Adriatic was from Monte Titano, nothing steadied him like holding his wife.

Kaya leaned against him, covering his hands with hers. "I like it here," she said, just loud enough to be heard over the wind.

They spoke in English, despite their monthslong stay in Calabria and now the Papal States. Paul wanted to resume his lessons in Egyptian, but he felt that was too intimate considering the state of their marriage. Or maybe it was only his feeling, this distance between them.

The distance he'd created and now had absolutely no idea how to breach.

He shook himself free of the thoughts that raced round his head with no end or answer. He kissed the side of Kaya's jaw, stepped back, and spread out the blanket.

"We can stay," he said casually. "San Marino is beautiful. Close enough to the water for a visit, not too many people around to bother us."

He looked at her as she knelt by the basket, taking out the chicken and cheese, the bowls of pasta they'd managed not to spill on their trek. And their bottles of orange and bergamot juice. No wine—never again. It still called to him, the sweet taste as it slid down his throat.

He'd spent the previous months battling that call.

No doubt he'd battle it for the rest of his life, but he'd win. One day at a time.

"True." She settled beside him, looking out over the plateau, seemingly unbothered by the constant wind. "I do enjoy the view. What would we do here?"

"Do?" Paul frowned. "What do you want to do?"

"I do not know." She picked up a plate and served chicken, pasta, tomatoes, and the last of the previous summer's zucchini. "What do people do?"

He opened his mouth but floundered. "Work, I suppose. But we don't need to work. Not to survive."

"No." She shot him a mischievous grin—he loved that grin—but she didn't acknowledge the jewels and gold sewn into the waist of her gown.

"Purchase a house?" Kaya shrugged and handed him a plate.

Taking it, he laughed and leaned over their food to kiss her. Azizi, curious and constantly hungry, lifted her head from the basket and woofed at them.

"None for you, precious," Kaya admonished. "You know better."

Azizi, undeterred, nuzzled Kaya's hand in an obvious plea for either affection or food. Or both.

"Go hunt," Paul ordered. The dog merely looked at him. "Or sleep." He laughed and scratched under her chin.

Azizi offered another playful yip and bounded off into the tree line. Paul shook his head. He'd never been the dog type. Then again, he'd never been the marrying type, either. Here he was, with a wife he adored and a dog he'd grown accustomed to in a shockingly short period of time.

"And there's plenty of places for Azizi to roam."

"She likes it here, yes. But is it right for us?" Kaya nibbled a piece of chicken, her head tilted as she looked back over the view.

Paul desperately wanted to know what she thought. Despite their short marriage, he'd once fancied he could read her mind. They'd talked about so much, shared dreams and hopes for the future, a thirst for adventure and knowledge. Those first months had been idyllic.

"How would you spend your days?" She paused and frowned. "How would I spend mine?"

"Yes, we've established that neither of us knows how to remain idle." Paul stopped and shrugged. "I've no idea. What do people do all day when not traveling?" He frowned and tried to remember his childhood.

As if reading his mind, Kaya asked, "What did you do before joining the Company?"

"Fetched and carried for the maids," he whispered.

He'd done so in the house his mum worked in. Staring out over the Adriatic, he tried to envision his mum or the master of the house. Possibly his father—Paul never knew and no longer cared. But there was nothing. He couldn't picture either person, not even the house. Not any longer.

How had the master spent his days? Paul tried to remember, tried to see past his hatred of that house, his loathing of the memories there and the friendship he'd formed with Harry Appleby that ended long before Harry died.

"Cultivating our wealth?" Paul shrugged. "You could host tea parties." He snickered again, trying, and utterly failing, to envision Kaya hosting a tea party. "Or the San Marino equivalent of a tea party."

"I don't even know what tea tastes like." She sniffed and scowled at him, but her dark eyes danced with humor. "Or *you* could. Is there a male equivalent of tea parties? Perhaps the ladies of San Marino would prefer you as their host."

Laughing aloud, he shook his head. "I have absolutely no idea and no desire to find out."

They ate in silence, but Paul watched her. She didn't pull away, though she sat just out of his reach. The ease between them today, as they enjoyed the quiet solitude, gave him hope. Perhaps all had not been lost. Perhaps he still had a chance to make things right with Kaya.

To show her he was the man she knew before San Grigori. The man he strived to be.

"I'm unused to being still," she said abruptly. "My days have always been filled with activity. Studies or practice." She met his gaze, but this time no humor shone there. Only the sadness of having left her family behind.

"If we stay in San Marino, I can write Roberto again and send along a letter to Cairo." Paul grasped desperately at straws, hoping to ease her sorrow. He reminded himself that one conversation—or weeks' worth, in their case—could not repair everything between them.

"We've just sent Marta there," she reminded him, her voice soft.

"All the more reason to write." But he heard something in her tone. Something that nagged at him...

Ah. There it was. Paul wanted to smack himself for not realizing it sooner. "You miss Marta."

Startled, Kaya met his gaze. The sorrow in her eyes told him all he needed to know. Since landing in Rome, Kaya hadn't mentioned Marta, but he saw now that she hadn't forgotten her friend. Her grief was not only for her grandfather, who was still in Cairo, but for the friends she'd made in Italy.

"She is safer with the Spanòs." Her voice broke, and she cleared her throat. "Away from that village and the people who did nothing to help her, when she gave everything to protect them."

"Marta is braver than most people." Paul shifted closer and reached for Kaya's hand. Her fingers tightened around his, but the slight pull of her lips looked tired and worn. "With the Spanòs, no one will ever question whatever story Marta spins."

"Do you think I am who I believe I am?" Kaya asked abruptly.

"What?" Paul blinked in the bright sun. Azizi had wandered back to their clearing and flopped next to Kaya. The dog curled into a tight ball and nestled her nose in her bushy tail. "What brought that on?"

"Would Derya and my mother have lied? Would Gidd have taken me in?"

Paul took a moment and swirled his pasta around his spoon. Chewing slowly, he said what he'd always thought.

"Tahir believed Derya. He trusted the letter your mother had on her when she escaped Istanbul for Cairo." Paul watched her, but Kaya didn't meet his gaze. She stared into the bowl of noodles as if it held the answers she sought.

"Derya maintained that story my whole life," she admitted.

"Whether Tahir believed her or not, he took them both in because they needed help. He could've taken you to an orphanage and kicked Derya out onto the streets. He could have contacted the Ottomans and let them know a woman claiming to be the daughter of the sultan was on his doorstep."

Paul tilted her chin and looked into her wary gaze. Words tripped on his tongue. Promises of love for this amazing woman, vows of protection, pledges to never leave her. He swallowed them all.

One step at a time.

"Tahir protected you for decades. He lied to one of the most powerful empires in the world. He lied to everyone to keep you safe. Trained you to keep yourself safe."

"Hm," Kaya hummed. "Yet after the way Appleby treated Marta, to keep her family safe, her parents shunned her. Banished her from the entire village." She looked south, as if she could see San Grigori, or even farther, to Villa San Giovanni. As if she could see Marta.

"She has a fresh start now," Paul reminded her. He hoped she heard the deeper meaning in his words. The fresh start they needed. "We gave her that fresh start with Olivia and the new babe. Money she never had, never would've hoped to have. A chance. A choice. What she does now is up to her."

Kaya nodded and closed the distance between them to kiss

him softly. "Yes. Thank you." She cupped his cheek and pressed her lips to his again. "We'll write Roberto and tell him our travel plans."

Paul heard what she didn't say. She didn't believe there would be word from Cairo. Tahir would never endanger her by acknowledging he'd received a letter, much less replying. He'd spent her entire life keeping her safe from enemies real and imagined. That wily old man wasn't going to stop because he had contracted her to marry an Englishman and they'd fled Cairo that same night.

"Perhaps San Marino is not right for us."

Kaya sniffed and shook her head. One hand was buried in Azizi's fur, and the other was still in his. "Perhaps not. Far too many brigands about."

Seven

Their inn in Domagnano was a small, well-kept establishment. The dining hall was large and spacious, the room comfortable and clean, and the stables swept daily by a pair of boys who'd rather chase each other, and Azizi, than see to their duties.

Kaya liked it here, the freshness of the area, the openness of the mountain. The distance from San Grigori and the memories that village held.

Sitting in the back gardens, Azizi snoozing by her side, she let the near-constant breeze wash over her. The late-morning sun shone down, warming her in the chill of spring. If she closed her eyes, she could block out the sounds of the stableboys and the clatter of the maids as they hauled their cleaning buckets about the inn.

She imagined she was back in Cairo. Derya in the kitchens, she at her studies in the gardens. Reading about great Egyptian generals and battle tactics. Kaya frowned and tried to focus on her gardens as they had been. Her lush sanctuary, not the dead vines and withering leaves.

However, that was all she could see, the brown vines. The air heavy with despondency and fear. Even her neighbors, unseen her entire life, had disappeared. Kaya never discovered what happened to them.

The clatter of buckets startled her, and she looked to the maids, who were hastening down the stairs, yelling in Calabrian. The breeze, momentarily chilly, made her sit straighter, her fingers digging into Azizi's fur.

Azizi's presence comforted her, and Kaya looked down at the dozing dog, smiling. Yesterday, atop the mountain, had been the first time in weeks they'd laughed together with such freedom, such ease.

"I love our time together," she told Azizi now. She whispered the words, so they died on the wind. She was afraid to say them too loud, though no one bothered her here. "And I would not trade you, precious."

Azizi opened one eye and bumped Kaya's hand with her large snout, as if she understood and agreed.

Paul had set out long before breakfast to inquire about a ship up the coast to Venice. They had not settled on a plan, whether to stay in San Marino or continue traveling. However, she had to agree: the number of bandits in the Papal States was truly alarming. Once they left the relative safety of the inn, they were constantly beset by would-be thieves.

Kaya had offered to accompany him. Paul had agreed, then hastily offered to go himself and allow her the morning alone. Confused, Kaya had agreed. Then that unease returned. So here she sat, in the rear gardens, alone, with only Azizi and her whirling thoughts for company.

Things had never been like this between them. Not even that first night, as they'd walked out of the gates of Cairo and into *al-ṣaḥrā' al-kubrá*. Quiet, yes. She had not known how to properly converse with a stranger, and Paul was never one for inane chatter. But not like this, where they knew so much about each other but still danced so awkwardly, as if strangers once more. She had thought their time walking east from Rome helped, but it was not as restful as that.

"Signora Conrad!" Marion Zanotti, the proprietress of the inn, huffed as she hurried from the kitchens.

Azizi lifted her head but didn't move from Kaya's side. "No, Azizi. Stay where you are."

The dog eyed her, clearly unhappy, but sat on guard. She didn't like Marion, and the feeling was mutual. However, the stable lads and the maids liked Azizi, and none of them gave Marion any cause to banish the dog from her inn.

Then again, their coin was too plentiful for her to banish her best—and only—paying guests.

"Your husband, he disappeared before the sun came up," Marion huffed, hands on her hips. "Is he returning?"

Kaya's heart skipped. It'd long been her fear, Paul abandoning her. He never gave her cause, of course. The moment her sheltered life became less so, she had learned painful lessons. Abandonment was one of them.

And these last months had been so hard, their finding each other again. Her finding herself.

"Of course," she snapped. Tempering her tone, annoyed with both her slip of control and that flutter of fear, she added, "He travels to Riccione." She tilted her head to study Marion and didn't rise from her favorite chair. "Why would you think otherwise?"

Marion huffed again. The set of her lips told Kaya more than her vitriolic words could. Ah. She had been abandoned. She'd had to make her way in this world alone and without resources. That explained much about Marion Zanotti, and Kaya was surprised at herself for not recognizing that sooner.

Except her dislike of Azizi. It did not explain that.

"We shall be staying at least through next week," Kaya said, quieter now. She settled back in her chair, all too conscious of the gold and jewels sewn about her waist. They dug painfully into her. "Thank you for your hospitality."

She hadn't necessarily meant it to be the cold dismissal it sounded like. But her thoughts whirled like a haboob, and they were just as relentless. That wasn't Marion's fault. No, that was—well, no one's, perhaps.

What she needed to do was speak with Paul. Truly, honestly speak with him. She had hoped their picnic yesterday might be the day they broke through the barrier between them, but the would-be thieves had not helped.

And the words she had spoken were not ones she wanted to admit. They'd spilled out, clunky and awkward, a fear she had skirted for months and not truly admitted to herself until she heard it. Who was she? Who was Paul? More importantly, what were they together? She thought she knew, but that was before San Grigori and the opium smugglers.

Before Paul's past caught up with them and threatened all they'd worked for.

The sun had shifted, moved beyond the high walls of the inn. Cold without its rays, Kaya stood from her broken solitude. So did Azizi.

"Let's walk, shall we?" Kaya asked, though of course she didn't expect an answer.

Alone, she and her dog walked from the rear gardens and toward one of the many mountain paths. Beyond the inn's walls, the sun shone brightly, but it did little to warm her. Paul would return, of course he would, and they—what?

"Marriage is not easy, Azizi." Kaya looked down to the dog, who easily kept pace with her. "Don't ever get married."

Laughing at her own absurdity, Kaya turned for the coast. She liked looking over the Adriatic. She'd always wanted to see the water, travel across the vast oceans. But her seasickness as they'd crossed the Mediterranean had told her all she needed to know about her relationship with the sea. Her time on the packet ship hadn't helped.

"Have you met any other wolves, Azizi?" Kaya asked as they climbed the mountain. "Domagnano was once known as a haven of wolves."

Azizi, sniffing beside her, offered no answer. That was all

right; Kaya enjoyed the silence. Even if it meant being alone with her own thoughts.

"*Grazie*, Mary." Kaya smiled at the serving girl and waited until she left the dining room.

Only she and Paul dined tonight, typical of their stay here. Spring was no time for the rich, who traveled to these warmer shores on their Grand Tours or honeymoons. That suited Kaya perfectly well. She had no desire to share this view with anyone other than Paul. And Azizi, of course.

Because one ought to have a guard dog.

Solitude and dogs aside, Kaya waited until she was certain they were alone. She did not wish anyone to overhear their conversation. In the months since leaving Cairo, she'd discovered the majority of people were suspicious of outsiders. Whereas she wished to know all she could and explore every nook of this world, most people mistrusted those they had not known all their lives.

Swallowing the last of her tuna and noodles, she broke off a chunk of bread and gathered her thoughts. Truly, she stalled for time. Nerves danced in her belly, but she forced herself to swallow the bite of bread.

"Do you regret what you had to do?"

Oh, no. Kaya closed her eyes and wanted to disappear under the table. That was absolutely not how she wished to begin their conversation. Where was the woman who knew exactly what to say as they'd gathered to stop the smugglers? That woman was capable.

"Yes." Paul didn't even pretend to misunderstand. He set his mug of juice on the table and looked across at her. His face was tanned from his walk to the port, and when his gaze met hers, the blue-green looked haunted. Sad. Desperate.

Kaya didn't know how to ease that desperation. Nor did she

know what to say. All her carefully planned words vanished in the face of his despair. She reached for his hand, then simply held it.

They touched so infrequently now. First it was because Paul secluded himself in the bedroom of Marta's cottage, willing the opium and alcohol from his body. Then it was because, well, Kaya wasn't entirely certain. He hadn't initiated anything, and she hadn't, either.

Which led them here, to this impasse.

"Shall we walk?" Paul asked, standing from the table. He tugged her hand, and Kaya willing walked beside him.

"Where would you like to go?" she asked as they exited the door by the stables. "It's far too dark to see the mountain paths."

"No, let's stay close to town."

"Town" was a generous term, but Kaya swallowed that nervous bubble of words. They did not need the distraction. Hadn't she told herself that on her walk this afternoon as she waited for Paul's return?

She cleared her throat and tried to remember what she wanted to say. Outside, the night had cooled considerably. Kaya didn't have her cloak or gloves, but she didn't wish to break whatever closeness they'd forged between them.

She could warm up later, by the fire. If she left now, she didn't know if they'd ever reclaim the closeness they'd once shared.

"It's my fault." Paul's abrupt words surprised her.

Slowing their pace, she tentatively slipped her hand through the crook of his elbow. Paul automatically covered her fingers as he always did. Something in her eased, and she looked up at him. The wind continued to whip fiercely around them, sending the ends of her hijab fluttering over his arms.

"What I did to stop Appleby." He blew out a breath and stared straight ahead. "The drinking, the secrets I kept. I hate that I had to do that."

"You—the secrets weren't... I mean, I understand." Kaya stumbled over her words, uncertain now that they faced what had happened. She wanted to take a firm stand, but she didn't understand so much of what Paul went through. The line between her certainty and understanding wavered. "You warned me that you were not a nice man, but you meant in your past. All I saw was the present. The man you wished to be."

"I hate what you saw." His words slowed, but Kaya didn't think he realized. "I never wanted you to know the sort of man I had been. It chokes me—" He scrubbed a hand down his face. "I hate everything I did in San Grigori." He turned to face her in the semidarkness of the tree line. "But ridding the world of Rogerson and Appleby was right. It was the only thing to do."

"Yes." She cupped his cheek and met his gaze. "Yes. It was."

"It won't stop the opium. I doubt anything will. But it helped the village. And Marta."

"She's far better with the Spanòs," Kaya agreed. "A fresh start for her and Olivia."

Kaya struggled to ask her question, the one that burned through her every day. Every night, when Paul held her but did not touch her. They hadn't made love since before they'd stopped the smuggling operation.

She missed him. Terribly.

Even when he held her, or she rested her head against his chest, the distance between them felt like lifetimes. As far as they now stood from her home in Cairo.

"What happens now?" she whispered into the wind. In the distance, she thought she heard Azizi, but the dog had disappeared during supper. She'd return before bed; she always did. "Will you always choose wine over me? Is the call that strong?"

"I don't know," he admitted. He took her hand and kissed her palm.

Shivering, she closed her eyes. She missed that touch.

"I'll try. Every day. It's easier when we talk." He stopped and seemed to struggle with what to say next. "It's...I don't know, but when I can tell you I want a drink, it—it eases it." He blew out a breath and stepped from her.

"Paul." She grabbed for his hand, stopping him.

"You shouldn't have to carry that burden, Kaya."

"No. Don't walk away from me. Please don't." She took his hand again and cradled it between her colder ones. Her heart thundered in her ears, and she gripped his hands too tightly. "Tell me."

"It's been weeks." He chuckled, a short bitter sound. "But I spent several of those trapped in a cottage in the snow."

"Did it help?" she asked, still struggling to find both words and footing in this conversation. But she didn't want it to stop. Not when they talked more, now, about what happened than in the previous months.

"Being trapped in the cottage Appleby abused Marta in?" His laugh was hard and acrid. "No wonder she didn't want to stay in that village."

"Being alone in the cottage." Kaya tried not to think about all that had happened in that house.

"Yes." He pressed his fingers to his eyes and sighed. "Yes, it did. Removed the temptation, so to speak."

"But you still feel it." She still did not understand his craving, but she desperately hoped to. Or at least hoped to help him avoid temptation.

"Every day." He lifted her hands and pressed them to his chest. "But two months has to count for something, yes?"

"Two months is better than two days," Kaya agreed, and another band eased from around her heart. "Yes. One day at a time. I won't let you fall, Paul."

"I will," he warned. "But I'll need you to catch me. And I hate to put that on you."

"Always."

Just then, Azizi, with truly spectacular timing, bounded from the woods with a happy woof. Laughing, Kaya let the moment fade into the night. Perhaps she had been wrong to believe they could solve everything in one conversation. But the relief and joy moving through her now told her all was not lost.

"You still wish to sail for Venice?" Paul asked as they

continued around the village, a sprawled-out construction that claimed Monte Titano as surely as the mountain claimed the view of the Adriatic.

"No." She laughed, far lighter than was warranted, given her loathing of the water. "However, I'm weary of these bandits. Marion claims they have the blessing of the local officials, but I find that difficult to believe."

"I don't." Paul snorted. "Greed is pervasive, and with so many aristocrats ripe for the picking, it's easy to see why people steal."

"Hm. If the landowners truly cared about anything save themselves, we would not need to fend off thieves with every turn." She hated the way the peasants were treated here, as if they were less than nothing. No, she didn't blame them for wanting more. Though if they could perhaps not attempt to rob them every time they stepped from the inn, Kaya would greatly appreciate it. "Perhaps it's best we leave, yes."

"It won't be better anywhere else," Paul warned, turning them back toward the inn.

"No, it won't," she quietly agreed. It never was.

The brightly lit inn came back into view. Despite the lack of travelers, several lampposts shone with candles, flickering in the wind even through their glass enclosures. The warmth of that light beckoned her, and she dropped a hand to Azizi's head and scratched behind her ears.

"I don't wish to settle in San Marino. It does not feel right."

"No, it doesn't." He stopped and turned to face her. "But I'm glad we stayed."

Leaning down, he kissed her. Kaya sighed into his kiss, letting the warmth from his touch spread through her. She missed this, missed him so much.

Never again. No matter what she had to do or say, never again would she let months of awkward silence and ignored conversations pass between them.

"I love you, Paul." She stepped back and took his hand. "Let's go to bed."

Eight

Paul took his time tasting her. It'd been far too long since they made love, and he wanted to savor every moment. Part of him wanted to rush, wanted to feel Kaya tighten around him as she climaxed, wanted to lose himself in her.

But not tonight. Tonight was for reacquainting and remembering.

With each tie he unraveled, each layer he removed, Paul worshiped his wife. Laying her skirts over the bench, he knelt before her. Gliding his fingers up her strong calves and thighs, he untied the ribbon that held up her stocking. He rolled it down, trailing his mouth along newly exposed flesh.

Words tumbled on his tongue. He missed her. He was sorry. He loved her. Paul swallowed them all. Tomorrow, in the sunlit day, he'd tell her. Tomorrow, he'd find the words he hadn't known how to speak before.

Tonight, he'd let his body tell her of his love.

He untied the second stocking, taking care to roll it down her beautiful leg, tasting the inside of her thigh. Kaya shuddered beneath his touch, her fingers curling in his hair.

"Paul."

He looked up, catching her dark eyes as they held his. "I love you, Kaya."

Her fingers clenched in his scalp, and she pulled him to her. Her mouth was soft against his, yet insistent. Hesitant but wanting. He thought he could lose himself in her kiss, in her taste.

Laying her on the bed, Paul quickly shed his own clothing. In his haste, he struggled with his boots, but he refused to let anything stand between him and making love with Kaya.

"Perhaps we should look for a boot maker." She giggled, a sound so unlike Kaya, Paul paused.

Staring at her, he noticed something he hadn't before. Or maybe it had been there during their travels around Sicily, but he'd forgotten it in the last months. Happiness. Joy. She smiled up at him, naked on the bedding. A temptation he had never been able to ignore.

I missed you.

Paul swallowed the words but smiled. Kneeling at the end of the bed, he kissed the inside of her thigh. "We have time." Light as a butterfly's touch, he trailed his fingers up to her heat. "All the time. Ships leave Riccione daily." He pressed his lips just below her belly button and felt her sharp intake of breath.

"Yes," she hissed. It wasn't in response to their newest mode of travel.

Her heat beckoned him, and Paul pressed a finger to her nub. She arched beneath him, crying out. Settling between her legs, Paul breathed deeply of her scent and kissed her wetness. Kaya's fingers dug into his shoulders, and she moaned his name, opening wider for him.

"Yes, come for me, Kaya." He thrust two fingers into her, leaning on an elbow to watch her as the pleasure shuddered through her. "That's it, sweetheart."

Kaya cried out, hands bunching the bedding beneath her. He built her orgasm up again, pressing hard to her clit, aching to bury himself in her but wanting this more. Wanting to watch her climax, her pleasure vibrate through her.

Gasping his name, she blinked open her eyes. They were heavy with pleasure, her arms limp at her sides as she gulped in air.

God, he'd missed that, watching her lose herself in his touch.

"Hmm," she hummed, a lazy smile stretching her lips even as her eyes slid closed again.

Paul laughed, his body tight for her. "Hmm?" he repeated. "That's all?"

"When I can remember how to form words…" Her voice trailed off, but her smile remained. That was enough for Paul.

Kissing her hip, he skimmed his hands up her sides and cupped her breasts. Her nipples, hard points, beckoned him, and Paul leaned down to taste them. "I'm not finished," he whispered against her fragrant skin.

He took each nipple in his mouth, teeth scraping over them, then rolled them between his fingers. Beneath him, Kaya sobbed his name, her nails scraping down his back to dig into his arse.

Paul hissed out a curse, his control hanging by a thread. Settling between her legs, he slowly guided himself into her. Kaya gasped, shifting to fully seat him. Damn, he'd missed being in her. Missed the bond between them.

He moved slowly, watching her as she touched herself. Jaw clenched, hands fisted by her side, Paul held himself in check even as he thrust harder and faster.

"Paul!" she cried out, coming as his control snapped.

His own climax raced up his spine, and just before he completely lost control, he pulled out and came on her belly. He rolled to the side, gasping for breath as his heart finally slowed. Beside him, Kaya hummed in contentment, her arms stretched high over her head as she sighed.

When he judged his legs able to hold him, Paul stood and searched for a linen. After he cleaned them both up, he grabbed his shirt and her chemise.

"I hope you aren't cold." Paul scowled at the foot of the bed, where Azizi was curled on the heavy wool blanket they'd pushed aside. "Your wolf has claimed the blanket for herself."

"Oh, precious." Kaya grinned and sat up, tugging her chemise over her head and searching for her dressing gown.

It'd been one of their first purchases upon arriving in Rome. If they stayed along the coast, she wouldn't need the heavy wool much longer.

Paul wanted to shower her with gifts. Anything she wanted, everything she desired. All his life, he'd wanted enough money to do with as he pleased, and now that they had gold and jewels, all he wanted to do was buy things for Kaya. They hadn't purchased much since Damietta, but perhaps when they settled, wherever they did so, he'd buy her every comfort imaginable.

With a gracefulness he adored, Kaya sank to the floor next to Azizi. He brought the stubby trio of candles to the bedside table and watched the light flicker over Kaya's face. She looked far more relaxed than this morning.

"You're a good dog," she cooed and scratched the dog's belly. "But we need that blanket. The nights are far too cold without it."

Azizi, one eye open as she soaked up the belly rubs, looked not at Kaya but at Paul. He thought, as he often had over the last months, that the dog judged him. And found him wanting.

Perhaps the sounds of Kaya's pleasure still echoing in his blood put to rest whatever Azizi thought of him.

"Come on, Azizi." Kaya tugged the blanket, much to Azizi's disgruntlement.

"I did ask about bringing a dog with us," Paul said abruptly.

"Yes?" Kaya sat on the bed beside him and shook out the blanket. Azizi yipped at it, trying to catch the end, but she shooed her away. "And what did they say? I presume they were agreeable, as you said you found passage."

Paul laughed and curled around her. Yes, right here. This was what he missed. The warmth of her body against his beneath the blanket. The press of her arse as she wiggled to get comfortable. Draping an arm over her waist, he pulled her tighter to him and kissed her shoulder.

He probably should have lit the room's small brazier. At the very least found the spare blanket they'd paid far too much for.

He did none of those things. Instead, he held Kaya tighter. It wasn't an unreasonable fear, thinking she'd pull back. One conversation and a brilliant night of passion didn't make up for the months of distance. The past that came back to grip him by the throat. His own recriminations.

"I only mentioned we had a dog, not the half wolf part."

"She's a Calabrese Shepherd," Kaya said primly, but he heard the laughter in her voice

"I did mention that, yes." Paul pressed his lips to her shoulder, unable to stop his own smile.

They lay like that awhile, and he felt her relax in his arms. Her fingers twined with his, her head resting on his arm. Paul thought he could lie like that forever.

Though they traveled light, they couldn't leave immediately. Kaya had promised Marion they were staying another week, and while she didn't mind paying for the days they would not be here, they still needed things.

Ginger, for one, in case Paul was wrong about her ability to handle the Adriatic Sea from Riccione to Venice. To be fair, she'd survived the journey to Rome, but she remained wary. She'd need to steep the ginger in boiled water for at least a day to properly infuse it for their trip—possibly longer. But Kaya refused to acknowledge that slight need to dawdle. Still, she was waiting on a new dress from the local seamstress, and Paul a greatcoat that didn't tear at the shoulders. Plus, no one moved on Sundays.

By midweek, however, they declined the use of a donkey and walked from Domagnano toward Riccione.

"You are much taller than the average local," Kaya laughed as they finally left Domagnano behind them. "Perhaps we should have waited on a better pair of boots for you."

He shrugged, shifted the long beam they carried for their tent, and shot her a grin. "I'll survive until we reach Venice."

Azizi walked beside them, as if she, too, knew how desperately Kaya wished to put distance between them and that small village.

"Did you encounter any difficulties on your walk to Riccione?" Kaya suddenly asked. "I hadn't thought about it until now, and you didn't mention anything."

"If by difficulties you mean brigands, no." He grunted and moved his shoulders. "I forgot how awkward this thing is." But he continued on, not even slowing. "Surprisingly," he added.

"Perhaps it is me, then, who attracts so many." Kaya tucked the end of her hijab behind her shoulder. "Or Azizi."

"You think we'll encounter a band today?" Paul chuckled. "No doubt. Shall we wager?"

"I do not gamble," she sniffed. But her words held no heat. She knew Paul offered in jest, just as she knew he understood her reasons for not gambling. "And that is a bad bet to offer."

"After lunch, then," he said, as if she'd agreed to that wager. "Azizi will wander off, and a band of thieves will wander in."

"You have very little faith in the local authorities." Kaya paused as they skidded down a path, strewing loose rocks along the way. Up was a far easier walk than down, but down was the only way from San Marino to Riccione.

"I've seen very few local authorities. Even the Fortress Guards we've heard so much about seem absent. Or at least uninterested in these thieves. I've got you." Paul's hand steadied her just when she thought she'd lose her balance.

They walked in silence for a while then, steadily making their way from Monte Titano. The day had dawned bright and clear, as it had for weeks, but it was colder than the previous week. The wind chilled her fingers and nose, but Kaya was eager to arrive at their next destination, so they continued on.

"Marion packed lunch," she said eventually. The sun shone high overhead, and she stopped to enjoy it. As warm as walking downhill made her, the sun felt good on her upturned face.

"Tuna and noodles?" he asked, skidding the last few feet to the base of the path.

"A most excellent guess." Azizi wandered into the trees, and Kaya watched her.

She always returned, but on their walk from Rome to Domagnano, she'd discovered the locals weren't fond of wolves. Even half wolves. Kaya disagreed, but she had no real way to keep Azizi beside her at all times.

"I think it's all she knows how to make," Kaya admitted, returning the conversation to Marion. "I don't think this is the life she saw for herself, but she's trying to make the best of it."

"Aye." He met her gaze and shrugged. It caused the wooden beam to shift at an odd angle, and he cursed. "Damn thing," he muttered.

Kaya hid a smile, even as Paul changed *damn* to *drat* with a side look of apology.

"We'll stop at the base of the next mountain?" Kaya peered ahead, uncertain where their path took them, except for east. It couldn't be much farther to the coast now. They'd set out after breakfast, and Paul assured her it was only a five-hour walk. "Enjoy our tuna and noodle lunch?"

"*Ciao, amici miei.*"

Kaya froze at the menacingly polite greeting. Then she slowly turned to look at the single man, a stout ruffian with a very impressive knife, and eased her khanjar from its sheath on her waist. Once. Once she had agreed not to carry her knife in so obvious a place. That once had led to her almost being kidnapped. Never again.

"Oh, for Christ's sake," Paul muttered. "It's not even noon."

Kaya's lips twitched, and she met her husband's gaze. "It is not even after lunch. You were wrong. Does this mean I win the wager I most assuredly do not approve of?"

Paul grunted and sighed. "Name your price, my princess."

The purse thief, who clearly had no cause to care about their conversation, brandished his knife in a truly impressive arc. Kaya remained unmoved, however, and flicked her wrist, showing her own—far more imposing—knife.

"One day, I would like to not be besieged by men trying to rob me," she told the man, who eyed her knife with something akin to envy. "Just one."

"Not today, sweetheart," Paul said, their pack already on the ground and out of his way. "I'm sorry about this."

Kaya could have told him not to bother, that she could easily handle one thief. But she did not. Paul protected her, and he took that duty seriously, as much as they both knew she could defend herself. But she liked it—far more than she expected. Knowing he loved her enough put his own life in jeopardy to protect her warmed her heart.

Privately, Kaya believed he liked showing off. Plus, she loved watching him fight. Even against a man who had only the size of his shoulders to scare his prey and not much else.

"Azizi!" Kaya called as Paul easily disarmed the robber. Paul kept the man's knife, and she turned and said, "You're amassing quite the collection."

"Bah. Some are not even worth the time to take them from these highwaymen. This one?" He eyed the blade, a carved beauty unlike any Kaya had seen since arriving on the peninsula. "It looks more like the kukri I've seen in Bombay."

A chill raced down Kaya's spine. Azizi barked, startling her from her memories. "You think he has something to do with the smuggling?" she whispered.

But the man was long gone. He'd disappeared into the mountains, as all the other disarmed would-be thieves had. Still, she looked in the direction he'd gone and wondered if the smuggling had, indeed, ended with the deaths of Major Rogerson and Harry Appleby.

"I don't know," Paul admitted just as quietly. "It's possible he took it from a ship, stole it from a passenger. They're not sold, far as I know, so he couldn't have legitimately purchased one." He struggled to reshoulder their pack with its long wooden beam.

Kaya listed it over his shoulders, hoping it settled evenly. "They're ceremonial, but deadly." He sighed. "I don't know."

"Let's find Riccione," she said, helping him adjust their pack. "I'm so weary of these attacks."

"Weary" was a far from strong enough word for what she felt just then. The cold crept down her spine, along with memories of those frozen nights as they'd tried to stop the opium smuggling.

"Aye," Paul agreed.

Unfortunately, their luck in encountering brigands was as good as ever. What was it Paul called them? Highwaymen? She'd have to ask him about that word. She hadn't heard it before.

At the base of the next mountain, a carriage had stopped on the side of the road. Two women, a well-dressed lady and a woman who looked like her companion or maid, and two footmen stood just off to the side of it.

Paul slowed, once more unshouldering the pack. He sensed it, too. The oddness of the scene, the too-quiet stillness of the people. This wasn't a simple broken axle or a damaged wheel. Azizi growled, drawing attention—the woman snapped her frightened gaze to them.

"We really need to stop finding trouble," Paul grumbled.

Nine

The woman, pale eyes wide and frozen in fear, held her companion, who was even now sobbing uncontrollably. She didn't move, just stared at them as if they were mirages in the desert. Kaya smiled, uncertain how to approach the clearly terrified women.

"Azizi, *tajid*." Her precious dog looked up at her. Kaya nodded. "*Tabie 'iitbae* Paul." Azizi snorted and disappeared around the carriage, close on the heels of Paul, who crept around the opposite side.

"Ciao," Kaya said quietly. The woman showed no recognition, though she surely knew that greeting. "Are you injured?" She stepped closer, a single small move.

The footmen moved to intervene. Kaya glared at them. Whatever had happened, they clearly hadn't protected their mistress, not with the woman's shaking, silent tears running down her too-pale cheeks. But the moment she tried to help, they stood at attention?

Men.

"There were two," Paul called. "Ran off when they saw Azizi." Kaya heard a muffled sound, then Paul's voice again. "Good dog, yes, you are."

"Do you need—" Kaya broke off when the woman sobbed, a great, gasping cry as she released her companion and raced to the other side of the carriage.

Kaya followed her and took in the mess. The door hung off its hinges, and belongings were strewn over the rocky land. A man, presumably the driver, lay dead on the road, a musket ball lodged in his throat.

"They took it!" the woman sobbed. She threw her remaining belongings into the road, scattering clothing over rocks and down the side of the ravine. "They took it!"

Kaya looked to the companion, who was still crying quietly, falling to her knees with a painful thud, in her own world of terror. The two footmen's expressions were blank as the woman tore through the already-scattered trunks, her cries growing louder.

"My miniature!" she cried.

Paul looked lost in the face of this woman's distress. Azizi sat beside him and howled in unison with the woman's cries. Uncertain, Kaya met Paul's gaze. He shrugged.

Kneeling beside the woman, awkward in offering comfort, especially to a stranger, Kaya tried to hush her. If for no other reason than to quiet Azizi. The wind whipped the window's curtains and flapped unmentionables along the road. Coins scattered over the dirt. It was as if the thieves had grabbed handfuls and left in a rush when she and Paul stumbled onto the scene.

"He took it," the woman sobbed, leaning into Kaya, hands covering her face. "He took it. He took it."

"I'll go after them." Paul sounded resigned. She looked up at him, and he shrugged. "What else can I do?" She nodded and offered the faintest of smiles. "They can't have gone too far. Keep Azizi with you, in case they have friends."

Kaya slowly untangled herself, leaving the woman sobbing over a painting. Not the clothing and coin the men stole. Or the jewels, given the woman's obvious wealth. Or the dead driver. A miniature. It must have held special meaning.

Kaya's heart twisted, and she wondered what she'd do to retrieve a miniature of Gidd or Derya. She had none, of course, but if she had, and they'd been stolen...she'd do whatever it took to recover them.

"Signora." Paul crouched before the woman and gently removed her hands from her face. "I'll find the miniature for you."

She nodded, her blonde hair falling around her face, the wind taking whisps and clinging them to her cheeks. "*Grazie*," she whispered. "*Grazie*."

"Who are you? What do you want from us? How do we know you aren't in league with those men?" one of the footmen asked, stepping forward as if he had been so brave moments ago, when they were being robbed, presumably at musket point.

"It's your job to protect your mistress," Paul snapped "You did not. If you had, I wouldn't have to leave my wife, track those men, and find her miniature."

The footman glowered and stepped back, sulking. Kaya glared at him, then instantly dismissed him. She had a feeling she'd have to watch her back—and the rest of this woman's possessions— around that one.

Paul took her hands and kissed her palms. "Stay safe, sweetheart." He dropped his voice and whispered in English, "Don't trust anyone."

Kaya snorted a laugh. "Only you, my untrusting husband." Then she sobered and said, "Come back to me, *ya rouhi*."

"You haven't called me that in a while." He cupped her cheek and pressed his forehead to hers.

"I've always believed it." It meant *my soul*, and she meant it with everything in her.

"How do we know you won't keep the jewels for yourself?" the other footman asked sharply.

Kaya sighed at the interruption, but Paul answered before she could. "If I don't, you can keep my wife."

She laughed and kissed him, unconcerned with the strangers watching them. "Come back to me," she repeated.

"Always."

Kaya watched him disappear into the trees, silent and graceful with both his knife and the one they'd taken from the brigand not a half hour earlier. Azizi let out a soft woof, but Kaya kept her beside her, resting a hand on her dark fur.

"Be watchful, Azizi," she said to the dog in Egyptian.

"What will you do if he doesn't return?"

The question startled Kaya. She looked to the ground, where the woman still knelt. She seemed to have composed herself somewhat, brushing her hair from her face and wiping the tears from her cheeks.

Kaya offered a hand to help her stand, then helped her sit in the open doorway of the carriage. The vehicle rocked uncertainly, but the woman didn't seem to notice.

What *would* she do?

That fear was still there, a cold tendril trying to wind around her heart. Kaya forced it away. Would she always fear being left alone? Abandoned? She looked to where Paul had disappeared into the trees. He'd return. He'd promised, and she believed him. She always believed him, even when she didn't want to. Because he promised her the truth. Always.

He promised to love her and protect her.

"Then I shall find his murderers and avenge him," she said.

The woman let out a startled laugh, a watery, faint sound, but it brought life to her wan face. "I don't understand." She stopped and eyed the khanjar on Kaya's waist. "Oh. Ah." She cleared her throat, looking embarrassed and uneasy.

"Let's see about your traveling companion." Kaya glowered at the two footmen, who had not moved. "Perhaps you could be of use? See to the driver and collect the belongings strewn about the road."

They didn't look happy. Kaya suddenly knew they'd keep the

coin for themselves as they did as she ordered. On the other side of the carriage, the poor woman had cried herself into exhaustion.

"Oh, Charlotte." The woman ran to her companion's side and gathered her into her arms, murmuring soothing words Kaya didn't catch.

Charlotte looked weak and terrified, but she offered her mistress a slight smile. She said something in a language Kaya didn't understand, and the two women spoke softly.

"Here." The woman said something else. Then, turning to Kaya, she said in Calabrian, "Please help me see her off this road?"

The pair of them slowly guided a shaking Charlotte off the road and into the tree line. Charlotte looked exhausted, her dark hair falling about her shoulders, her cheeks tearstained. She collapsed onto the small boulder and didn't look as if she wanted to move again.

"If your footmen will help, we have a small tent we can shelter beneath until my husband returns." Kaya edged around the side of the carriage, but the footmen were, indeed, cleaning up the mess. Azizi stood guard between Kaya and the carriage, as if she, too, knew the worth of those men.

"I am Countess Hannah von Almey of Schloss Schönwalde." She smiled up at Kaya. Her cheeks finally had some color in them, though her hands bunched her skirts and her gaze focused on the path Paul had disappeared down. "Given the informality of the situation, please call me Hannah."

Inclining her head, Kaya said simply, "Kaya Conrad. My husband, Paul." She gestured in the direction of the trees, then nodded to Azizi, who watched the footmen with a distinct growl. "And my dog, Azizi."

"A most unusual name." Hannah paused, her gaze flicking to Azizi, then Kaya, then back to the trees. "A most unusual dog."

"It means 'precious,'" Kaya told her, crossing the short distance between the carriage and the edge of the road.

She left an exhausted Charlotte alone and sat in the sunlight.

Her position also held the better vantage point, should anyone set upon them—Paul, brigands, another carriage even, though Kaya had seen few vehicles since they left Rome. The mountains roads were rocky and uncertain.

She twisted the satchel and laid it across her lap, then slipped her khanjar from its sheath and kept it within easy reach.

"Have you been best by brigands before?" Kaya looked at the driver, who no one had bothered to even cover. The poor man.

"Not since leaving Rome." Hannah shivered, wrapping her arms about her despite the warm sunlight. "You seem familiar with them."

"Unfortunately." Kaya snorted and stood, khanjar gripped firmly in her hand. "Have you a blanket for your driver?"

Startled, Hannah met her gaze, then looked to the dead body. "Oh, Fritz." She stood and rummaged in the carriage. "I'm sorry, I didn't—I'm not usually so—" She sounded on the verge of tears again, her voice shaking as badly as the hands that handed Kaya the blanket.

Kneeling beside the driver, Fritz, Kaya whispered the prayer for the dead and covered him until the footmen could bury him. Taking another moment, she closed her eyes and said a prayer for Paul.

What *would* she do if he didn't return? After tracking down his murderers and exacting revenge, of course. Travel onward? Where? Why? She enjoyed traveling because she and Paul did so together. If he didn't return, and she could not find him—alive— would she return to Villa San Giovanni? Marta and the Spanòs were there, the only other people she knew. What then?

"Frau Kaya?"

Startled from her whirling thoughts, Kaya stood. She shook off questions about a future that might not manifest. Questions would do her no good, this dwelling on possibilities. She smiled at Hannah. "Let's set up the shelter; I'm sure you'll all be more comfortable beneath it."

The footmen, who followed her direction well enough,

looked skeptical about the tent. Kaya offered no explanation, though she knew it was far from the usual covering. A much smaller version of the ones the desert tribes used, this shelter had seen them safe from the desert sun and the cooler Calabrian nights.

Azizi sniffed the fabric, then snorted and curled beneath the shelter.

"Charlottes, yes?" Kaya asked as she helped the woman stand. Her knees gave out, and she collapsed against Kaya, but she recovered and walked beneath the overhang without a word.

"What did they take?" Kaya asked as Charlotte and the footmen gathered beneath the tent, out of the bright midday sun and the harsh wind. Hannah stood beside the carriage in the middle of the road and watched for Paul's return.

"A portrait of my son." Her voice broke, and her hands covered her belly. "It's all I have left of him."

"I'm sorry." Kaya didn't say more, had no words for such a loss. However, she knew grief, knew it intimately, and she reached out to take Hannah's hand. "Paul will find them. He has peculiar skill for such things."

"You have encountered bandits before." Hannah nodded, but only spared her a glance. Her fingers tightened around Kaya's, as if drawing strength from her.

"Almost daily since we crossed into the Papal States," Kaya admitted. "It's been most annoying."

Hannah laughed, a quick sound that seemed to surprise her more than Kaya. "Annoying? Yes, I imagine it is. You know how to protect yourself?" She nodded to the khanjar though she barely looked from the deserted path.

"Yes. My grandfather taught me."

"Very unusual. Your husband, he takes no issue with this?" Hannah frowned and slowly dragged her gaze from the trees. "Your grandfather taught you?" she repeated, then shook her head. "How unusual," she said again.

"He—" Kaya floundered. Once again, her insulated life had

left her with very little understanding of propriety. Derya never mentioned a word about women not knowing how to defend themselves, though Kaya had learned that particular taboo soon enough.

Paul had never spoken of her abilities. Not in any sort of unusual way, only asking curious questions. The why and how of her training. Kaya frowned. Even on their first night together, walking out of Cairo long after curfew, he'd never mentioned a word about her weapons.

"Is the fact I carry a dagger supposed to bother him?" she asked Hannah.

Hannah smiled and shook her head. "I've no idea. I know no woman who carries a knife such as yours, and so openly, let alone one who is comfortable being left by their husband on the open road."

Kaya wanted to snap that Paul hadn't left her, but she knew that probably wasn't what Hannah meant. Comfortable? Well, not entirely. As much as Kaya wished to explore the world, she found she did not wish to do so alone.

Despite her awkwardness with simple conversations, she enjoyed talking with others. Instead of answering, Kaya opened the carriage door and sat inside its frame. It was far from comfortable, but she had no desire to stand on the road for however long it would take Paul to return.

"He does not often leave me alone," Kaya admitted. She resisted reminding Hannah that the only reason he had done so now was to search for the men who'd robbed her. "He protects me as I do him."

Hannah looked at her then as if seeing her for the first time. "How unusual." It seemed to be her favorite saying—or perhaps only in regards to Kaya.

"That he protects me?" Curious, Kaya wondered what husbands actually did if not protect their wives. That was why Gidd had contracted her to marry a man like Paul. His reputation might not have been pristine, but he'd die defending her.

Kaya preferred that to a man with a spotless reputation—not that she knew any. Or even what a spotless reputation might entail.

"Yes." Hannah offered a small smile and wandered to the carriage, though she still faced the road. "Where are you traveling to?"

Hesitating a bare moment, Kaya saw no reason to lie. In their travels, she'd learned the hard way that people did not often tell the truth, or they asked innocuous questions to garner information. Small talk, Paul called it. She detested it.

"Riccione," she said honestly. "We sail for Venice."

"Oh!" Hannah brightened and offered a true smile, her gaze firmly on Kaya. "I, too, am headed to Riccione. Are you walking?"

The question, a slight from anyone else, held only curiosity, and Kaya relaxed. She'd endured enough suspicious merchants and proprietors to last a lifetime. "Yes, we prefer to walk. Also, Azizi does not like carriages."

At her name, Azizi perked up but didn't move. One of the footmen stood and stretched, then wandered over to tend the horses.

"I'm sorry about your driver," Kaya offered.

"He's been with me for years." Hannah sniffed back tears and looked wistful. The breeze blew her tangled, loose hair about her face. "Fifteen years ago, he saved my life during another roadside attack. Fritz was a good man and a steady friend."

Pieces of Hannah's life slotted together, and Kaya understood the woman's terror. Whatever happened fifteen years ago had stayed with her, and it haunted her even now. She wanted to offer comfort, but she didn't know this woman well enough to offer more than she already had.

"It's several hours' walk to Riccione. Perhaps once Signore Conrad returns, you will join me in my carriage?" Hannah paused and eyed the vehicle. It listed on the uneven road, and the door hung askew. "It looks sturdy enough."

They'd lost precious time here, and now they would be lucky to see Riccione before sunset. Having encountered more than her fair share of bandits, and having no desire to spend the night outdoors, Kaya weighed the question for only a moment. "We'd be happy to. But I'm afraid Azizi will need to ride with us."

"Azizi," Hannah repeated. "Arabic?" Surprised, Kaya nodded, and Hannah smiled. "A beautiful name for a beautiful dog."

"Have you traveled far?" Kaya asked cautiously. She'd been careful not to reveal her heritage. Not even to Marta, with whom Kaya enjoyed her first friendship. Most people already looked at her suspiciously.

"I've come from India and the great Hindu temples." Hannah's voice softened. "On our way back, we detoured to Rome. But I've learned many languages. Well, I know enough of several of them to be polite."

Smiling, Kaya settled into silence. She quite liked Hannah, even enjoyed this small talk with her. When she told Paul, he'd no doubt laugh. Eyeing the sun, she wondered how long he'd been gone. The bandits didn't have much of a start on him, but she disliked that he hadn't returned. She also disliked him leaving without her.

Hannah waited in the center of the road, watching. Kaya leaned against the carriage door and let her mind drift. What would they find in Venice? It sounded like a beautiful city, with its canals and gondolas, but she didn't wish to settle there, not with that city-state's complicated citizenship rules.

From Venice, where would they travel? West to France? East to Russia? North to Austria or Prussia? Her eyes closed as she imagined her and Paul in each of those places, and Kaya wondered if Hannah was traveling home after such adventures as India and Rome.

She wondered what it might be like to have a home to return to. She tried to picture her house in Cairo but could only see it on that final night, with Gidd standing at the door as he said goodbye to her.

No, she couldn't return there.

Azizi let out a sharp bark. Standing from the carriage door, Kaya steadied herself for an attack and readied her khanjar. She waited for Paul or more purse thieves. Beside her, Azizi was alert, but she didn't seem ready to attack. Hannah appeared at her other side, anxious and hopeful.

Paul strode from the trees, disheveled and limping. Kaya ran to him but saw no blood or bruising.

"Paul." She wrapped her arms around him, uncaring what anyone thought, and held tight.

"You were right," he whispered against her neck. He spoke in English and sounded tired, far too worn-out to have fought only the two men who'd robbed Hannah. "I should've waited on a new pair of boots."

Pulling back, Kaya looked down at his feet, which were clad only in his stockings. "What happened?"

"Found their camp." He sighed and rested his forehead on her shoulder. She wrapped her arms around him. Comfort and home. "Several of them sat around the fire. It looked more like a base than anything. The two men from last week were there, but not the one whose nose I bloodied."

"Did you find it?" Hannah asked, edging toward them. She looked terrified but eager.

"Oh, aye." Paul held up a cloth bag that looked heavy, as if it held more than only a miniature portrait. "Found your jewels, too. Coin." He sighed. "Right profitable ring they had going."

"I'm glad you returned," Kaya whispered. She brushed his cheek, and he leaned into the touch. "And I'm glad you are unharmed."

Hannah had dug through the bag for the portrait and now held it to her chest, sobbing. "Thank you," she cried. "Thank you."

"We're riding in Hannah's carriage." Kaya tugged him onto the road, away from Hannah. She wanted privacy for the two of them, and she wanted to offer Hannah privacy as well. "We'll find you a new pair of boots in Riccione."

"Hannah?" Paul repeated, eyebrows rising as he met her gaze. He looked to the woman, who was still crying over the painting, then to her. "Made a friend?" He shook his head. "For a woman who does not like small talk, you make friends everywhere we go."

Ten

The port city of Riccione boasted several inns. The Locanda di Riccione sat on a cliff overlooking the Adriatic—a stunning view. The sea stretched before them, a gorgeous blue full of small fishing vessels and larger sailboats. The breeze brought a freshness they'd missed since landing in Rome, and the sun shone down from a spotless sky.

Hannah had already reserved several rooms there, and though Paul couldn't fault her taste, it was absolutely not where he would have chosen. The inn sat directly in the center of activity.

Situated on a bustling street, with a nearby market and direct access to a private port and the beach below, the inn screamed luxury. And wealth attracted bandits. Of course, so did walking across the country, but this inn clearly catered to a higher-end clientele and would no doubt be a target for ruffians.

He saw only two guards, which made the hair on the back of his neck raise. Two? In this area? Where every step brought men with knives wanting to rob you? Paul scowled. Either the proprietor had stationed additional guards around the perimeter, or he paid off the local bandits.

Or maybe he was a part of the local scheme.

Paul grunted and knew, just knew, it was the latter.

"Keep alert," he muttered to Kaya. "I have a bad feeling about this."

She smiled up at him tightly. "That, my dear husband, is nothing new." But she nodded, a quick movement. "This is no anonymous inn where we can slip in and out."

He hated putting Kaya in such a position, but she'd accepted Hannah's, Countess von Almey's, invitation, and Paul would never tell her no. Even if he cringed at each call from the copious dinghies at the marina or the constant stream of people wandering about.

Signore Ferrari eyed them curiously and scowled down at Azizi. Paul silently passed a few coins to the man, who took them without comment.

"We'll meet for dinner." Hannah chatted quickly, her eyes darting around the foyer. "I want to get Charlotte settled and Fritz—oh."

Nodding as politely as he could, Paul rested his hand on Kaya's back and edged her away. He needed a moment, just the two of them. "We'll meet you in the dining room," he promised.

Kaya nodded and called to Azizi. On the stairs, she whispered, "I do not think I like this *pensione*. It does not feel welcoming."

"Let's settle into our room." Paul shook his head. "We won't stay long—a night, maybe two. I'll find a ship that's sailing for Venice first thing in the morning."

Kaya waited for Azizi to enter the room, then pressed Paul against the closed door. She kissed him, humming against his lips, her hands cupping his face. Just as suddenly as she'd kissed him, Kaya stepped back and turned for the windows. "I love you."

Paul blinked at her and nodded. "Hell of a way to show me."

She laughed stepped onto the balcony. "This is not at all secure. As much as I enjoy the sea breeze, I don't like that it's open to anyone."

Stepping beside her, he looked over the balustrade. Below, in the rapidly dimming sunlight, the courtyard looked serene. And dark. No torches lit the area, and the shadows moved with the wind.

"It's not too far up," he agreed. "Anyone determined enough could climb."

Azizi sniffed along the corners, and Paul watched her. Just in case she found something. But the dog only snorted and went back into the room.

"Let's head downstairs." Kaya closed and locked the balcony doors, then drew the curtains over them. "As much as I enjoy Hannah's company, I find myself wanting an early night."

He grinned and kissed her cheek. "What an excellent idea."

Two hours later, they'd enjoyed a wonderful meal and the gorgeous view. Not in the dining room, but outside on the terrace. Paul had declined the wine, to Hannah's curiosity and Signora Ferrari's suspicion.

Now Paul watched Kaya admire the view as they awaited dessert. It seemed as if the inn often hosted a large number of guests, no doubt during the summer season. They'd eaten outdoors on the spacious patio, beneath a large awning over-looking the sea. Tonight, only a few braved the cool evening. The sun had long disappeared, but the owners had lit the patio with dozens of torches, which now flickered, somewhat alarmingly, in the wind.

"You can almost see Šibenik from here," Hannah said wist-fully. "It's a lovely town, so picturesque!"

"It's across the sea?" Paul asked, eying Kaya, who stood at the stone banister, her face raised to the wind. At Hannah's nod, he shook his head. "No, we sail for Venice."

"Oh, it's not a far detour," Hannah promised. "But Venice is beautiful, too. Not as magnificent as it once was, I'm afraid, but the canals are stunning."

"I'm sure it's lovely," Paul allowed. Kaya turned then and walked back to their table. "But I don't think we'll be sailing for anywhere other than Venice."

Kaya's eyes widened. "No." She offered a small smile and sat next to him, moving her chair just a bit closer. "Venice is far enough."

He took her hand beneath the tablecloth and warmed her chilled fingers in his. They hadn't much cause to sit and converse with others, and Paul had to remind himself about proprieties.

"Are you sailing for Venice?" Kaya asked.

"Oh, no. Bibione then up the Tagliamento River." Hannah sighed wistfully. "I return...home."

Paul didn't respond. Kaya had said little about what she and Hannah had discussed while he'd tracked the thieves and reclaimed her possessions. He'd seen the miniature portrait, of course. Why those men had decided to take that, he could only guess. It held little financial value. Perhaps it was because they wished to harm Hannah as much as possible.

The boy in the painting, no older than five, had Hannah's blonde hair and her smile, and a vibrancy he hadn't seen in the woman for all her laughter and chatter.

"Perhaps we can breakfast together," Kaya offered, much to Paul's shock. Or perhaps it wasn't shock. Kaya befriended the most unlikely people. Street children trying to sneak into opium dens, women abused by smugglers and abandoned by their families.

She had a kind heart, his Kaya. An innate understanding of others' loneliness despite her sheltered life. Rather, because of it.

"Oh, I'd like that very much." Hannah beamed at Kaya as if she'd offered far more than breakfast. "Perhaps you would be willing to show me your knife?" She looked earnest, her gaze darting between husband and wife. "I confess, I've never met a woman so adept with a weapon."

"You said you didn't have any trouble," Paul muttered. He sipped his coffee to hide his scowl.

"We did not," Kaya assured him. "Though I do not trust your footmen, Hannah. They do not seem the guarding sort."

"I hired them in Rome; however, I've already let them go," Hannah admitted. She looked down at her hands and frowned.

Her fingers twisted together in a nervous knot. "I had been warned of thieves on the roads, and I thought Fritz needed help." Her voice broke at the utterance of her driver's name. "I wanted to give him a proper burial but could only find Catholic priests here." She peered at them hopefully. "Do you think there's a Lutheran priest about?"

"I'm sure not," Paul said. Kaya squeezed his hand. He didn't roll his eyes—barely. To Kaya, he muttered in English, "Yes, all right, I'll ask around." To Hannah, he offered, "I'll see if Signore Ferrari knows of any, but we're in a Catholic country."

They were in the Papal States. It didn't get more Catholic than that, and Paul had no idea what the countess expected. However, the alternative was to purchase a tin- or lead-lined coffin and transport Fritz back to wherever Hannah lived.

"I'd be most grateful." Hannah's eyes lowered again, and her voice cracked. "Do you think they were involved?"

"Your footmen? As part of the band of robbers?" Kaya asked, her fingers tightening around Paul's.

"It's possible," he allowed. He shook his head and finished his coffee. "But then, I think a lot of the bands in these mountains are connected. There are far too many of them to work independently without fighting amongst themselves."

"Fritz paid with his life," Hannah whispered. "And poor Charlotte. When we landed in Rome, she fell ill for weeks with a fever. I'm grateful she survived. She will never wish to leave Schloss Schönwalde again—not that I blame her. It's been far, far too long since we returned."

Paul struggled to continue the inane chatter, but he only wanted time with Kaya. Real time, the two of them reconnecting. The problem was, despite having made love again, and even now holding hands, he felt the distance between them. Or perhaps that was his own expectations.

He felt Kaya should keep her distance and he needed to win her back.

"With no driver, how will you travel to your schloss?" Kaya

asked. He heard the hesitation in her voice and wondered at it. It worried him.

"I'll hire a coach." Hannah waved it off and eyed them speculatively. "Do you walk everywhere?"

"Yes," Kaya confirmed. "We enjoy the scenery, and I often stop to draw the landscape."

"How lovely," Hannah agreed with a wide smile. Then she frowned. "Though I wonder if that's why you encounter so many robbery attempts."

"No doubt," Paul muttered. But the thought of sitting in a cramped coach with no room to maneuver, should something happen, sent chills down his spine. Worse yet if they hired a post chase, or the Papal States' equivalent of one, and he and Kaya sat cheek-to-jowl with a group of strangers.

Heaven forbid he have to speak with so many strangers.

Kaya squeezed his hand in what was probably commiseration, but Paul took as a signal to leave. They said their goodbyes and retreated into the inn. The sudden silence and lack of wind momentarily startled him. He'd grown used to the sound and feel of the wind on his face, and now he needed a moment to readjust.

"Do you want to walk along the shoreline?" Paul asked, despite his concern about the number of people still wandering the beach.

"No, let's walk the path along the mountain." She smiled and tugged him toward the open doors into the main courtyard. "It's a lovely night, and I don't want to retire yet."

"I can fetch your sketchbook if you'd like?"

"Not tonight. Let's just walk."

Azizi, who rarely left Kaya's side, appeared just as they exited the inn. Signore Ferrari, a stout, wildly mustached man in his sixties, had eyed their dog and frowned. Paul added a couple extra coins to the counter, which had disappeared without so much as an acknowledgement. They'd encountered no trouble with Azizi staying in their room, however, and that was all that mattered.

"Do you wish to see Šibenik across the Adriatic?" he asked, tentative and annoyed with himself for his uncertainty.

"Across the sea?" She let out a breath of laughter and leaned her head on his arm. "No. Venice will do nicely."

"You're worried." It hit him then, the reason for her hesitation, and he wanted to kick himself. It wasn't only he who trod new ground. They both did. "You're worried about the trip."

"I'd rather walk, yes." She shrugged, her shoulder rubbing against his arm. "Or even hire a carriage, though with the mountains I've no idea how Hannah made it from Rome without more mishaps."

"I don't know," he admitted. "Perhaps she doesn't draw trouble the way we do."

"Paul." She breathed out a soft laugh. "No one attracts trouble the way we do."

He grunted. "I certainly don't look for it. I'd be perfectly happy with a quiet life, just the two of us." He paused and looked down at Azizi. "Three of us," he amended.

They stopped just outside the inn's circle of light. She didn't move from his side and kept her head against his arm. He liked this, the quiet moment between them. The peace and affection.

Along the rocky path, he spotted the purple flowers Kaya had been so fond of drawing on their initial walk.

"There are those purple flowers you love."

She stiffened at his side. Scrambling to figure out what he'd said, Paul peered at her in the uncertain light.

"Apparently," she said slowly, "those are poisonous."

Paul jerked. "What?"

"Marta." Her voice slid but didn't break. "She used them to poison Appleby."

"What?" Paul had a lot of questions. But then, she and Marta had spent a lot of time together during their winter exile. He snapped his mouth closed. A hot current of satisfaction rushed through him. "Good."

"*Good*?" But then Kaya nodded. "Yes, I agree. I do not know what might've happened to the kidnapped villagers if she had succeeded before we found them. However, she grasped matters in her own hands, and I admire that very much. She had been slowly adding the poison to his food." She met Paul's gaze, her own unreadable in the half-moon light.

"Good," he repeated, not sure what else such a revelation warranted. Appleby had abused and used Marta, and no one in her entire village stopped him. Her own parents had not stopped him. "Marta is very resourceful and smart. She'll do well in Villa San Giovanni. I'm sorry we didn't arrive sooner to finish it."

"Do you believe in fate?" Kaya asked.

The question caught him off guard. "Fate? That everything is preordained? Or that things happen because they're supposed to?"

"Yes. That things happen for a reason." She smoothed her hands down her skirts. The nervous gesture surprised him, and he blinked at her. "That we were supposed to be there, in Villa San Giovanni, when we were."

"Perhaps." He worked through the possibilities. "If we had arrived later, we'd have missed Rogerson's shipment—the supposed last for the season, what with the snow." Paul grunted and ran a hand down his face. "Missed him and our chance to stop the smuggling. And if we had arrived sooner—"

"Then what?"

"I don't know," he said honestly. "We might've missed Appleby. Or stopped Rogerson sooner. Or—" Paul broke off.

"Perhaps we were meant to arrive when we did," Kaya agreed.

"Yes," he admitted, and he turned her away from the flowers. "Yes, I suppose I do believe in fate." He took her hand and walked slowly back toward the inn. "Fate let Tahir's letter find me. I hadn't left Bombay since he'd been there, but I'm not sure he could've known that. Fate had me accepting his offer."

She laughed. "You accepted his offer so you could rob him!"

Paul grinned down at her. "True. But I didn't."

"Only because you didn't have the opportunity." She sniffed. "If you recall, I held a knife to you when you broke in."

And that was the start of his fall, Paul knew it. Other men loved women who sang prettily or offered witty commentary. Paul? He'd fallen in love with a woman who held a knife to his kidneys. Typical.

"How do we regain the closeness between us?" Kaya asked suddenly. "What we shared before Appleby."

His mind raced, but he kept his mouth closed. He didn't want to blurt out just anything, though he wanted to assure Kaya that nothing between them had changed. Except everything had.

"I had hoped never to show you that side of myself," he admitted.

"You said." She let out a huff of breath. This wasn't the first time he'd said that, but she didn't know how to move beyond it. "You are no longer that man, Paul. Please stop looking back."

"I'm afraid I can't help it," he said quietly. "I have many regrets. I regret not doing more in Bombay while I was there. I knew how the British treated the locals; I saw it every day. But I was too—" He'd been drunk, or in the opium dens, or too concerned with the next mark he and Basu planned to cheat at cards or dice.

Paul could've taken a stand, said something. Saved Basu. Even now, almost a year later, Basu's dead eyes looked up at him from the street, haunting his every step. He would never forget his hopelessness as he stood with the rest of his battalion as Major Rogerson ordered them to fire.

He hadn't fired, but didn't not stopping the mad major from killing innocents also count against him? Paul had no idea what he could've done. A lowly sergeant couldn't have stopped the slaughter, and even questioning Rogerson would've landed him in chains, but following his conscience would have counted for something.

All he could do now was atone for those sins. Stand up, stop others from harming innocents. Speak up.

"I look back and see the man I was and all the ways I could've changed then." He ran a hand down his face, suddenly wary. He couldn't change the past—no one could. But he regretted it. "I have many regrets, Kaya." He picked up her hand again and kissed her palm. "Many things for which I need to atone. Repent. But I've never regretted loving you."

"Nor I you," she whispered. "*Ya rouhi.* We shall walk together, then. Wherever the path takes us."

"Anywhere you wish." He kissed her tenderly. "My soul."

Eleven

The next morning, Kaya smiled at Paul as he held out her chair. She sat beside Hannah in the dining hall. She wanted to sit on the patio again, but Hannah seemed to prefer indoors. Kaya suspected it had something to do with the theft yesterday, given Hannah's reaction to it.

In the end, it didn't matter. The three of them shared a pleasant meal of fruits and breads with fig preserves and coffee. Hannah chatted brightly, as she had since Paul returned with her stolen items.

"I have a few things to see to," Paul said as their conversation wound down and their coffee cooled.

Kaya met his gaze and nodded. He was going to ask about the Lutheran minister and their passage to Venice. They'd argued last night about him leaving her. He disliked doing so, but she had grown more comfortable being alone. It was not her favorite, of course; she'd rather him by her side, but she knew how to defend herself and was far from helpless.

"Be safe."

He lifted her hand and kissed her fingertips. "Don't find trouble."

"I shall remain here and not wander."

His lips twitched, and he looked around the dining room. "Where's Azizi?"

"Wandering." No doubt hunting for her own food. "She'll return."

He leaned down and looked her in the eyes. They may have argued last night, but they'd made love afterward, holding each other in the soft bed and laughing about the comforts they enjoyed.

"Kaya." He said nothing more, but she knew. It shivered down her spine and around her heart. He'd return to her. Kaya wondered if there would ever be a time when she didn't fear his desertion. It was a silly fear, given all they'd been through in the previous months. However, years stretched before them.

The way his blue-green eyes watched her, told her the truth. He'd never leave her. Kaya smiled and nodded, hoping he understood. Hoping this was the next step in repairing what had torn between them.

"*Rihlat amna*," she whispered. Safe journey.

With a final nod, Paul kissed her fingers and left.

Kaya watched him, his long, sure strides, the confident tilt to his chin. The new boots they'd had hastily made. She smiled and turned back to her new friend.

"He's devoted to you." Hannah's voice startled her. "I've never seen a man look at a woman so." She smiled wistfully and met Kaya's gaze. "How long have you been married?"

"Eight months," Kaya said.

"If the shine has not worn off by now, I doubt it ever will."

Kaya had no idea what that meant, but she nodded and stood. "Shall we retire to the courtyard? It'll be easier to show you my khanjar there."

Hannah seemed suddenly nervous. "Oh. Ah, yes."

"If you no longer wish—"

"No, it's not that, only...ah." She cleared her throat; she was wringing her hands. Two spots of red colored her cheeks, and her eyes darted around the nearly empty room.

"Are you nervous about being without a chaperone?" Kaya asked in understanding. She was quite familiar with that. The world was dangerous, she'd learned. The constant judgment of others, the threats of violence and robberies. Most especially, the world was dangerous for women. "I'm sure we can ask Signore Ferrari if—"

Hannah interrupted again. "Oh, no. It's only...well, are you certain we won't be set upon by bandits?" Hannah once more twisted her fingers together. Then she caught herself and straightened her shoulders, tilting her chin just slightly.

"I've been set upon by bandits so often in the last weeks, I'd be surprised if we weren't." Kaya said that before she'd thought her words through, and she hastily amended, "However, I can't imagine they'd attack so close to the inn. We're near a busy part of town, and there are guards. I'm sure we'll be perfectly safe."

Hannah looked only partially convinced, but she nodded and straightened her hat. Kaya eyed it, the wide brim reminding her of the blue hat she wore in Damietta. She hated that thing, much preferring her hijab.

"Have you always known how to protect yourself?" Hannah asked as they crossed the foyer into the still-shaded courtyard. The sun barely brushed the ground here, but at least the building stopped the constant sea wind.

"Yes. My grandfather taught me when I was very young." Kaya paused, but there was no reason not to tell Hannah. Well, perhaps not the entire story, but a portion of it "I had snuck from the house, and no one realized until I clumsily snuck back in."

Wide-eyed, Hannah grinned. "That was when he decided to train you?"

Gidd had taught Kaya to protect herself should the Ottoman Empire discover she was the daughter of a sultana and an Egyptian guard who'd married in secret, and very much against the wishes of the sultan. "He was a firm believer in precautions."

"I'm impressed," Hannah admitted, though there was no

undertone in her voice. "Women are not often taught to protect themselves."

"Perhaps we should be. Relying on men is never feasible." Kaya's voice darkened. "Especially if the men we are forced to rely upon are those who hurt us the most."

Hannah looked surprised. "Surely not Paul!"

Kaya blinked at her. "No. No, I didn't mean him." She'd meant Marta and her now-dead husband, who had not treated her well. "Paul is a wonderful fighter. Very graceful. He would never hurt a woman."

Something in the way Hannah looked, or perhaps in the way her hands continued to twist together, made Kaya stop. She'd been hurt. Terribly. Unsure how to tread with this new information, Kaya pulled her khanjar from its sheath.

"I've never seen one like it," Hannah admitted, though she didn't touch the handle. "It's beautiful. So elegant." Her blue eyes met Kaya's, earnest and a touch desperate. "Will you teach me?"

"If you wish." Kaya hesitated, not at all certain where this conversation was heading. "However, we sail for Venice this week. And you are off to Bibione."

"You didn't ask." Hannah offered a watery laugh. "Neither you nor your husband asked."

Completely at a loss, Kaya shook her head. Were all conversations so scattered? "Asked?"

"About the portrait." Hannah's light blue eyes filled with tears, but she blinked them back.

Just then, Azizi bounded up and nudged Kaya's hand for her usual greeting. Distracted, Kaya petted her dog, praising her for being a good girl. But her gaze remained on Hannah. The sun crept over the building, lighting the courtyard, and, though the day was still chilly, it brought warmth with it.

"I don't understand." Kaya stared at the woman, scrambling for reason. "Was I supposed to ask about it?"

Hannah laughed and waved a hand. "Most would. So many are curious, sticking their noses in where it doesn't belong. But you, the both of you, are so different. I've never met anyone like you."

Kaya eyed her cautiously. What did noses have to do with curiosity? How did one stick their nose into something? "Is...is that good?"

"Yes. I'm so glad I met you. You've changed how I see things in only a day. Most people wouldn't help a stranger without compensation." Hannah shook her head. "You did, and I'm grateful—more grateful than words can express."

"You're welcome." Kaya tried to keep that from sounding like a question. Honestly, she had no idea what to say, but Derya hadn't raised her to be rude or ignorant. "I'm pleased we could help."

Hannah laughed again. "I'd like you to travel with me, to Brandenburg. My final destination."

That was not what Kaya had expected. She paused, confused and curious. Travel with another? It had never occurred to her to do such a thing. She and Paul managed quite well together, and introducing Hannah—anyone, really—felt odd. Not wrong, just strange.

"Why?" she asked.

"The portrait." Hannah pulled out the miniature and looked at it. No, she cradled it, holding it as if it were more precious than all the jewels Paul had also recovered. "It's my son, Karl Friedrich Christian Albrecht von Almey. He would've been almost twenty by now."

Kaya's heart twisted, and she thought of Olivia and Teresa. She prayed the hardships they'd gone through so early did not affect them later in life. Teresa with her opium-addled brother, and Olivia with the knowledge of how a man had treated her mother.

"I'm sorry," she whispered.

"Thank you." Hannah looked up from the portrait. "We were traveling, Karl Fredrich, my husband, and I, along the country road near Breitlingsee. We were stopped and robbed. My husband, he—" She shook her head and took a moment to compose herself. "He was not like yours. He paid others for protection."

Words dried in her mouth, and Kaya swallowed hard. She knew, of course, that most women did not know how to defend themselves. Derya had not, nor had her own mother. It simply was not done. They relied on men for protection. She didn't know what to say, so reached for Hannah's hand instead.

"They killed him. Killed my precious Karl Fredrich." Hannah's free hand curled around her stomach. "After they robbed us, they attacked. It wasn't enough they took our coin and jewels, but they hurt us as well. They killed my husband."

She shook her head, and even now Kaya saw her pain and fear. Her anguish. When had she last released her well of grief and spoken of the tragedy?

"They stabbed me," she whispered. "And killed the child I carried."

Hot rage nearly blinded her, but Kaya remained still and silent. Azizi wound around her skirts and sat between them, as if she understood Hannah's terrible words. Or sensed her pain.

"Fritz." Hannah's voice broke. "He was our driver then, too. They wounded him, but he was so strong. So determined. I don't remember much, but later Charlotte told me what happened. She was with me then, too. They both were." Hannah wiped her cheeks and offered a wan smile. "He put me in the carriage and drove me to the nearest farmhouse."

I'm sorry sounded so inadequate, so Kaya merely squeezed Hannah's hand tighter. Her throat closed, and she had to clear it several times before she trusted herself to speak. "He sounds like a strong, faithful man who cared deeply."

"I'm sorry," Hannah said abruptly. "I shouldn't burden you like this. I only wish you to understand why I want to learn. And why I'm inviting you to stay in my schloss. I don't want to be afraid anymore. Not like then, and not like yesterday."

"All right," Kaya heard herself say. "I'll teach you.

"There she is!"

Signore Ferrari's harsh shout startled Kaya. Fingers tight on her khanjar, she whirled toward the man. He stormed through the dining hall, boots clicking on the polished wood floor, face flushed in anger.

"You!" he screamed at Hannah. "You killed her!"

Kaya had no idea what he meant, but she stood before her new friend, ready to protect her. Azizi stood in front of Kaya and growled, baring her impressive teeth, muscles bunched and at the ready.

"My wife!" Ferrari cried, falling to his knees.

Just then, Kaya noticed several Fortress Guards marching behind Ferrari. The two who normally patrolled the inn marched formally in the back. Kaya's stomach sank, and she looked down at Azizi. "I have a bad feeling about this."

Paul shook the captain's hand and turned for the inn. He disliked leaving Kaya alone, especially for so long, even with Azizi. However, finding a Lutheran minister hadn't been easy. In fact, he hadn't found one, per se. He'd found a dodgy Catholic priest who looked to be heavily in his cups, but he swore up and down he knew the Lutheran funeral rites.

He'd mumbled something about, "Not the first foreigner who needed them," and that was the only agreement he offered.

But he was the only man of the cloth Paul had managed to find who hadn't threatened to have him hanged for heresy, so Paul paid him and sent him to the inn. He wasn't sure what surprised him more: the fact that no one knew non-Catholic funeral rites in a heavily visited holiday area, or that this man truly did know the funeral prayers.

Finding a ship's captain he deemed trustworthy enough to sail for Venice had been far easier.

Paul made his way along the wharves. Though it was another

beautiful day on the coast, Paul hurried his steps back to Locanda di Riccione. He hoped Kaya and Hannah were getting on well, solidifying whatever tentative friendship they'd formed over the last day. She wanted to make friends, and thus far, her experience hadn't been as lasting as Paul knew she wished.

The moment the inn came into view, Paul realized he shouldn't have disregarded the sinking sensation that had followed him all morning.

"Kaya!" he shouted, then instantly whistled for Azizi.

Both of them stood in the foyer of the inn, Azizi baring her teeth while Kaya watched the room, khanjar in hand. She looked ready, braced for a fight, but also calm, waiting. Relief made his knees weak, and Paul raced to her side.

"What happened?" He kept clear of her line of sight, standing on her left as he scanned the room. "Fortress Guards?" A dozen at least. And a priest, though not the one he'd paid.

"Signora Ferrari has been murdered." Kaya glanced at him and took his hand. "I'm happy to see you," she whispered. "It's been a most trying morning."

He'd been gone mere hours, and now he cursed himself for spending so much time searching for a priest when Kaya clearly needed him. "I'm never leaving you alone again."

She laughed, a weak, soft sound, but the smile she turned on him was loving and genuine. "I'm not sure that's practical; however, I tend to agree." She sighed and stepped closer. "Signore Ferrari has accused Hannah of murdering Signora Ferrari. I'm uncertain what evidence he has, but the Fortress Guards have arrested her and transported her to the local *carceri*."

"I was gone four hours," Paul muttered. "All right. What makes Signore Ferrari so certain it was Hannah?"

"They argued last night, I believe, she and Signora Ferrari, though I don't know about what. I have not yet been able to speak with Hannah, but the signore was loudly insistent." Kaya snorted. "After you left, Hannah was nervous. I thought it was because of the robbery attempt, but now I'm uncertain. However,

Signore Ferrari was so insistent Hannah had killed the signora, I'm beginning to believe he murdered his wife and laid the blame on Hannah."

Paul blinked at her. "That's a bold claim. I don't know the laws here, but I imagine we'll be allowed to visit her." With enough coin. "Have you spoken to Charlotte?"

"Yes. She's packing a small bag for Hannah, but I'm afraid she's not much help otherwise." Kaya shook her head sympathetically. "She's still very upset from yesterday's, ah, encounter, and her Calabrian isn't the strongest. Apparently, she had a fever when they arrived and lay abed for several weeks."

"I imagine." Paul pinched the bridge of his nose. "All right." No, he didn't know what their next move was. "All right. We'll take a bag to Hannah, leave Charlotte with the footmen—" Paul stopped. "Where are the footmen?"

"Hannah dismissed them last eve." Kaya sighed and shook her head. "Apparently, she didn't trust them after they did little to stop the bandits or prevent Fritz's murder." She met his gaze. "I'm afraid this is a rather tangled mess."

"Tangled, indeed," he agreed sardonically. "We have two choices." He already knew what Kaya's choice would be, but he continued anyway. "We can pack up, sail to Venice, and not look back. Or we can stay and help Hannah."

"We're staying."

"I knew you were going to say that."

"Then why bother to ask?" Kaya tilted her head and eyed him. "Why would you think otherwise?"

Paul opened his mouth, then shook his head and chuckled, though there was precious little to laugh about. "I have no idea. All right, I'll speak to the condottiero and see about visiting Hannah. I'm not sure if she'll be allowed a lawyer, or what the laws are here, but hopefully we can at least speak with her."

"I'm not leaving until we discover who killed the signora." Kaya frowned, then returned her gaze to the milling guards in the foyer. "Whether it's Hannah or another, I'm not leaving."

Of course she wasn't. He supposed this was another notch in his atonement. Before, he would've left, disappeared into the night—or day, in this case—and not bothered to worry about the prisoner ever again. But he liked Hannah. He just preferred to keep Kaya away from prisons, military guards, and murder.

It was not the easiest task.

Twelve

Kaya had experienced many things since leaving Cairo. A mix, she supposed, of good and bad, which was generally the way life went, so far as she could tell. She had not, however, ever thought she'd experience a prison.

They took Hannah's carriage. Charlotte sat stoic and stunned as they made the trip, though that might've been the language barrier. Charlotte had no one to speak with about Hannah, and Kaya had no way to offer her comfort. So the two of them sat in silence as Paul drove.

"Perhaps not the wisest time to have dismissed the footmen," he muttered as he helped Kaya and Charlotte from the carriage. "Not that they were any use."

"I'm surprised the directions the condottiero gave you were accurate. Given his distaste, I half expected him to direct you off a cliff." The captain of the guards had looked anything but helpful, but he had begrudgingly agreed to Paul's request and given detailed directions to the prison.

"He had nothing to lose," Paul said as he took the bag from Charlotte and settled one hand on Kaya's back. "Plus, I'm certain whoever is guarding Hannah will demand a bribe."

Charlotte had only blinked when Paul took the small pouch

of coins he'd retrieved from the bandits yesterday. He'd tried to explain that they were for Hannah's welfare, but Charlotte didn't speak English and only a smattering of Calabrian, and neither Paul nor Kaya spoke Prussian.

Perhaps they ought to try Marathi. Hannah had said they'd traveled there. Kaya made a mental note, but they were at the doors. Now certainly wasn't the time.

"We're here to see Countess von Almey." Paul used his haughty tone. The one he used when speaking to inn proprietors who looked down on them because they traveled by foot rather than by carriage.

Kaya didn't bother with the pair of guards, who stared at Paul as if they didn't speak Calabrian, either. Instead, she watched the area, her fingers brushing her khanjar. Just in case. New locales required a certain level of surveillance. Especially a prison.

Not that she knew that. "This is one experience I could have definitely done without."

Paul cast her a sardonic smile and tilted his head slightly in agreement.

No one else lurked around the street, and it seemed these guards didn't require a bribe. They opened the doors and silently let them enter. The building was drab brown stone on the outside and not much cheerier on the inside. Because it was on a corner surrounded by taller buildings and a forgotten road that abruptly ended, little light entered the grimy windows. A tall desk with a smattering of candles lay directly in front of the foyer, and a single man sat behind it.

Kaya looked around and frowned. "I'm not impressed with this place," she muttered to Paul as another guard led them deeper into the building.

"Eh, it's cleaner than what I've seen." He grinned at her. "Cleaner than the military stockades, too."

She snorted and rolled her eyes. "I'm sure," she said primly.

They waited while the guard opened the heavy wooden door and disappeared. Charlotte ran to Hannah, and the pair embraced, talking rapidly and crying. Kaya and Paul stayed by the open door, and Kaya tried not to breathe too deeply.

"The stench is truly atrocious." She wrinkled her nose but doubted anything would help. "How much did you pay the guards?"

"Far too much, the greedy bastards." Paul shook his head. "But if it makes them remember her at mealtimes, it's worth it." He moved to lean against the doorframe, then stopped and straightened.

"Best not." Kaya agreed to his silent grimace. "What do you mean, remember her?"

"I don't know how Italian prisons work, but in England you have to pay for the prisoner. If there's no one to pay or bring food, they'll freeze or starve."

"Barbaric," Kaya spat. "Are all prisons like that?"

He shrugged and stepped further into the small, dark cell. "No idea." He glanced at her. "And I don't want to find out, either."

She couldn't fault him there. "Hannah," Kaya called and stepped toward her new friend. "We've brought a few things." She nodded to Charlotte. "And Charlotte packed some items." She lowered her voice. "And coin, in case you might need."

"Thank you." Hannah wiped her cheeks and shook her head. Her fair hair fell from its once-immaculate bun, and her face was stained with tears and dirt. "I don't know what happened. I don't understand."

Kaya waited, but, other than a few tears, Hannah said nothing more. "Signore Ferrari is most insistent you killed his wife."

"I did not!" Hannah snapped, spine straightening, chin raising. "He's wrong. Desperate. I don't know, but I had nothing to do with Signora Ferrari's death."

"All right." Paul looked around, then shrugged and set the small case on the single chair by the window. The tiny window sat high along the wall, and no light penetrated the cell, but at least some of the breeze came through.

"Start from the beginning. What happened? You argued?" Paul folded his arms, feet braced. Kaya looked to the door, but no one lurked there. Still, she felt it best to keep quiet.

"Argued? Bah." Hannah waved an impatient hand. "The footmen were angry I dismissed them; they were loud and drunk. The signora didn't like it and didn't care that they were no longer in my employ. We argued, but it was a triviality."

"Apparently not," Kaya said softly. "Why were the footmen angry? Did you not pay them the agreed-upon wage? Did they demand more? Had you promised them long-term employment?"

Hannah eyed her. She looked angry, but only on the surface. Beneath that, Kaya could see her fear and uncertainty. Understandable, as Hannah had only finished telling Kaya she wished to protect herself when the guards arrested her.

"No. Our agreement was they'd see us safely from Rome to the coast. They did not see us safely," she added hotly. "Poor Fritz paid with his life. However, I paid them their wage, and even a small bonus for their return, should they wish."

"Where are they now?" Paul asked.

Sniffing in dismissal, she waved her hand again. "I do not know. They are no longer in my employ."

Kaya nodded. "All right. Don't say anything; we'll find a lawyer or someone to represent you." She eyed Charlotte, who looked worried and annoyed to be left out of the conversation. "Please tell Charlotte we'll handle everything. Does she speak Marathi?"

Hannah blinked in surprise. "Yes. We spent a lot of time traveling around India." She said something to Charlotte in Prussian, then looked at Kaya.

"I'm sorry we didn't think of Marathi before," Kaya said apologetically. "We both speak the language." Though Paul, who had spent more than a decade in Bombay, no doubt spoke it more fluidly than she. Gidd had taught her, but that had been a while ago. "We promise we'll look after Hannah and see about her release."

"Thank you." Charlotte nodded in relief, no doubt pleased they could finally include her. "How do you plan to release the countess?"

Hannah eyed them both speculatively, whether at this new tidbit of information or in curiosity about her release, Kaya didn't know.

Paul shook his head. "We'll work on it. Someone knows something; they always do."

"We'll be back," Kaya promised.

"Thank you. Oh! Did you find a priest for Fritz?"

"Aye, he should be at the inn now." Paul sighed. "But I'm sure Signore Ferrari turned him away. I'll see if I can find him again and give Fritz the proper rites."

"Thank you," Hannah said again and smiled. "I truly—you don't know what that means to me." She offered a watery laugh and nodded at the bag. "This as well. I've never been in prison."

Kaya laughed and squeezed her hand. "Hopefully you won't be for long. We'll work on finding a way to release you."

"Thank you." Hannah shook her head. "You barely know me. Why go to all the trouble?"

"We like to take care of our friends," Paul said.

Kaya stifled a laugh. They were practically strangers, but she appreciated his words. She wanted Hannah to be a friend. "We'll see if we can return tomorrow. And hopefully we'll have more information about what happened."

"Thank you," Hannah said. She gave a final hug to Charlotte and a sincere smile to Kaya, and then they left.

The guard banged closed the heavy door, and Kaya tried not to jump. She most definitely hoped never to be in another prison again.

"What?" Paul stared at her as if he'd never seen her before. "Where?"

"Brandenburg. I believe it's near the Baltic Sea." She honestly had no idea where it was, only what Hannah had told her. It sounded much farther north than she envisioned them traveling.

Colder, too. But then, Kaya hadn't really thought about it. They traveled wherever they wished. Neither had ties to anyone save each other. Traveling to Brandenburg, wherever that was, or across the Continent was all the same.

"Why?"

Kaya didn't know whether to laugh at his simple questions or be annoyed by them. She settled for a smile and a quick wave of her hand. They walked along the shoreline, watching the boats out at sea. These were not the fishermen they'd seen before dawn, but visitors enjoying a ride on calm waters on a clear, sunny day.

Azizi stayed close by, suspicious of anyone who ventured too close. For so loving and affectionate a dog, she did not like strangers. Kaya didn't blame her. She, too, was unused to so many people. It crept down her back, that unease of being seen.

"Hannah, she—the portrait miniature is of her son."

"Aye, I guessed as much." Paul shook his head and pinched the bridge of his nose. "What does that have to do with us traveling with her?"

She tightened her hand on his arm and shot him an annoyed look. Paul dropped his hand and met her gaze.

"He was killed in a robbery similar to the one yesterday. She's lost her driver and has let go the footmen she hired in Rome. She has no protection, and she's scared."

Paul looked down at her and waited. He didn't object—not that Kaya could think of a reason why he might, other than he didn't trust Hannah. And he didn't trust anyone other than Kaya. And Azizi.

"Why?" Paul held up a hand to stop her and shook his head. "I don't mean why does she want us to travel with her. I mean why do *you*."

"I don't know," Kaya admitted. The wind gusted hard, pushing her a step ahead. She looked out over the sea, and the endless blue stretched before them. So many possibilities lay in every direction; they only had to choose one.

"Do you not wish to travel to Prussia?"

"I've never thought about it." Paul shrugged. "Thought we'd stay closer to the coast, perhaps the South of France." A slight smile tugged his lips. She wondered what that meant. "Maybe buy a small cottage by the ocean."

Kaya tilted her head. "I've never heard you mention that. Why there?"

"Oh." He waved a hand, then curled it around hers, which was still resting in the crook of his elbow. "Not necessarily there. In Bombay, we talked about that, John, Oliver, and I. When we had enough coin, we'd leave Bombay and settle in the South of France, along the coast, with wine and women and drink ourselves into a stupor every evening."

She wrinkled her nose and twisted her lips. "How very exciting."

Paul laughed and tugged her closer. He was not one for properties, her Paul, and he didn't seem to care how scandalous affection in public looked. Even with his wife.

Kaya liked it.

"I never said it was exciting. Only that it was a plan." He shrugged. "Not a very good one, either, I'm sorry to admit. But the South of France was not Bombay, and that was all that mattered."

"Do you still wish to travel there now?" Kaya considered that change, heading west rather than north. She didn't necessarily want to travel to France, but she could not pinpoint why. Only that if Paul had wanted to settle there for the wine and the women, she did not want any part of it.

"Not especially. If you truly want to travel with Hannah to Prussia, that's fine. I don't foresee a reason we shouldn't." He stopped and held her by the shoulders. His fingers brushed her cheeks, and he kissed her forehead. The soft, intimate touch curled through her, and Kaya relaxed. "In case you hadn't realized, I'll go wherever you go."

"I'm glad." She took his hands and turned him back toward the inn.

"That I'll follow you?" His rich laugh warmed her, and she thought they were another step closer to closing the distance between them.

"No. Well, mayhap." She shot him a mischievous grin and watched his answering one from the corner of her eye. "I'm glad we agree. It doesn't matter where we travel." She lowered her voice as they neared the inn, though only a single guard stood at the top of the stairs.

She didn't necessarily trust the man, though Kaya hadn't heard either guard utter a single word. Not even when they'd arrested Hannah. Now that she thought back on it, that seemed odd. Perhaps they deferred to the Fortress Guards, but not even a word of gossip? Strange.

"How did you find a Lutheran minister?" She asked suddenly, slowing their steps. She didn't really wish to return, but neither of them enjoyed crowds. The streets around the inn were bustling with mid-afternoon shoppers, and several couples sat outside coffeehouses.

"One of the priests who didn't threaten to have me hanged directed me to Father Roberto." Surprised by the name, though it was a common one here, she blinked up at Paul. "Yes. Omen or not, I thought it a good sign. This priest didn't ask questions, and I didn't offer answers." Paul's voice lowered as they started up the stairs.

"You do find a way," she sighed as they passed the guard. "You have a gift."

"For bribery? Finding the most disreputable people in any given area?" He stopped and offered a sardonic bow. When he looked up at her, he winked. "Thank you, my lady. I do try my best."

"It's a talent," Kaya insisted. "Who else would have managed to find a Lutheran minister in such a Catholic country? We are in the Papal States, after all."

"I'm not sure how much a minister he is," Paul allowed, steering her toward the terrace. "But Father Roberto insisted he knew the Lutheran prayers."

"I hope it will be enough to ease Hannah's mind. She's worried over Fritz. Apparently, he had been with her for decades." Kaya closed her eyes against the wind and let her mind wander. What would it be like to share so many years with Paul? She'd loved Derya and Gidd, but those relationships felt so very different than the one she had with Paul.

Not only because of the intimacy, of course.

Now all she had was Paul. Paul and Azizi and herself. The stab of longing didn't surprise her—jealously and longing were old friends. Now the world lay before her. People and knowledge and adventure. A future she never thought she'd live.

"Do you want to travel with Hannah for her sake?" Paul asked suddenly. "Or yours?"

Caught off guard by the question, Kaya turned her back to the ocean view and weighed her answer. Somehow, despite her walking boots, sand had wedged its way to her feet.

"I don't know," she admitted. "It feels right, joining her."

Scowling, she tried wiggling her toes, but that only made it worse. She'd had enough of sand as they crossed *al-ṣaḥrā' al-kubrá*. Perhaps she was not meant for the beach.

"You make friends in the oddest places, Kaya."

"Do I?" She tilted her head. "Or maybe I know the oddest people. I married you, did I not?"

Paul's laughter startled Azizi, who woofed in agreement, and Ginevra, one of the maids. Kaya merely smiled. "Let's sneak up to our rooms. I want to make love to you."

His eyes darkened, and he took her hand. "Your wish is my command."

Thirteen

"We don't have much to go on," Paul said as they settled in their room.

So far, Signore Ferrari hadn't kicked them out, but Paul wanted to be ready in case of such an occurrence. Packing their scant belongings, he nodded to the balcony doors. "Open the doors?"

"I thought you did not like the openness and insecurity." But she opened them anyway, letting in the softly scented breeze from the Adriatic. "The courtyard is empty."

"I need to listen for the guards," he said quietly, so his voice wouldn't travel. "I don't like any of this."

"Do you believe Hannah?" Kaya turned and sat on the bed. She leaned down to scratch Azizi's head, who purred and slowly sank to the floor belly-up.

Paul chuckled at Azizi's antics and shook his head, refolding their tent as tightly as he could manage. "I'm getting better at this," he muttered, tightening the buckles on his pack.

He eyed the long wooden beam they used to carry the tent but left it by the pack. If they had to move fast, they'd need to leave it. Straightening, he rubbed his knee. Damn, he'd twisted it harder than he thought yesterday. Tracking those thieves in too-tight boots hadn't done it any good. The walk back, without those boots, had been worse.

"I don't know if I believe Hannah," he said, in answer to her question. "I can't imagine a woman who showed such fear at a robbery would suddenly turn vicious and murder a near stranger."

Kaya cocked her head. "Is that possible? Have you heard of that before? Someone freezing in terror when they are attacked but attacking others?"

"No," Paul admitted as he limped to the bed. "I haven't. Is it possible?" He shrugged. "Most anything is, so far as I can tell, so who knows."

"I can't see her stabbing Signora Ferrari so many times." Kaya frowned and knelt before him. "Do your new boots bother you?"

"No. Well, yes, they aren't broken in." Paul tugged off his boots and stretched. He suppressed a groan when his knee twinged. "What were you saying about Hannah and the signora?"

"Anger." Kaya took his calf in hand and massaged it.

Paul groaned, feeling the knots loosen from his calf clear to his shoulders. "Damn, you've got magnificent hands, sweetheart." His eyes slipped closed at her touch, and, not for the first time, he wondered how he'd ever survived without her. "Don't stop."

"It takes a lot of anger to stab someone so many times. There was blood everywhere." She sighed and moved to the back of his knee. "Let me know if this hurts."

It did, but he didn't want her to remove her hands. "It feels amazing," Paul said honestly. "What about the blood? You didn't tell me that part." He opened his eyes and met hers. "I didn't see any in the hallway."

"Things were a bit rushed," she reminded him dryly. "And I'm certain the maids scrubbed the walls as soon as the guards took Signora Ferrari's body away. No sense worrying the other guests." She stopped. "Not that there are other guests."

"I'm still surprised Ferrari hasn't kicked us out." Paul sighed, body sinking further into the bed. "For associating with Hannah. We arrived together and dined together."

Kaya's strong hands kneaded into his thigh, and he felt his eyes roll into the back of his head. She shifted, and her beautiful, warm hands left his leg only to move to the other. Starting at his calf, she kneaded the muscles until he thought he might melt into the bedding.

"Hmm," she said, but he couldn't tell if it was in agreement or not. "If you were to argue with someone, what might prompt you to kill them?"

Paul jerked up. "Just outright murder?"

She nodded, her eyes serious even as her hands moved from knee to thigh. He was as hard as a rock, aching for her, and she wanted to talk murder?

Paul would never understand his wife, but, God, did he love her.

"I'm not sure I would," he admitted. "Not—it's hard to explain." He shook his head and tried to think of an example. "A lot of men, well, people, are quick to anger over the most trivial slight. Cheat at cards? That calls for a knife duel. Or a stab in the back. Or even an ambush in the back alley on your way home."

She eyed him in disbelief. "Over cards?" Shrugging, she straightened and undid his trousers. "Go on."

"Some might say it's a matter of pride, but really it's to show you're the bigger, badder man." Paul shoved his trousers down and scooted farther onto the bed.

"So it could be that quick." Kaya knelt over him, settling on his thighs. "We should discover if anyone else spoke with Signora Ferrari after the argument."

"You really want to talk about that now?" Paul asked, slipping a finger into her wet heat. "I can think of far more interesting things to discuss. Right now."

"Discuss?" She smiled, that slight twitch of her lips that showed her mischievousness. "I did not realize we were discussing things." He pressed against her clit, and Kaya's breath caught. "Right now."

"We can discuss many things." Paul slowly circled her nub, watching her eyes close and her head fall back. Kaya arched into his touch, her fingers curling into his shoulders. "We can discuss how your head falls back when I do this."

He curled his fingers within her, his thumb pressing hard to her nub. She shuddered, her hips grinding down on his hand, her blunt nails digging into his skin.

"Or this." He rubbed hard on her nub, watching her breath heave out of her open mouth. Kaya lifted her head and opened her heavy-lidded eyes to watch him. "Or when you shatter around me, or the absolute gorgeous sounds you make when you do."

"Paul," she breathed, but her hips moved faster as she sought her release.

"That's it, sweetheart. Come for me."

Kaya did, the moans he so loved falling from her lips as she tightened around his fingers, her orgasm crashing through her. He loved watching her like this. As much as he ached to bury himself in her, watching her fall apart from his touch made him want her more.

"Christ, I love you, Kaya." Paul lifted her hips, and she settled over him, taking his cock deep into her.

"Are we discussing that now?" she asked, cheeks flushed as she moved over him.

"I can think of a thousand ways to show I love you," he admitted, urging her faster. "But I can only say I love you. It's a very small way to tell you what you mean to me."

"Paul." Her face softened even as she tightened around him, her orgasm winding through her.

"Come for me, Kaya." He found her nub beneath all her skirts and watched her come again.

Rolling them over, and nearly falling off the bed onto Azizi, Paul kissed her. He moved faster, harder, as his own orgasm tightened through him. Sinking his teeth into her shoulder, he withdrew and came.

He stayed like that for a while as his breath slowed and his heart stopped its mad race to beat out of his chest. Kaya's hands stroked up and down his back as her own breathing slowed.

"You can massage me anytime," he mumbled into her shoulder.

Kaya laughed, a breathless sound, her fingers tangling in his hair. She gently tugged until he looked at her, then she kissed him. "I shall keep that in mind, should we need to discuss things again."

Paul smiled against her lips. "I'm always open for discussion," he promised. Just then, Azizi barked, and Paul looked over the bed. "And you, you have impeccable timing, as always."

His beautiful wife laughed and shifted beneath him, pushing at his shoulder. "I don't want her wandering outside alone. Get dressed." She kissed his cheek. "We'll go for a walk with her."

Laughing at the notion that Azizi would be safer with them, Paul did as she asked. "I still don't like it here." He tugged on his boots and scowled at the tightness of the leather. "Can you hear anyone in the courtyard?"

"No." She looked at him over her shoulder. "But then, I was also busy."

Paul grabbed her about the waist and kissed her. His fingers tangled in her loose hair, and he felt her melt into him. "I enjoy this kind of busy," he whispered against her lips.

"I am most glad to hear that." The tips of her fingers caressed his cheek, and she looked so serious for a moment, Paul wondered what she wanted to say. "Let's walk," she said instead, and he knew that wasn't what she'd originally planned. "I wish to talk further about Hannah."

They made their way out in silence, listening for any sound from either the courtyard or the hallway, but the inn remained eerily hushed. Not a sound from the maids or the stableboys, which made the back of Paul's neck itch.

Outside, with the sun deceptively bright and the breeze a warm caress, he thought Signora Ferrari's murder had not touched this place. But a heaviness hung over the inn, an air of foreboding in each shadow and rustle of the leaves.

"You haven't heard the maids talking?" Paul asked as Azizi ran ahead of them, deeper into the woods. "Nothing about an argument with anyone other than Hannah? With Signore Ferrari? One of the other guests? Not that there are other guests, you're right. Anyone?"

"I haven't spoken to them. However, they were silent this morning as they served breakfast. I wonder if they knew something." She squeezed his arm and rested her head against his shoulder. "Could one of them have done it?"

"I don't know. I've never investigated a murder—or any other crime, to be fair—but I'm sure we can safely count anyone as a suspect."

"Charlotte?" Kaya nodded. "I suppose. If she was angry enough over the robbery, perhaps something in her broke." Paul didn't need to see her to know she frowned. Disbelief coated her words. "An odd and extreme reaction, however, considering how she and Hannah clung to each other afterward."

"And how she and Hannah interacted with each other in the prison."

"Mm-hmm," she agreed. "How do we plan to ensure the authorities release Hannah? Is that possible? People are released because others ask?"

Paul laughed. "No, not in my experience. But maybe if we find the true killer."

"And if that is Hannah?" Kaya asked hesitatingly. "Or Charlotte?"

He shrugged, uncertain. "Then I suppose we leave Riccione as quietly as we entered. Given what you said about Signore Ferrari, perhaps we should look into him more." Frowning, he tried to work it all out. "But you said he was insistent Hannah killed her?"

"Most insistent." Kaya stopped in a small clearing and looked up at the cloudless sky. "He didn't hesitate to accuse her."

"People grieve differently, I suppose, but none of this makes any sense." Paul could only come up with two plausible answers, given the limited information they had: Signore Ferrari had killed his wife, or Hannah had.

"If Hannah did not kill the signora," Kaya said slowly, turning in a small circle, her head still tilted skyward, "then Signore Ferrari knows who did and accused her anyway—which is odd, if he only wished to push blame onto someone else."

"Considering there were others to blame?" Paul nodded and listened for Azizi. He spotted her not too far from Kaya, one eye on something she hunted and the other on them. For all her wandering instincts, she knew when something was amiss, and she'd keep close.

"Why blame the wealthiest among us when no one would have cared if one of the footmen were to blame?"

Kaya shook her head and stepped from the circle of sunlight, blinking up at him. He held out his hand, and she took it without hesitation. He kissed her palm.

"I adore the way your mind works." He grinned then shook his head. "Hannah dismissed the footmen, and no one would have blinked if one of them had been accused of murder. They aren't from the area, and they're servants, so they would have been treated differently."

"Same with Charlotte, though I'm certain—if she is not our murderess—that Hannah would have fought for her release."

"And us." Paul shrugged but knew he was right. "We would have been the easiest targets. We arrived in a carriage, but it's not ours. We've had run-ins with the locals since we set foot in Rome."

"I do not know," Kaya admitted and tugged him deeper into the shade of a tree. "Does this mean Hannah did kill Signora Ferrari? Or that her husband did and framed her?"

Paul frowned and shook his head, pulling her to sit on a fallen tree. "I've no idea." Sighing, he scrubbed a hand down his face and shook his head again. "I'm certain we're missing something, but until we speak with the maids and stableboys, I'm at a loss."

"What shall we speak about then?" Kaya laughed and leaned against him. "Have you given any thought to joining Hannah in Brandenburg?" She paused. "Assuming she is not, in fact, a murderess?"

"What do you want to do once we reach Brandenburg?" Paul asked instead. He doubted anyone was eavesdropping on their conversation this far from the inn, but they continued to speak in quiet English in case. "The same question applies there as it does here, or in San Marino."

"Do?" Kaya tilted her head, eyeing him in the shadows. "Hannah has asked us there so I may train her in the use of a weapon."

"Aye, and it'll take several weeks to arrive, I'm guessing." Paul had no idea how long such a journey might take. He sighed. "Given our previous luck, we'll no doubt also encounter...trouble."

Kaya snorted. "Paul, we encountered trouble in the middle of the desert."

He grinned. "It's a talent."

She eyed him speculatively, and he wondered what she thought. Eight months was not a long time, not when they had the rest of their lives together. But in those eight months, he'd learned more about her—and himself—than he thought possible.

"You think our meeting Hannah was meant to be."

"No," she said slowly. "Not preordained or predestined, as we spoke of before. Fate. Simply timely." She frowned and waved a hand as she tried to find the words.

He noticed her doing that more and more, a mannerism she'd picked up from Marta. During their first few months together, Kaya held herself very still, very close. No unnecessary movements, no nervous habits. Away from her strict upbringing, she had grown. Paul loved that. Loved that he was able to witness such growth.

He shifted on the tree and tucked her head against his chest. He loved that she changed him, too.

"Perhaps things are not predestined," he said quietly as Azizi came bounding up to them. "But yes. I do believe we are where we are meant to be."

"What does one do in Brandenburg?" She smiled, curling her fingers around his. "Perhaps we shall purchase our own schloss and—" She frowned. "Engage in whatever activities one engages in while living in a schloss."

Paul laughed. He startled several birds, who rustled in the trees. Azizi sent him a huffy snort but otherwise didn't leave Kaya's side, good dog that she was.

"I don't believe one engages in anything while owning a schloss. One merely enjoys one's wealth."

Kaya frowned. "How tedious."

"Work is overrated, sweetheart." Paul stood and helped her up as well. "It's hard, backbreaking, with long hours and little pay."

"Then why do so many engage in it?"

Laughing, he shrugged. "Food. We all have to eat."

"A most rational reason."

"The best reason of them all." They exited the wood and made their way into the still-silent courtyard. Paul doubted anyone else stayed at the inn—he'd seen no others when they arrived yesterday, and no one had joined them in the dining hall for breakfast. The lack of guests bothered him, but Paul couldn't pinpoint why.

"Speaking of, I'm starved. Let's find dinner." He eyed the sun, which was slowly sinking into the sea, and estimated another hour, hour and a half of light. "Then we'll speak with the maids. I don't want to be out of our room after dark."

"No?" She looked up at him curiously. "Why not?"

Paul shrugged, unable to find the words to convey the sinking feeling slithering down his back. "I don't trust this inn."

Kaya snorted. "You don't trust anything, my love."

"And that keeps you alive," he reminded her with a wink.

Fourteen

The next morning, as Kaya sought out the inn's maids, she realized two things about herself. She enjoyed speaking to new people—maids, stableboys, innkeepers, countesses, it didn't matter—but she did not like doing so under false pretenses. She supposed that had more to do with how thoroughly Gidd and Derya had lied to her than anything.

Now, with Azizi by her side, she walked toward the rear of the inn, where the maids and stableboys liked to sit and talk.

She and Paul had breakfasted alone, the air hovering over the inn somber and quiet. Bea, the kitchen maid who had helped Signora Ferrari, had served them with a nervous bob and refused to make eye contact. The bread was slightly burnt and the coffee a little overdone, but otherwise there was no real change after the murder.

Kaya paused just outside the small cottage that served as a storage room. She let the warm sea breeze wash over her. The sun shone down and chased last eve's chill away. She stretched onto her toes and lifted her arms as freely as her dress allowed.

Promising herself she'd practice her movements and footing later this afternoon, Kaya rested her hand on Azizi and braced herself. From here, she could only hear jumbled whispers, which seemed to stop as soon as they reached the open door. She stepped around the corner and nodded to the group.

"Oh, Signora Conrad." Ginevra, the second-floor maid, jumped up as soon as she spotted Kaya. "Can I help you?"

"Hello, Ginevra." Kaya smiled then included the other four—two more maids and two stableboys, all of whom Kaya knew by name. "I wanted to say how sorry I was about Signora Ferrari."

Ginevra looked shocked for a moment, then she nodded. The two stableboys edged closer to Azizi, and Kaya smiled. Either they knew very little about what happened, and the women had been filling them in, or they wanted to leave before the conversation progressed. Either way, Kaya knew the women before her had some sort of information.

"Go on, go play." She told Azizi the same thing in Egyptian, and the three of them bounded out of the small cottage and into the wood.

"*Grazie*," Ginevra said, but she still looked as if Kaya had caught her doing something she ought not to have done.

"Will Signore Ferrari keep the inn open?" Kaya asked the three women. Bea continued to look at the ground. Rosa, the downstairs maid, flicked her gaze from Ginevra to Kaya and back again.

"I believe so, *sì*." Ginevra swallowed. "*Sì*," she repeated. "I think so."

"If he does not, what will you do?" Kaya asked, not entirely certain where this line of questioning would wander. Was this how people retrieved information?

"*Cosa farò*?" Ginevra paled further. "I need the money, my mama...we need the money."

"Ginevra." Kaya closed the distance between them and took her hands. "All right. It's all right. I'll help. What do you need? Is your mother ill?"

"My youngest brother, he needs constant care." Ginevra broke off with a sob then straightened. "You will speak with Signore Ferrari? See he keeps the inn open?"

"Aye," Kaya said, already planning to speak with the man. "I'll see he does. Rosa?" She turned to the other maid, who hovered uncertainly beside Ginevra. "Find a place to help her clean up. We'll talk to Signore Ferrari."

Rosa nodded uncertainly and moved off, one arm around a shaking Ginevra. Before she moved out of earshot, Rosa turned around. She was a small, quiet woman whom Kaya hadn't heard utter more than two words.

"Be careful, Signora Conrad. These woods are not safe."

Kaya nodded and offered an encouraging smile. But her fingers brushed her khanjar, and the warm day suddenly turned cold. Did Rosa mean not safe from bandits? Something else she and Paul had not encountered? Yet?

Signore Ferrari?

"Bea?" Kaya turned to the other woman. "Do you need help in the kitchens? Shall I speak to Signore Ferrari about finding help?"

"I'll manage." Her clipped words belied the wan look on her face. "Ginevra needs the work, so I won't say this in front of her."

Kaya nodded and kept silent, though she heard Azizi and the stableboys moving closer.

"Signore Ferrari is a spendthrift and a bastard." Bea made a strange movement with her hands that Kaya had seen before—mostly directed at her while they traversed Sicily—but didn't understand. "Be careful. I'm sorry about your friend. Don't let her confess to anything."

"Thank you." Kaya nodded and scrambled to say something more, something to draw Bea out. "Do you know who killed Signora Ferrari?"

"No," Bea said. Kaya heard the truth in that word, but there was also something else she couldn't place. "But I doubt it was the *contessa*. She may have been a *latifondista*, but she was kind. I doubt she has that sort of rage in her."

"I'll have my husband speak with Signore Ferrari. If he closes the inn, I'll see all of you are given references and money. Jobs, if I can." Kaya held Bea's gaze, who watched her as if she didn't understand her words.

"Ginevra was right," Bea said as she turned to walk away. "You aren't like the *latifondista* who normally stay here. Be careful, signora. There are dangers all over this city, and they don't care how kind you are to the rest of us."

"I'll be careful, Bea," Kaya promised. The cold slithering down her spine did not abate, and she whistled for Azizi.

Kaya waved to Tino and Nestor as they laughingly rejoined Bea on the path back to the inn. Resting her hand on Azizi's head, she looked down at the dog, who was panting from her playing.

"That was not at all how I'd envisioned that conversation," she said in quiet Egyptian. Though Kaya was confident they were alone, she didn't wish her voice to carry. "I suspect they know more than they say, but I can't blame them for remaining silent. Come, let's find Paul."

Kaya finally found Paul, but only after she let Azizi sniff him out. He was on the balcony off the dining room, arms folded, hatless, as he watched the shore. His hair, longer and curlier now than when they'd first met, blew slightly in the wind, and she longed to run her fingers through it.

She loved his hair, but the very public balcony wasn't the place to indulge in their private moments.

"What are you looking at?" she asked, joining him at the balustrade.

"Nothing," he admitted and smiled down at her. "Thinking."

"Did you discover anything from Signore Ferrari?" She tugged on his arm, the left one, as always. Standing on his left hindered her own movements, should they need to move quickly, but both of them always tried to keep free their dominant fighting hand.

Especially in uncertain situations. Which they found themselves in more and more.

"He's wailing like a child who lost his favorite toy," Paul grumbled. He kissed her forehead. "I'm not sure if that's grief or acting."

"You do not believe he grieves for his wife?" Kaya tilted her head and leaned a hip against the railing. She met Paul's gaze as their fingers twined together.

"I suppose everyone grieves differently," Paul admitted. "And, to be truthful, I've never seen anyone grieve over another. Not—" He broke off and held her tightly. "Those I used to know did not grieve another's death."

He stopped again, and suddenly Kaya knew what he meant. She was going to say the words aloud, but her throat closed. He'd never mourned anyone, but if something should happen to her...

"I know," she managed around the understanding and love that was choking her. She knew because she felt the same. She'd mourned Gidd and Derya, and no doubt would until the day she died. But if something happened to Paul, Kaya didn't know what she'd do.

Her conversation with Hannah came back to her. They stood in the road, the sun shining brightly down on them as they waited for Paul to retrieve Hannah's miniature. Hannah had asked what she'd do if Paul *didn't* return, and Kaya had no real answer. Finding the murderers was one thing. Afterward? She honestly couldn't say.

"Bea, the kitchen maid," Kaya began, though her heart raced with uncertainty. "She warned me to be careful. That there were many dangers here."

"She's not wrong," Paul snorted and hugged her close. "I don't want you leaving my side. I know." He tightened his hold on her. "I know. You are more than capable of defending yourself."

"You believe her?" Kaya did. The foreboding that shivered over her skin told her to heed Bea's words of warning.

"I believe there's more here than we're aware of." Paul pressed his lips to the top of her head, and Kaya closed her eyes, hugging him tighter. "And I know that if something were to happen to you, I would not handle it well."

"Perhaps Signore Ferrari is not acting, as you suggest." Kaya swallowed around a dry throat. "Perhaps he truly grieves his wife."

She couldn't see Paul crying and wailing over her death, but she all too easily saw him burning the inn down if the same fate befell her. Kaya shivered in the warm afternoon and pulled back just enough to meet his gaze.

"We shall not separate to speak with others," she agreed. "I don't want anything to happen to you, either."

His kiss was harsh and hard, but in it she tasted all his love, his passion and hunger, and his driving need to keep her safe. Kaya kissed him back, pouring in every ounce of her own love for this brave, wonderful man. She never wanted to let him go, and she marveled that there had once been a time she seriously considered leaving him.

"I suppose," she said, pressing her lips to his once more, "you are stuck with me."

Paul laughed and wrapped his arms around her. He embraced her in warmth and security and the sureness of his love. "I wouldn't have it any other way."

They stood like that for a while. Kaya closed her eyes and simply enjoyed being in his embrace. There had been a time, not many weeks ago, when she worried she'd never feel his arms around her again.

"What else did you discover?" she eventually asked. "When you spoke with Signore Ferrari."

"That he fully believes Hannah murdered his wife." Paul loosened his embrace and leaned against the balustrade, tugging her next to him. He faced the inn, his back to the beach. He was constantly scanning for danger. Or eavesdroppers, in this case.

"Did he say why? He had to have a reason."

"He claims he found them."

"Found them?" Kaya frowned. "I don't understand. Found them where?"

"In the hallway." Paul glanced at her and shrugged. "He wouldn't say if he caught them arguing or if he saw Hannah standing over the body. He kept repeating he found the countess with his wife."

"How strange. Either he's speaking of an earlier incident, the one Hannah told us about, or he's lying." Kaya sighed and nodded at Paul's unspoken statement. "Or Hannah is."

"At this point, I'm not sure I believe either of them." Paul looked to Azizi, who had curled beside them, eyes closed, ears perked and alert. "Did any of the maids say more than be careful?"

"Ginevra was most upset over possibly losing her position. Her family needs the money." Kaya thought back to their conversation and shook her head. "Rosa, she didn't say anything. I'm afraid none of the women knew anything."

"And the stable lads?"

"Played with Azizi, though all five of them were whispering when I arrived at the cottage."

"It looks as if we'll have to figure this out on our own, though with no information to aid our search, I'm not sure how." Paul shook his head and lifted her hand to kiss the back. "Seems we've found trouble again."

"That seems to be a daily occurrence." She leaned against him and closed her eyes. "Helping is never wrong. No matter the outcome."

"I didn't say we wouldn't help Hannah." Paul chuckled. "Merely that we can't go a day without finding some sort of trouble."

"Yes. That, I can't explain." Kaya straightened and took his hand, pulling him toward the doors. "Let's see if we can find something to eat. Then you can speak with the stableboys, and I'll see if Bea needs help in the kitchens."

"I don't think we'll find our answers there." Paul held open the door for her and waited while Azizi stretched and followed.

"Most likely not," Kaya agreed. "But it's been a day. I'm not giving up so soon."

"Oh, Signora Conrad!" Ginevra stumbled to a halt just as Kaya and Paul crossed into the dining room. "There's a priest here to see you."

"A priest?" Kaya repeated, somewhat daftly.

"Oh. Yes. That's for...I'll handle it." Paul leaned in and whispered, "It's for Fritz, the driver. I forgot all about him."

She had as well, both poor Fritz and the priest Paul had found who swore he knew the Lutheran funeral rites. So much for staying together and not wandering off alone. But Fritz's funeral seemed more important, and Kaya wanted the opportunity to speak more with Ginevra.

"I'm glad the priest did not." Kaya squeezed his hand and shooed him off. "You take care of the priest; I'll see to luncheon."

"Kaya," Paul warned. "Be careful."

"I always am." She sniffed and grinned. "You as well—trouble follows you."

Paul offered a sardonic bow and disappeared out the door. Kaya turned to Ginevra and smiled. The maid looked better, not as pale and upset, though not her normal cheerful self. That, Kaya understood, especially if Ginevra's wage supported a family.

Well, she and Paul could at least take care of that.

Nodding to the other woman, Kaya gestured for Ginevra to walk beside her. "How is Bea making out in the kitchens alone? Does she need help with today's luncheon?"

Ginevra blinked at her and nodded. "Rosa and I help where possible, but we're expecting guests to arrive next week. There's so much to make ready."

Kaya had no idea what making ready the inn entailed, but she nodded. "I'll speak with Signore Ferrari about finding help, even temporary, until he decides what comes next."

"You will?" Ginevra smiled again. "Thank you, signora."

"What of the guards?" Kaya tilted her head toward the outside, where the two men appeared and disappeared with bewildering randomness. "Are they permanent? Or only for the holiday season?"

"They're so the rich guests feel safer." Ginevra shrugged and waved her hand. "Signore Ferrari feels it adds a level of security that competitors do not offer."

"Do you know anyone who needs a position and can help Bea in the kitchens?" Kaya could cook; she and Derya had spent time doing so, though their meals were only ever for the two of them. And Derya was not the best of cooks. As an *odalik*, she saw to Kaya's mother's needs in the court, not the preparation of meals.

"I think her sister might help," Ginevra said. "Does this mean you believe Signore Ferrari will keep the inn open?"

Kaya had no idea but hadn't the heart to say that. Ginevra didn't need the added worry. "Let's take it one day at a time, shall we? I'll speak with him about finding more help for Bea, and then we'll find out what his plans are."

She had no idea how she'd do that, or what she'd do if he planned on closing the inn, but it was best to solve one problem at a time.

Fifteen

Paul thanked Father Roberto and waved him off with a hefty change purse. The priest may have been slightly shady, but he had returned to the inn after being turned away yesterday. Of course, that might have had something to do with the payment Paul had promised, but whatever it took—he wasn't one to quibble.

Too much.

He needed to stop thinking like that, as if he never had enough. He and Kaya carried more than enough in jewels and gold, and they had spent only a small fraction of their wealth. However, a lifetime of scrimping and saving—and spending the moment he received his pay—hadn't prepared him for reasonable spending.

Though he wanted to find Kaya and ensure nothing bad had happened to her, Paul took this opportunity to speak with the stableboys. He doubted they'd be of much help, as they wouldn't have seen anything from the stables, but it was worth the stop. Paul turned to eye the distance between the inn and the stables, but it was too far. The inn boasted three floors and what looked like several additions, which expanded the building to odd angles.

The dirt path between the front of the inn wound round the

building, through the torches Signore Ferrari lit at night, and skirted the tree line. Though in a busy area of town, the back butted the trees and offered privacy. Was there a back path? Cursing himself for not scouting their sleeping arrangements more thoroughly, Paul debated backtracking now. But he heard the two lads talking to the horses, and he wanted to speak with them now before they ran off to their other duties.

The sun disappeared behind the building, spreading golden fingers of light along the path. Paul blinked and tugged his hat lower to shield his eyes. Slowing his gait, he listened to the conversation. It centered on horses, the maids, and whether Signora Conrad would keep her word about talking to Signore Ferrari and keeping the inn open.

He blinked. *What* had Kaya promised them?

Sighing, Paul looked heavenward, but he knew no help would come from there. Instead, he stepped into the stables.

"Oh, Signore Conrad!" One of the boys—Nestor, Paul thought—stopped whatever he was doing with the nearest horse. "Shall I saddle a horse for you?"

Paul shook his head. He had no idea how to ride a horse and wouldn't know where to ride one now, even if he wished to. "No, thank you. Nestor, is it?" The boy nodded and resumed brushing the horse. "I'm trying to help my friend. The countess we arrived with?"

Nestor hunched his shoulders and brushed the poor horse harder. "I didn't see nothing."

"I'm sure you didn't," Paul agreed. "That's not why I'm asking. I want to know if anyone else came to the inn. Any other guests."

The boy glanced at his friend—Tino, Paul thought—and they both shook their heads. "Nothing."

"All right." Paul only half believed them, but he let it slide. "Do either of you happen to know if the prison accepts *legame*?" Their expressions were blank at the word. Paul tried to think of a different one but had nothing. He didn't know the word for "bail." "Money, or a deposit, or something of great value to the prison instead of the prisoner?"

Both boys shook their heads, frowning.

"Once you're in prison, you don't get out," Tino said with a quick glance at the open doors. "You either hang, or they find the person who did it." He paused and shrugged. "Still might hang you."

"Ah." Paul nodded, and this time, he left.

That tidbit of information did not help their cause one damn bit. His backup plan, which was somewhat hasty, even he had to admit, was to spirit Hannah from the prison—bond, bail, or not —and leave the Papal States.

Apparently, that wasn't possible.

All right, then. Back to the original plan of finding the real killer. Unfortunately, Paul had nothing, other than there were no additional guests, Hannah had a terrible alibi, and Kaya had promised they'd somehow help keep this inn open and operational.

They really did manage to find trouble wherever they went, didn't they?

Paul scrubbed a hand down his face and turned to walk round the opposite side of the inn. He still wanted to scout out any other paths, no matter how little-used they might have been. The trees marched along this side of the building as well, leaving only enough space for two people to walk abreast. He looked up, but these rooms were along the outside of the inn, not the courtyard theirs overlooked.

They were shuttered, even amid the promise of wealthy guests arriving next week.

Continuing down the barely trodden path to the front of the inn, Paul hoped Kaya had a better plan than breaking Hannah out of prison. He really didn't want to be a fugitive. Again.

He found her in the kitchens, chatting with Bea, who stirred a huge pot over the fire. The weather seemed the topic of conversation, with Bea animatedly explaining the warmer summers and the full season of wealthy visitors.

Paul hated to interrupt when it was clear Kaya had earned Bea's trust. He resisted sighing and rolling his eyes—perhaps Bea's lively chatter had something to do with what the stableboys had said about keeping the inn open. Had Kaya offered to purchase it?

Paul had a feeling that was exactly what she'd promised.

"Kaya." He stepped fully into the kitchens and nodded to Bea, who instantly quieted. "Have you eaten?"

"Bea is nearly finished with the noodles; it's early for luncheon here." Kaya tilted her head and glanced quickly to the side. He couldn't tell if that meant she'd discovered something, or if she wished for more time to speak with Bea.

Perhaps both.

Either way, Paul nodded and smiled at Bea, who looked at the pot as if she expected it to sprout wings and fly away. The sea breeze cooled the room and sent the fire flickering, but other than the multitude of open windows, it was a plain room covered in shelves and hooks.

There was nowhere for him to stand without intruding, so he shrugged and retreated. He didn't wait long for Kaya to join him in the dining room. They sat near the open balcony doors, that same sea breeze cool on his back. Outside, he could hear the sounds of the fishermen and locals, but he wasn't close enough to interfere with their conversation.

"Bea apologizes for the late meal, but with Signora Ferrari gone, she's alone." Kaya waved a hand. "I promised to speak with Signore Ferrari about additional help, but I haven't been able to find him."

Not the solution he'd expected—maybe she hadn't offered to purchase the inn after all. "I'll see if I can speak with him before we leave."

"Leave?" She sat up straighter. "I am not leaving—"

He held up a hand. "I meant leave for the prison. I wish to speak with Hannah again."

"Ah." She nodded regally. "All right, then. Thank you, Bea." She smiled at the maid, who'd wheeled the serving cart to their table. "Please leave it; we'll be all right."

Bea smiled, cast Paul a nervous glance, and bobbed quickly. Paul reached for one of the plates and served them both steaming vegetables. Kaya spooned the noodles onto their plates and poured their juice.

"Have you seen Charlotte today?" she asked.

"I have not." Paul frowned. "The horses were stabled, and I saw the carriage parked further in the building." He tried to think where they'd walked today, if that path would've crossed Charlotte's. "I doubt she's returned to the prison—not on foot, not when she has a carriage available."

"Perhaps she's in her room." But Kaya looked troubled as she nibbled a piece of greenery. "What about the priest?"

"Father Roberto is taken care of. He said the rites, buried Fritz in the plot Signore Ferrari had agreed to before...well, before all this, and was handsomely paid. I've no idea if he said the Lutheran rites, but if Hannah asks, he was most respectful."

Kaya turned slightly in her chair and peered at him curiously. "And was he? Respectful?"

"Most," Paul repeated. "I also discovered that the Papal States have no concept of bail."

Sipping her juice, Kaya frowned. "Bail?" She paused then shook her head. "I don't understand."

"It's when you're in jail, and you post your bond. If you're wealthy, sometimes that's just your word." Kaya snorted, and Paul had to agree. "You can offer money, a land guarantee, a business, things like that."

"And so posting provides...?"

"Freedom. You post your bond, and you get out of jail until your trial."

"Interesting. I've never heard of the concept. And you say there's no bail here?" Kaya ate another bite and slowly chewed.

Paul knew her thoughts were racing in the direction of offering money in exchange for Hannah's freedom.

"When I spoke with the maids earlier, they warned me not to let Hannah confess." Kaya offered him the bowl of noodles, but he shook his head. "Is a confession needed here?" He shrugged. "That's possible. When we see her this afternoon, we'll warn her, though I doubt very much she'll confess. She's already claimed to have had nothing to do with Signora Ferrari's murder."

"We're no closer to discovering who actually killed the signora than we were last night. What about a lawyer or a solicitor?"

He pinched the bridge of his nose. "It looks bad for Hannah; I'm not going to lie."

"I had hoped we'd discover a piece of information we could use, but I'm afraid you're correct. A heaviness hangs over this inn, and it has only increased since Signora Ferrari's death." Kaya paused and met his gaze. "Her murder."

"Let's collect Charlotte." He stood and drained his juice. The lemon juice wasn't as pleasant as the orange they'd had at Marta's, but Paul still found it refreshing. "I want to be back from the prison before nightfall."

"Bea!" Kaya called as she crossed the dining room. "Have you seen Miss Charlotte, Countess von Almey's companion?"

"Yes, miss, she's in her room. I brought a tray to her this morning. She's distraught."

"Thank you. I'll see to her. We're returning to the prison; would they permit us to bring food?"

"Mayhap." Bea shrugged and returned to their table. "I'll wrap up some vegetables. The guards, they'll either eat the food or let you pass."

Paul sighed. Not the most reassuring phrase he'd heard. "Please also ask Nestor to hitch the cart. Easier on these hills," he added.

Bea nodded and left, and Paul turned to Kaya. He didn't know why he thought now was the right time, but he pulled the Egyptian coins from his waistcoat.

Her eyes focused on them, and Kaya hesitatingly reached out. Her fingers caressed the edges, and she met his gaze for a brief heartbeat before focusing on the coins again.

"Where did you find these?" Her voice cracked, but she continued tracing the coin's edges.

"Found them in your dress, when I opened the seams in San Grigori." He watched her face: awe and sadness and just the faintest of smiles. "I kept them—not sure why. But I thought you might like to hold onto them."

"We can't use them," she said practically, and he nearly laughed. "We should've traded them in Damietta."

"Perhaps," he agreed. "But then you'd have nothing of your home. These might not be miniatures of Tahir and Derya, or even something of your parents, but it's Egypt. And it's still your home."

"I have nothing of them." She frowned and met his gaze. "Nothing except memories. And memories eventually fade."

"True," he agreed. "But you can draw your memories. Perhaps not faces." They both grinned at that. Kaya was a fantastic still-life drawer, but her portraits needed work. "But your house or gardens."

"Perhaps."

He tipped his hand and let the coins slide into her open palm. Her fingers closed around them, and she met his gaze once more.

"I know you miss Marta and Olivia." His lips quirked. "Bravo, even. And the walk from Rome was hard and awkward." Paul paused and fumbled with his words. He knew what his heart wanted, but translating that into words proved harder than he imagined. His nerves didn't exactly help, but then, they'd spent weeks—months—dancing around the core problem. "We didn't exactly talk about everything."

"We did," she corrected. "However, one conversation does not fix anything."

Paul inclined his head in acknowledgment. "Be that as it may, I want us to make new memories. Together. I want you to look forward to our future." He brushed his fingers over her cheek. "I want our memories from here on out to hold only happiness. Happiness and honesty. No more secrets. I want whatever children we may or may not have to know and love us."

"You've never spoken of children before." Kaya opened her hand and stared at the coins. "I think I shall teach our children my heritage and culture."

"How to protect themselves," he agreed. "And how to fight for others. You've taught me much in our time together, and I want our children to have that...that—I'm not sure of the word," he admitted.

"You have it as well," she whispered. "You wouldn't have done all you had with Appleby if you didn't." She sat straighter and smiled, hiding her hands in her lap. "Do you know the first moment I realized what a good man you are?"

He blinked. "No."

"In the desert, after the haboob, when we encountered the slavers." She snarled the word but didn't stop. "You fought. You didn't hesitate; you just attacked. You didn't know anything other than what you saw, and you didn't care about whatever excuses those men might've offered. You leaped into action and fought them."

"And that's what made you think I was a good man?" He shook his head. "Only you, Kaya, would think that."

"No," she countered. "You think very little of yourself. However, I agree. Any children we have, I want them to learn just that. Protect yourself, protect those weaker than you. Help where you can."

"You're an amazing woman, Kaya Conrad." He kissed her cheek. "And I am the luckiest man alive to have married you."

"Life happens for a reason," she whispered, looking back at the coins. "And though I might've been furious at Gidd for contracting our marriage without so much as a warning, I'm lucky, too."

"I love you."

Sixteen

Kaya watched Hannah's reaction to the wrapped vegetables. Despite the lack of cutlery, she devoured the now-cold food as if it were a court feast. Did they not feed their prisoners, even with the coin they'd left? What of the others, who didn't have the wealth Hannah possessed?

Shifting slightly from Paul so they could both keep an eye on the door, she listened to him recount his discoveries.

They'd gathered Charlotte, and the three of them had used the cart rather than the larger and less maneuverable carriage. Azizi had been left in the room, and she'd huffed and pouted as Kaya locked the doors. Poor thing. Kaya still felt guilty, but she most definitely didn't want her in this prison.

Now the four of them stood in the cool, dark room, the stench lingering so heavily Kaya felt as if they could reach out and touch it. They spoke in Marathi, which worked surprisingly well for both conversation and privacy.

"And you believe the maids know more?" Hannah frowned, staring at the dirty linen. "In my experience, the staff often do. They hear things, see things." She sighed and met first Paul's then Kaya's gaze. "However, I had little interaction with any of them."

"When did you meet Signora Ferrari?" Kaya needed to hear

what happened again. From Hannah's perspective, the interaction had lasted bare moments. Yet no one could deny the signora had been repeatedly stabbed in a brutal, angry murder. "Was it when you retired? Or before?"

Hannah frowned, staring at the remnants of the vegetables. "Before. We were not in the hallway, but the foyer."

"Why were you in the foyer?" Kaya had no clear timeline of events, and that bothered her. Only a handful of hours had passed between when they'd arrived at the inn and when they'd dined with Hannah. Kaya and Paul had walked with Azizi around the property, and she didn't know all that had happened in the meantime.

"Ginevra, the maid, she said the Ferraris wished to speak with me." Hannah frowned harder. "I thought it odd that at least Signora Ferrari didn't come directly to my room. I followed Ginevra and met Signora Ferrari in the foyer. Her husband was not there."

"When was this? We arrived, you and Charlotte entered your rooms, and then you both met us for dinner." Signora Ferrari had been found the next morning, and they'd breakfasted late. The sun had long since risen by the time Hannah had joined Kaya and Paul on the balcony.

"Oh, not long after arriving." Hannah shook her head and sat in the chair. "I left Charlotte to unpack and relax—she was still so upset—and followed Ginevra. That's when Signora Ferrari told me about the footmen. But I had dismissed them shortly after arriving. The stableboys had barely unharnessed the horses."

"So you argued the day we arrived." Paul was frowning now, too. "You argued with the signora, then we dined. What about after?"

"It had been a long day." Hannah sighed and offered a rueful smile.

Charlotte echoed that sentiment and added, "We retired early."

Kaya glanced out the door once more. Satisfied the coast

remained clear, she crossed to crouch beside Hannah and took her hands. "You must understand, we're only trying to help. We need all the information in order to ensure your innocence before the judge."

"I do appreciate that." Hannah squeezed Kaya's hands, and hers were cold despite the heat of the day.

Paul's hand rested on her shoulder, and Kaya stood, slipping her hand into his. "You rested; did you or Charlotte leave the room afterward?"

"No, not at all," Charlotte said.

Hannah shook her head. "Not until breakfast the next morning. Charlotte refused to leave the rooms, even for a morning walk. As I'd already made plans with you, I promised to send up a tray."

Kaya didn't want to say it, but a glance at Paul told her he thought the same thing. Hannah, who must have picked up on the sudden discomfort hovering in the air, sat straighter. She clutched the linen in her hands and glared.

"No. Charlotte had naught to do with any of this. She was upset over the robbery and needed time to recover." Hannah reached for Charlotte's hand and stood, scraping the chair over the rough flooring. "They threatened her," she snapped. "If you had not arrived when you did, I'm afraid what might've happened." Hannah's voice broke.

Charlotte had paled. "I understand why you ask," she whispered. "But I had nothing to do with the signora's murder, and I'd never let the countess take the blame for anything I did."

"She would not hurt a fly, let alone murder." Hannah's voice cracked, and her boldness crumbled.

Kaya, quite at a loss, hugged her close and looked helplessly at Paul. He shrugged and opened his mouth, only to shrug again. Some help he was.

"Let's say, Charlotte, you stayed in her room until word spread about your arrest." Paul walked to the door and checked it again. He seemed satisfied that their bribe, outlandish as it was, would allow them as much time as they needed and a modicum of privacy.

"That means Signora Ferrari was killed sometime between dinner the night before and that morning. Signore Ferrari isn't saying a word about anything." Paul scowled and rolled his shoulders. "The maids are mum, and the stable lads know nothing."

He paced away to stand at the door, his arms folded. Kaya wanted to ask what he was thinking, but she knew him well enough to know he was trying to sort through Hannah's story. Also that he wished they'd continued sailing up the coast. Genoa or the South of France sounded wonderful right now.

"I'm never leaving this prison, am I?" Hannah sniffed and looked up at the window, high along the wall. "They're going to hang me."

"I've been advised that you say nothing, not even to a priest in a confessional." Kaya didn't know what that meant, but Bea had reiterated it when Kaya helped her in the kitchens with luncheon. "Any admission, no matter to whom, could sign your death warrant."

"I'm not guilty!" Hannah repeated hotly. Then, in a softer tone, "You believe me?"

"I believe you," Kaya promised.

"Why? We are practically strangers, despite what your husband said about helping friends." Her voice was stronger now, but still quiet. She glanced at Paul—rather, the open door—but no one bothered them.

"I explained to him about traveling to Brandenburg," Kaya said for lack of a better explanation. "He's agreeable." She paused but saw no reason not to share Paul's desire to live someplace warmer. "He'd prefer the South of France, however."

Hannah grinned, her eyes sparkling. "I've never been! We should travel there first." As quickly as her demeanor brightened, it fell again. "Though after this experience, I think I shall prefer staying at home for some time."

"I don't blame you," Kaya agreed. Where would she have

stayed after such an ordeal? She and Paul claimed no permanent home. They traveled, walking the countryside and enjoying the experience.

She thought about the Egyptian coins Paul had given her. Egypt was no longer home. Kaya looked to Paul, who was now speaking with the guard in the faux jovial tone he always used with those he planned to scam. Shaking her head, she returned her attention to Hannah and Charlotte.

"What's he saying?" Hannah nodded to Paul and the guard.

"No doubt worming his way into the guard's good graces with talk of wine and gambling." Kaya made a face. "He's very skilled in that area."

"In gambling?" Hannah's voice dropped, and she leaned closer. "I don't understand."

"Paul—he did not have the most conventional upbringing." Kaya resisted adding that she wouldn't know convention if it landed at her feet. Neither of them was conventional, but she believed it made things between them far more interesting.

"I see," Hannah said in a tone that told Kaya she didn't see at all. "And his time in Bombay?"

"He—he prefers not to speak of it." What little she knew involved Harry Appleby and more unsavory stories than Kaya cared to remember. "We all have our pasts. It's what we do now to show who we are that matters."

Hannah watched her for several long moments. "You're very wise, Kaya Conrad." She smiled and squeezed her hand. "I'm so glad I met you."

"Happening upon you was a happy coincidence," Kaya agreed. "And I don't regret it at all."

"Kaya." Paul appeared at her elbow and nodded to Hannah. "We should leave. Renzo here"—he nodded to the guard—"he's wary of the condottieri."

Kaya blinked. That was a bold statement from a lowly guard. She leaned closer and asked in English, "How much did you pay him?"

"More than enough." Paul grinned. "Also promised him a bottle of wine from the inn."

Kaya eyed him, but Paul didn't look distraught or worried over the mention of wine. He seemed oddly relaxed, though still cautious. Smiling at her, he lifted her hand and kissed just above her glove.

"I'm all right," he promised. To Hannah he said, "We'll return on the morrow with more food, though Renzo promised to have at least a small tray delivered."

"I appreciate that, Herr Conrad." Hannah's lips twitched in a semblance of a smile, and she looked genuinely grateful. "I am most appreciative of all you've done," she added. "And if—well, if the worst should happen, please see Charlotte safely to Brandenburg? I think she'll be happier at home."

"All right," Kaya agreed. "However, we haven't given up. Something about the signora's murder is wrong."

"Agreed," Paul muttered, his hand on Kaya's back, urging her along. "It's all very neat, accusing the new occupants of the inn, who arrived with a dead driver after bandits attacked. Very neat." He jerked his head. "We need to leave, before the condottieri arrive."

"Hannah, don't say a word," Kaya warned. "If you must talk, tell of your home, but say nothing of your time in the Papal States."

Hannah looked uncertain but nodded. "Until tomorrow."

Kaya leaned over and kissed her cheeks as Marta had done. "Stay well."

She and Paul waited just outside the door while Hannah and Charlotte said their goodbyes. Charlotte was a tall, quiet woman. After yesterday's events, Kaya didn't blame her for not trusting anyone, but she hoped they could work together to free Hannah.

Charlotte eventually exited, looking tired but ready. "Thank you," she said as they walked down the hall. "For bringing me today. The countess is a friend as well as my employer, and without you, I'm uncertain I could've learned anything that would help her."

"I'm glad we could help." Kaya smiled.

They left the prison, Paul nodding to Renzo as they walked down the hall. Once outside, Kaya breathed deeply and wondered if she'd ever erase the stench of that place from her memory. She sincerely doubted it.

"I'll ride in the back." Charlotte offered a wide smile. "It's a beautiful day, and I don't wish to intrude." Without another word, she climbed into the back bed and turned to face the rear.

"Why does Renzo not trust the captain?" Kaya asked as Paul helped her onto the cart they'd borrowed from Signore Ferrari.

The grieving man seemed to only half listen to Paul's request. The cart was smaller and easier to maneuver than Hannah's carriage, and it allowed Kaya to sit atop next to Paul rather than inside alone. It also offered a clear view of their surroundings.

"Hannah misses home," Kaya said as they paid the lad who'd watched the horses and started down the street. "However, I believe she's happy we agreed to travel with her to Prussia." She sighed and leaned against him. "Provided she isn't found guilty here."

"She finds more trouble than we do." His laughter rumbled through him, and Kaya smiled, though she didn't move her head from his shoulder. "Are you positive you'd rather not find a small cottage in the South of France? Monaco or Nice, Marseille perhaps?"

"I think we'd be very happy in either of those places," Kaya conceded. "The two of us and Azizi. It sounds beautiful and warm. I like the water."

"Even if you'd rather not sail upon it?" He laughed again, and she wondered what had him in such a good mood.

Pulling back, she kissed his cheek. "Hannah mentioned returning home and staying for a while. Would Monaco or Nice be home for us? Or merely another stop on our wanderings?"

"I don't know," he admitted as they left Riccione proper and headed for the inn.

The sun had started its descent behind the mountains, and Kaya closed her eyes against its brightness. She peeled her gloves off and dropped them to the floor. She didn't know if they could be salvaged. She definitely didn't want to know what the hem of her dress looked like.

"Do you want to settle someplace?" he asked, steering the horses along the rough road, dodging pedestrians.

"I didn't," Kaya admitted, straightening and turning slightly to face him. "I wished to explore the world—or as much as we could, given my unfortunate seasickness."

Paul grinned and slowed the horses. He leaned over to kiss her, caressing her cheek with a fingertip. "Anywhere you want, sweetheart. France, Brandenburg, St. Petersburg, or Paris."

Not England, she knew that. He never wanted to return to England. Not after all that had happened, his childhood, the East India Company. Kaya understood and closed the distance between them, kissing him again. Though they'd mended so much of their relationship, there was a faint uncertainty underlying their talk of the future.

"Let's see to Hannah's freedom first, then at least travel with her from Riccione north."

"If you wish." He nodded and cupped her face. "I only want you happy."

"I'm happy with you," she admitted as the horses whinnied and someone cursed at them to move. She took his hand and repositioned herself beside him. "Where did you learn to drive horses?"

"Ah." He cleared his throat, and Kaya tried not to laugh. "Not exactly a skill they taught, I admit. Basu and I...well, we—aye, we stole a pair," he admitted with a sigh. "I can't remember our reason, probably for a lark and nothing more." He frowned. "I think John was with us. Anyway, they were attached to a cart, one of the Company's, and they knew what to do better than we did."

"And after all that, you remembered how to drive them?" Kaya snorted. "That must have been some lesson."

"No, not exactly." He looked sheepish. "More like I hoped the horses would know what to do. I just guided them along the proper roads."

Kaya laughed, feeling free and happy despite her new friend's quandary. Resting her hand on Paul's leg, she nodded toward the pair of horses. "Are they rare? Gidd never talked about them, and until Sicily I'd never seen them."

"Not rare, no, but expensive to keep. Not everyone has a horse. In Bombay, they used cattle in the fields, and the rich usually have their servants carry them in chairs. I'm sure there were other methods of transportation, too, besides walking."

Kaya couldn't picture it. They carried the chair *and* the person around town? Fascinating.

"Horses are expensive," Paul repeated, more slowly now.

"You said. I presume feeding them requires money. And so does keeping them someplace. San Grigori had no horses, and Marta never mentioned needing to care for any."

"No, she wouldn't have. Horses wouldn't be practical in those mountains." He still sounded distant, as if figuring something out. "Donkeys like Bravo, yes. Horses, not so much."

"What's wrong?"

"There were four horses in the stables," Paul said, his fingers clenching the reins. "Four. Hannah's pair and two others. I had assumed they belonged to the inn, that Ferrari used them for this." He gestured to the cart. "They'd need supplies, and it's easier with a cart and horses. But why horses?"

"Instead of a donkey like Rogerson used?" Kaya frowned as she followed his logic. "Did you ask the stableboys?"

"No. I didn't think of it then, but it's bothered me, and until now I didn't realize why." He transferred the reins to one hand and pinched the bridge of his nose, shaking his head. "I can't imagine what they use the horses for when donkeys are far more practical."

"Status?" Kaya asked. "So many look down on us for walking rather than using horses or carriages."

"Possibly. This is a popular inn with the summer residents. If they sailed into port, they'd need to be picked up. Perhaps they use the horses and a carriage...but I didn't see the carriage."

"I thought you said you saw Hannah's. Oh, you mean another one? That's odd. Did you see the cart in the stables?"

This mystery deepened with every moment, and Kaya couldn't say she liked it. Though hardly knowledgeable about horses, carriages, or carts, she followed Paul's logic easily enough.

"Four horses, two stableboys, one carriage, one cart." He opened his eyes and met hers. "To be fair, I didn't go beyond the doorway, where Tino and Nestor saw to the horses."

"I'm afraid our collective lack of understanding about horses and their care is a deterrent. However, I'm not convinced that's important."

"Possibly not," Paul conceded. "We've been here only a few days, and we don't know anything about what the inn is like during the high season." He shook his head. "Still, I'm certain there's something off."

"Should we ask the boys again? You didn't seem to think they had any information."

"Perhaps I asked the wrong questions." He glanced at her as the inn came into view. "Which reminds me, wife mine. Did you promise to buy the inn?"

"Only as a last resort," she said primly. "They were worried Signore Ferrari would close the inn. They need the work."

He laughed and hugged her to his side. "You are a most unusual person, Kaya Conrad." He kissed her temple. "And I love you all the more for it."

"I don't see what's so unusual about wanting to ensure people can eat," she grumbled but smiled. His compliment warmed her.

They pulled into the inn just as the three maids ran out, wide-eyed and pale in the rapidly darkening afternoon. Kaya's stomach sank.

"What's happened?" Paul called.

"Signore Ferrari," Bea said, her voice breaking. "He's dead."

Seventeen

"Well then." Paul shook his head and sat beside her. Kaya reached for his hand, a natural movement, and let the warmth of his skin against hers warm her numb fingers. "This was not the news I expected."

"Nor I," Kaya agreed. "I had hoped for a slightly happier return—perhaps to news that Signore Ferrari had rescinded the charges against Hannah and agreed to keep the inn open."

"I suppose we should discover if he has any heirs, a will." Paul kissed the top of her head. "See who inherits the inn now."

She agreed but hadn't the energy to speak the words aloud. It'd been an hour or so since they returned, and the sky had fully darkened. The breeze chilled her, and Kaya thought she should fetch her shawl, but she hadn't the energy for that, either. So they sat on the balcony, enjoying the privacy and silence and fresh air.

Huddling closer on the low stone wall, Kaya shifted until Paul's arm wrapped around her, warming her through her dress. Her eyes closed, and she let her mind wander in tired circles.

"I hope one of the staff knows," she said sleepily. "It'll save us from seeking out this person. Though I imagine if the Ferraris had children, they'd work here."

"I agree, but who knows?" He shrugged, then stilled and hugged her closer. "Do you want to go inside?"

"Yes, but I don't wish to move yet." She didn't need to see Paul to know he smiled. She buried her face in his shoulder. "It's been a long day. A long couple of days."

"At least we can be certain Hannah had nothing to do with Signore Ferrari's murder." Paul paused. "Two murders in the same inn, so even if it was Signore Ferrari who killed his wife, someone killed him."

"Revenge?" Kaya shook her head. "But from whom? One of the staff? A child they may or may not have?"

"And, for argument's sake, say Hannah did kill the signora. Someone still killed Ferrari." Paul yawned. "Are you hungry?"

"A little, but I don't want to disturb Bea."

He slipped off the wall and grasped her hips, lifting her off. "I'll see if they have anything ready. I'm sure Azizi is tired of Charlotte's company."

"And hungry herself." Kaya paused and stretched. She needed to do her exercises; her muscles had stiffened over the last few days. "Both Azizi and Charlotte. Though it was very nice of Charlotte to check on her while we found out what we could."

"I suppose we've ruled out Charlotte as the murderess." Paul shrugged and tugged her hand. "Though I suppose we haven't ruled out anyone, really. Charlotte could, in theory, have killed Ferrari before we left, though I admit that's a stretch."

"You mean it could have been more than one person? Someone killed the signora, and someone else killed Ferrari?" Nodding, she tightened her fingers around Paul's. "That might make the most sense, but we still have no suspect. And the condottieri haven't arrested anyone for Signore Ferrari's murder."

"I hate leaving you, but it seems to keep happening." He raised her hand and kissed her wrist. "I'll see if there's any food, and you check on Charlotte. And poor Azizi."

She smiled and kissed his cheek. "I'm afraid staying together isn't advantageous to our investigation."

Paul scowled. She knew he didn't like it. However, he turned for the kitchens, and if his step was more hurried than usual, well then, she didn't blame him. Being alone, without witnesses, was proving dangerous.

Kaya watched him disappear into the back and turned for the stairs. She couldn't hear Azizi howling but suspected she was antsy to leave the rooms. Sure enough, the hallway remained silent until Kaya stepped up to Charlotte and Hannah's rooms. Before she could even knock, Azizi began barking and scratching at the door.

The dog's antics made Kaya laugh despite the situation, and when Charlotte finally opened the door—amid many sharp words to poor Azizi—Kaya held out her arms for the dog. Azizi leaped up, knocking Kaya off balance. She was very large and heavy. Paul claimed it was her wolf side, and Kaya believed him.

"There's my good girl," she cooed in Egyptian. "Did you miss me?"

Azizi licked her face, and though Kaya grimaced, she accepted the greeting. Ushering her back inside, where Azizi bumped her side for pets and scratches, Kaya turned to Charlotte.

"You look tired. Azizi, did you keep Charlotte awake?"

Charlotte looked at the dog in exasperation. But she patted her head before retreating farther into the rooms, where a chaise sat near the windows. "She was most happy to see me; however, I'm afraid she didn't like being locked in the room."

"She likes roaming," Kaya agreed. "I'll send Bea up with a tray; you rest."

"Thank you, Frau Conrad."

"Kaya, please." She might never grow used to being called "Mrs. Conrad," no matter the language. Charlotte nodded from the balcony but didn't turn again.

Torn between sitting with Charlotte and walking with Azizi, Kaya eventually decided to leave the room. She sensed Charlotte wanted to be alone, and she didn't wish to make the other woman uncomfortable by prolonging the awkward silence.

"Thank you again," Kaya called as she motioned Azizi toward the door. "Please find us if you need anything"

"Thank you," Charlotte whispered.

They met no one as Azizi bounded down the stairs with Kaya following at a slower pace. She didn't know where the stableboys disappeared to after their duties, and she had no idea if any of the staff lived on site. She thought that was probably the case, given their limited number, but she had no real experience with paid employees.

"Go on," she said to Azizi. "Go off. But be careful." Kaya sighed. "It's not safe or welcoming here."

As Azizi disappeared from the small circle of light by the front of the inn, Kaya wrapped her arms around herself. She'd neglected to grab her shawl, and it was even cooler now than a half hour past. Especially without Paul's arms around her.

In the flickering torchlight, with the cool night closing in, Kaya pulled her khanjar from its sheath. She couldn't say she'd ever been prone to nervous jumping. However, she'd also never stayed at an inn where two mysterious and currently unsolved murders had occurred.

Slowing her breath, she moved through her first set of exercises. Gidd had taught her these moves immediately after she'd sneaked from the house in a vain attempt to see *en-Nīl*. Basic exercises that kept her limber and ready for whatever happened next.

Though she wished to close her eyes, Kaya kept them open and sweeping the area, even as she progressed to the more difficult moves. She bent her knees, her khanjar slicing silently through the air. No sound from Azizi, but she ignored the wind singing in her ears and focused on other sounds coming from the wood.

Small animals raced through the underbrush, and the occasional owl hooted though she couldn't see anything. She could almost imagine she stood in her back gardens in Cairo, preforming these same moves in the dark quiet of the house.

"God, you're beautiful."

Paul's voice startled her. She jumped, snapping her dagger

around, aiming at the voice though she knew who it belonged to. Kaya blinked in the darkening night, her heart jumping at the sight of him. He stood before her, blue-green eyes dark in the shadows but fierce and hungry as they met hers.

"I didn't hear you approach," she admitted, sheathing her dagger. This was the third time he'd snuck up on her. It was getting to be a habit.

"I'll take that as the highest of compliments." But he didn't give her a chance to respond. Instead, he pulled her into his arms and kissed her with all the hunger he'd watched her with.

Kaya sighed into his touch. The world rushed back, only to recede like the sea with his touch. She could drown in his kiss, in the taste of him, in the passion that sparked whenever he touched her. His lips were cool in the night air but warmed her clear through. She whimpered against his mouth and tugged him closer.

"Bea promised to bring up a tray. Where's Azizi?"

"Wandering," Kaya breathed. She swallowed and wet her lips before turning and whistling for the dog. "What about Charlotte?"

"I'm not inviting her to our bed," he growled, pulling her closer. His mouth crashed against hers, taking and taking, and Kaya surrendered. She might never get enough of his kisses.

Only Azizi's bark brought her back down to earth, and Kaya shook her head to steady herself. What had she been saying?

"We should see to Charlotte first," she said, voice breathless and uneven. "See how she fares. I meant to ask Bea for a tray, but I'll bring it up. I'm not leaving our room once we're there. You're mine tonight."

"Every night," he promised, twining their fingers together. "Always."

Kaya nodded, satisfied. Perhaps, she thought as they reentered the deserted inn, the additional company had been better for them than she thought. All traces of awkwardness had disappeared, and she could honestly say what she and Paul shared now felt more akin to what they'd shared before San Grigori.

She accepted a small tray from Bea with a grateful nod and turned back for the stairs. Paul took the tray and hurried her up, and Azizi raced to the top and waited for them, as if playing a game. Kaya laughed, petting her head and praising what a good girl she was. Once more, Azizi licked her, and Kaya thought maybe she could grow used to that affection.

They waited only a moment before Charlotte opened the door and accepted the tray.

"Do you think they'll release the countess now?" she asked, sidestepping Azizi, who sniffed around her legs.

"Azizi, no." Kaya pulled her back, lest the large dog knock Charlotte over.

"They can't charge her with Signore Ferrari's death," Paul agreed. "And as he was the only witness to his wife's murder, it's possible."

Of course, the first charge was bad enough. However, with this new, ah, incident, Kaya could only think that the condottieri needed to have a second look at the so-called evidence.

"Thank you. Good night." Charlotte nodded and closed the door.

Kaya didn't blame her for not wanting company.

"She was with us all afternoon, though of course that doesn't rule out her murdering Ferrari before." Paul grunted as they found their own rooms. "However, I fail to see her motive in killing either Ferrari."

"I agree. I can't see that happening. Why? Unless she finds pleasure in such acts, but I still don't understand why she'd allow her mistress, with whom she seems very close, to take the blame." Kaya closed the door as Paul preformed his usual security check, walking to each window, searching the corners and shadows for any eavesdroppers or would-be purse thieves.

"I believe she was wearing the same clothing as early this morning." Paul checked beneath the bed, his voice muffled.

"I noticed that." Kaya set one of the chairs against the door handle, a measure Paul insisted upon. "If Signore Ferrari was killed in the same manner as Signora Ferrari, there'd be quite a lot of blood."

"I believe we're alone in our rooms." He stood from the floor and pulled her to him. "And I believe I'm going to make love to you."

"Bea will be here shortly with the food."

"I don't care." He kissed her, hands framing her face, and backed her to the bed.

In his embrace, Kaya felt small and delicate. Strange that she could hold her own against most attacks, but Paul protecting her made her feel safe.

And she loved that. Loved him.

He kissed down her neck, and she shivered, her hands tugging at his shirt even as she arched against him. Paul laid her on the bed, kneeling before her as he took his time tasting her. He nipped at the sensitive juncture between her shoulder and neck. She shuddered again, body aching for his touch, arousal pooling between her legs. His hands, large and warm through her gown, cupped her breasts.

"Stand up, my love."

Slowly, Paul turned her around, his mouth now kissing along the back of her shoulders. His fingers, long and far more elegant than they had any right to be, undid the laces of her dress. He never stopped touching her, his mouth tasting each exposed patch of skin, his hands working quickly to uncover more.

Each time Paul undressed her, it was more arousing than Kaya imagined such a move could possibly be.

Breathing heavy, her skin aching for his touch, breasts heavy, she let the dress pool at her feet. Clad only in her chemise, she met Paul's gaze. He watched her with a burning hunger, and it sparked through her, hot and sure. He stepped back, gaze steady on hers, shedding his jacket.

Which was, of course, when the knock sounded through the room.

Kaya giggled, even as Azizi barked at the intruder. "Bea, no doubt," she said shooing him toward the main room. "I'm not dressed for company." She winked at him, stretching out on the bed.

"Do not move," he growled, pressing his lips hard to hers.

He disappeared, shushing Azizi and saying something to Bea that Kaya couldn't hear. The door slammed closed, and it was another moment before he returned to her. He'd no doubt placed the food on a high enough ledge that the poor, constantly starving dog couldn't reach.

"Where did you hide the food?"

Paul scowled and tugged his shirt over his head. "The bureau."

She laughed and tugged off her chemise. Paul's breath left him in a rush, and Kaya reveled in that. He sat on the bed, pulling off his boots and unbuttoning his trousers. With every layer that disappeared, Kaya wanted more. She ran her fingers down her belly, watching Paul watch her.

Mouth dry, heart pounding, arousal warming her blood, she stared at him. She'd never expected to enjoy watching a man unclothe quite as much as she loved watching Paul.

His chest was hard and well-defined, though several scars marred his perfection. His arms were far more muscled than they had a right to be, but she knew his strength. They'd carried her, held her, fought with and for her.

Hot arousal rushed through her, and she held out a hand to him. Her fingers itched to touch him; her mouth watered to taste him. Kaya drank him in, letting her gaze roam over his now-naked body. A thin smattering of hair covered his chest and legs, but she was unable to look away from his cock.

His mouth covered hers again, possessive and passionate, his tongue sweeping over hers. Kaya opened to him, even as she shifted so he lay beside her. Her fingers brushed down his chest, his lean hips and waist.

He knelt to shift positions, urging her further up the bed. But they moved awkwardly, and she banged her head against the wall. Kaya laughed, surprised, even as Paul looked chagrined.

"Are you all right?"

"Fine," she promised, heat pooling low within her. "Kiss me again."

"Your wish is my command." This kiss was slower and softer, and he drew it out until Kaya thought she'd come from that alone. His fingers brushed over her wetness, a teasing touch.

Gasping, she widened her legs, opening for him, angling her hips in a silent plea for more. Paul pressed kisses to her jaw, down her chest, and over each breast before taking one nipple into his mouth. His fingers never left her core, however, and all sense of anything but him disappeared.

That pleasurable burn coiled through her, and with every arch of her hips, every flick of his fingers, she felt herself ride it higher.

Her hands tangled in his hair, his beautiful curls slipping through her fingers. She opened her eyes and watched him. He knelt between her legs now, cock hard and proud against his stomach. Kaya licked her lips and nodded.

"Scream for me, Kaya." He cupped her hips, angling her higher. He pressed his mouth to her, and Kaya cried out. Pleasure shook through her, a crashing wave of desire. Paul took his time, tasting her pleasure as thoroughly as he had her mouth.

Hands fisted in the bedding, arching against him, Kaya let herself go. Fell into the glorious pleasure of being with him. She crested that glorious wave, crying out as he'd commanded.

Panting, trying to regain her breath, Kaya watched as Paul positioned himself over her. He eased into her, teasing her with short thrusts.

"Paul," she gasped, her nails digging into his back.

He buried his face in her shoulder, and she felt him smile against her skin. With a sure thrust, he seated himself fully.

"Yes," she hissed, wrapping her legs around his waist, drawing him deeper.

He leaned up, jaw clenched and face set, and she realized how little of his control remained.

Oh, she wanted to snap that control. Her nails scratched down his back, dug into his backside as he moved. Another orgasm tightened through her.

"Kaya," he moaned, a warning as well as a promise.

"Come for me, Paul."

Her mouth crashed against his, her teeth scraping his lip. She felt the moment his control snapped. He thrust harder, and her own fingers found her nub, rubbing hard as her pleasure tightened within her. Suddenly, she was hurtling over the edge, wordlessly crying out.

Paul moved harder, and she knew he was close. Kaya held him even as her orgasm shuddered through her. He pulled out, jerking against her, his face buried in her shoulder once again.

Then he collapsed beside her, breathing hard, fumbling for a cloth to clean them both. As soon as he'd finished, Kaya pulled him atop her, welcoming his familiar weight. She lazily kissed his shoulder, his chin, eventually finding his lips as her breathing evened out.

"Shame our visit to the seaside wasn't as relaxing as we expected," she said, eyes closed. "It's quite lovely here."

He snorted and pulled back. "Someday, we'll find a quiet week, just the two of us."

"We'd be bored in a day," Kaya predicted.

"I plan on ravishing you every day, and I promise you"—he kissed her hard—"I shall never bore of that."

Eighteen

"I much prefer staying in bed," Paul grumbled as they entered the dining room the next morning.

Charlotte still hadn't left her rooms, no one else had arrived, and the entire place held an air of abandonment. Paul thought it felt like the abandoned houses from his youth. Still standing, but unable to find their place in the world.

"I'd normally agree, but I'm afraid if we stayed in bed, something else would happen here." Kaya nodded as he held out her chair. "This is a place we need to keep a constant eye on, lest it fall down."

"Might not be a bad idea to tear it down, start from scratch." Maybe perform an exorcism.

"Paul." Kaya glared at him as if he'd said the exorcism part aloud. "We need to discover who will own the inn now that both Ferraris are...gone. And what will happen to the staff."

Something shivered down his spine, and he narrowed his eyes at his lovely, beautiful wife. His lovely, beautiful wife who also believed in helping everyone they came across. He knew it was part of her culture, but he had a feeling that this time it would involve more than merely giving extra food to a child.

No, it would be more like finding an opium addict deep in the dens of Villa San Giovanni.

Paul knew, he just knew, that it would involve securing the future employment of the inn's five servants, one way or another. Resting his elbows on the table, and ignoring Kaya's glare, he held his head for just a moment. He needed time to come to terms with this new realization.

This was part of his atonement. Helping when he once would have shrugged and left. Uttered a "Not my problem" and never once looked back.

"All right." He mumbled it to the table and straightened. "All right. I'll ask the condottieri if he has any information. I'm certain he'll at least know the family."

Paul doubted the man wasn't from here. Most people—at least, those who were not somehow attached to the military—stayed in the same area where they were born. Unless something happened, like with Marta, they never saw more than a few miles, he'd guess.

And here he never wanted to see the entirety of England, let alone his home, ever again.

"This bothers me," Kaya whispered, though no one was about. "Why murder the couple? What reason could anyone have?"

"Passion—maybe one was having an affair." Paul ticked the reasons off on his fingers. "Ferrari killed his wife, and someone decided to exact revenge. Maybe Signora Ferrari was not the original intended victim, and whoever killed her returned to kill him." He sighed and dropped his hands. "Honestly, there are so many reasons, I doubt I have enough fingers to count them all."

That produced the desired smile. Bea shuffled in just then, wheeling the breakfast tray. She looked tired, even more so than yesterday. Her hair wasn't in its usual tight bun but hung in a haphazard braid down her back, and her hands shook. Paul frowned and caught Kaya's eye. She turned to Bea and tilted her head.

"Bea, you need rest. So much has happened these last few days."

"I'm all right, signora." She glanced up, then back to the food. "As long as you pay, we'll serve."

And with those simple words, Paul knew what Kaya wanted. He grimaced but reasoned she was right. Someone had to help these people. The Ferraris certainly couldn't, and everyone needed to eat.

"I'll speak to the condottieri," Paul promised, accepting the coffee. "Do you know if the Ferraris had any heirs?"

Bea's head shot up, and a spark of what was probably hope lit her dark eyes. "No. They had no children. None that survived," she whispered and crossed herself. "The shipments are set to arrive today, food for the guests who will arrive next week."

"I shall look over the manifests," Kaya promised. "While Signore Conrad sees to possible heirs, I'll organize things here. We shall keep this inn open so you—all of you—can continue to receive your wages."

Paul looked at her in a new light. He'd never thought about the rest of her training. He knew she was amazing with her khanjar and far more skilled in tactical maneuvers than anyone else he knew. Even in the Company's army. Especially there. Somehow, he never imagined that education would bleed into other parts of her life.

"You will?" Bea squeaked in surprise. "Thank you, Signora!"

She leaped across the table, upsetting the cart, and hugged Kaya. Poor Kaya, who was unused to people touching her, looked startled but gingerly hugged Bea back. Bea bobbed a curtsy and backed away, a large smile on her face.

"I do believe you might've made her the happiest I've ever seen anyone." Paul lifted Kaya's hand and kissed her fingertips. "You consistently amaze me, Kaya."

"For helping?" She tilted her head but smiled.

"Yes. Most don't. Or they do because they believe it gives them an advantage with God once they die."

"That is—" She frowned. "I do not know what that is. I'm not sure I understand. Derya always taught me that we must help those who are less privileged. But I suppose we've seen the opposite: those who help only themselves without caring who they harm."

"What do you plan if the Ferraris have no heirs?" Paul stopped and realized there was another problem. "Or if either of them have lost the inn by gambling."

"Oh. I had not thought of that. If that's true, what else is there to do?"

"Purchase it from the deed holder and hope we don't have to stay." Paul tried to think it through, but he knew next to nothing about the laws here. "If someone holds the deed, through gambling or some other means, they'll charge an exorbitant price to buy it back. If that's not the case, we can reasonably assume control, but again, I'm not sure of the laws for that. Not sure who we'd pay."

"I do not wish to stay," Kaya whispered before she bit into her bread. "This is not where I wish to spend our lives."

"I agree." Paul was relieved to hear that. Her words lifted a burden from his shoulders. "You still wish to travel with Hannah?"

"I like her. I think we can become friends."

He heard the wistfulness in her tone and knew she missed Marta. However, Marta needed to find her own footing. Perhaps once they settled—in Brandenburg or wherever—they'd write and see if Marta and Olivia wished to join them.

"Then let's finish breakfast and visit her." Paul drained his coffee. "I'm afraid there's little else here to discover about either murder. I'm not sure what to do next."

"Speak with the condottieri," she said, sipping her juice. "And I'll see about the manifests and payment. And then, well, I suppose we can see if any of the staff has heard anything. Perhaps they saw Ferrari arguing or someone leaving the inn."

"We'll ask around. I really don't like leaving you alone," he grumbled.

"I know." She leaned across and pecked him on the lips. "But I want to figure all this out and leave."

"I can't disagree with that sentiment."

Kaya had been serious when she told Paul she wanted to leave not only the inn, but Riccione, the Papal States, and the whole peninsula. The inn made her uncomfortable, and she didn't think it was the two murders. Well, not only the two murders. Something haunted here. She didn't want to tell Paul, didn't want to worry him, but she felt as if they were being watched.

Not by the servants—they weren't responsible for her unease. She thought perhaps it was the two footmen who'd accompanied Hannah, but Charlotte, Ginevra, and Rosa confirmed they'd left immediately after Signora Ferrari confronted Hannah.

She supposed it was possible they hadn't returned to Rome, or wherever they'd meant to. Possible they'd stayed to exact revenge on Hannah, but Kaya found that overly complicated. As she sat in Ferrari's office, waiting for the manifest papers to arrive with the shipments, the doors open to the sea and the sounds of the town, she wondered what she'd do.

"I don't know, Azizi," she said to the snoozing dog. "I suppose sneaking around and framing the woman who dismissed me would make for satisfying revenge, but that seems too problematic. Perhaps they stayed, or one of them did, long enough to murder Signora Ferrari."

Azizi snored and rolled onto her back. Kaya smiled and reached down to rub her belly. Paul still hadn't returned from his visit to the condottieri and his quick stop to see if Hannah needed anything more. Kaya wanted to see her new friend but felt it better to keep her promise to the staff about their future.

"No," she continued thinking aloud, with only Azizi to hear.

"I can't see them staying. Doesn't seem worth their time or energy. Assuming Hannah didn't kill the signora, I'd say there's one murderer here."

Hiding in the shadows, watching. That was it. As if whoever had killed the Ferraris now lurked here, waiting and watching. Kaya shivered in the warm breeze and slipped her khanjar from its sheath. Fanciful or not, Gidd always taught her it was best to be prepared.

Nothing in her experiences since leaving Cairo had convinced her otherwise.

But men lurking in the shadows? No matter how outlandish she thought it might be, Kaya had a sudden urge to ask Bea when she returned with the coffee. Surely, if mysterious men were lurking, Azizi would warn her. At the very least bark at the shadows, which Kaya suddenly found suspicious.

She rubbed her forehead, a headache brewing behind her eyes. She never had headaches, and if they were anything like this, she never wanted one again. Perhaps she was merely tired. They hadn't gotten much sleep since arriving at the inn. Well, since arriving in San Grigori. And she and Paul had spent so much time working to mend their relationship. To merge the man he once was with the man he strived to be.

Perhaps traveling with Hannah was not ideal, but the appeal pulled at her, drawing her toward Brandenburg and Prussia.

"Signora." Bea stood uncertainly in the doorway, the coffee cart in front of her. "The shipments, they haven't arrived."

"All right." Kaya stood, glancing at the mess of bookkeeping Ferrari had left. She couldn't read much of the writing; she spoke the language well enough but couldn't read it well at all. From what she gathered, the extra stores were to arrive sometime this week, though no firm date had been mentioned.

"Signore Conrad hasn't returned?" Kaya asked, though she knew the answer. If Paul had returned, he'd have found her no matter what.

Bea shook her head, not moving from the door. Kaya

frowned. The moment she'd promised to see to their continued employment, Bea had been overjoyed. When she brought the earlier tray with juice and fig preserves, she'd been smiles and laughter. Now, the poor woman looked nervous. Kaya narrowed her eyes.

"What is it, Bea?"

Bea opened her mouth, but no sound emerged. Kaya shivered and grabbed her khanjar just as Azizi sat straight.

"I'm sorry," Bea whispered, her voice breaking. "I'm sorry."

A tall man with a nasty little smile on his face stepped from behind Bea. He held a knife in one hand. From the looks of it, it was one she and Paul had taken from one of the numerous bandits they'd encountered on their trek from Rome.

"*Albaqa'*, Azizi," she ordered the dog, not entirely certain she'd obey. Or that Kaya wanted her to. She dug her fingers into Azizi's fur to keep her still, just in case.

"You interfering little bitch," the man snarled. His voice sounded scratchy, as if he had a cold, but she suspected that was his normal tone. "Where's your husband?"

"Out for a walk," she snapped, weighing her options. If she attacked from this distance, he'd have enough time to hurt Bea. If she ordered Azizi (who stood, muscles bunched and ready) to attack, the same outcome applied.

"Mouthy, too," the man spat. Kaya scowled at him, disgusted. "I'll fix that."

"I am not broken," she snapped. "Who are you, and what do you want?"

"What's mine. Ferrari owes me money."

"For?"

"Protection, signora," Bea sobbed. She shook but didn't move, even as tears fell down her cheeks. "He didn't pay the protection money."

Kaya had no idea what that meant, but she suddenly realized two things: This man, or someone he commanded, had killed both Signora Ferrari and her husband. And he was the eyes watching from the shadows.

"And you believe I have this money? I am neither Signora Ferrari nor her husband; I do not own this inn, and I have nothing to do with the money you may or may not be owed."

"Where's his coin box?"

"I don't know," she admitted. She hadn't found it yet. The amount she'd already paid for the first delivery had been small enough that she was easily able to afford it, and for that she was grateful.

"Liar."

Still gripping her dagger, Kaya swept her hand over her shoulder. "Do you see the box? I don't know where it is."

"You'll have to do then."

"Why?" Her heart sank, and she knew separating from Paul had been a terrible idea. If he moved more than ten feet from her sight in the next fifty years, she'd be shocked.

"Payment."

"No." Kaya knew that was the wrong thing to say, but it popped out before she had the chance to swallow it.

He grabbed Bea and held the knife to her throat. "Then I gut pretty little Beatrice here."

The fact he knew Bea's name alarmed Kaya far more than the measly knife he held to her throat. What had Paul said about people knowing each other? Not traveling more than a few miles from their birthplace?

"All right." Hand resting on Azizi's head, she hoped the dog would stay until Paul returned. "Only me. Not Bea."

"I think I'd rather both of you," he said in an ugly purr that made Kaya want to vomit.

"If you touch one more hair on her, I'll gut *you*," she snapped.

He laughed, his face creasing in wrinkles that made him look far older. It was that same ugly sound, and she wondered if he knew anything but ugliness. From the lines on his gray face, she'd wager he did not. "Feisty. I like it. I'm going to enjoy you."

Not likely, but she didn't offer another word to the man. To Azizi, she whispered a quiet command to find Paul. To Bea, she nodded and offered a tight smile. Head high, she crossed to the man and looked at him haughtily.

"Well?" She gestured for him to move. "I presume you don't wish to travel in the dark, and it's already midafternoon."

Had Azizi left already? Doubtful; she only wandered from Kaya's side when she was hungry, and certainly never in a situation like this.

"Azizi!" Kaya called without looking away from this horrid man. "*Al-athour ola* Paul."

The man raised a hand to smack her, but Kaya stepped back. She didn't flinch as he scowled, cursing her with several rather colorful words. She wanted to comment on their variety, if only to anger him further, but her heart tripped over itself, and cold fear slithered down her spine.

"Bea, it'll be all right," she promised the woman.

Kaya doubted that, but she let the man grab her arm and force her out of the inn.

Paul urged the horses up the last hill. The sun backlit the inn as it sank further behind the mountains. He'd been gone far longer than he intended, but the condottiero had mysteriously changed his mind and released Hannah.

She now sat huddled on the seat beside him in the inn's little cart. Confinement hadn't sat well with her, but she'd walked from the prison with her head held high and not one backward glance. The moment they left Riccione proper, she'd collapsed, shoulders sagging, head in her hands.

Paul had no idea how to comfort her, so he settled for driving the horses as well as he could through the path they'd taken far too many times over the last week.

"We're nearly there," he promised. "I'm certain Ginevra and Rosa will see to a nice bath." The stench of that prison wasn't coming out of her clothes anytime soon, but he refrained from mentioning it. Or that he knew that from experience. "And I know Kaya will be thrilled to see you. Charlotte, too."

Hannah sat straighter and wiped her cheeks. "I'm afraid this is far from an auspicious beginning."

He snorted. "Countess, it was far from an auspicious beginning when we met."

She smiled and offered a watery laugh. "You may be right. And call me Hannah, please." She cleared her throat and tucked her hair into what was left of her bun. "Did the condottiero say why he let me out? Not," she rushed to say, "that I'm ungrateful, but it seems strange, given his insistence."

"Probably because Ferrari was also murdered. I'm sure the condottiero believes, as we do, that it's connected." Also, Paul doubted the poor man had any experience solving murders. He'd looked slightly bewildered and lost when confronted with Ferrari's death.

Or maybe he knew who murdered the couple. Paul shivered in the cooling night. He had a sinking feeling that was true, though he doubted many murders happened here.

"No doubt he'll be back in the morning with more questions."

Then Azizi leaped from the shadows, growling and startling the horses. Paul froze. Azizi did not leave Kaya's side except to hunt. Dropping the reins, he jumped from the seat and raced for the dog. She backed away, and for one horrible moment, Paul didn't know if she growled in warning for him or someone else.

"Azizi, where's Kaya?" Paul said, inching closer, hands out. He spoke in Egyptian, as that was the language Kaya had trained her in. The dog backed away another step. "Who took her?" he snarled, uncaring that the dog couldn't answer.

Whistling to Azizi to follow, he ran into the inn. Bea sat in a chair in the foyer, cheeks tearstained, fingers tangled around her skirts. The rest of the staff surrounded her, all looking lost and scared.

"Where is she?"

"They took her," Nestor said. He looked as pale and frightened as the rest. "The local gang. They demanded protection payment, and Signore Ferrari refused. We were so proud he stood up to them, but then the poor signora."

"Where is she?" Paul repeated, advancing on the hapless group. "Which direction? Where is their camp?"

He didn't bother to ask why her; he knew. If it was a choice between keeping these people safe and using herself as bait, Kaya would protect them each and every time. Fury blinded him for a moment, and he took a breath. He loved her fierce passion to protect. Even with this clawing fear choking him, he wouldn't change that about her.

But he was never letting her out of his sight again. Ever.

"They're in the mountains to the north," Nestor said, his voice shaking. "I can show you."

Paul narrowed his eyes at the boy. "How do you know where they are?"

"Everyone knows," Nestor admitted, but he looked determined. "They don't hide."

Paul accepted that. However, he would not bring this boy into whatever danger lurked in the mountains. Paul quickly completed his inventory—he carried only two knives, but also planned to bring a very anxious Azizi. More than enough.

Paul started for the door but instantly turned around. "Did she have her khanjar?"

"The *pugnale*?" Bea asked in a quavering voice. But she sat straighter and watched him with clear eyes. "*Sì, sì*, she had that. She saved my life, Signore Conrad." Her fingers flitted over her neck, and Paul saw a faint mark there. Someone had held a knife to Bea's throat.

Paul hoped his expression looked understanding, and he nodded. "She does that, Bea. I'll bring her back."

Once more, he whistled for Azizi and disappeared out the door. As much as he'd have preferred a more detailed map to where this little gang hid, he didn't want to place anyone else in danger. And he certainly didn't want anyone slowing him down.

On the north side of the inn, he slipped his knives from their hiding places and nodded to Azizi. She raced off, her long wolf-legs eating up the ground. Paul raced after her, heart pounding. He didn't think, just followed, refusing to let his panic take hold.

He had no idea how far they ran or in what direction; he

merely followed Azizi, who ran like the hounds of hell were on her tail. Whatever the dog wanted in the future, Paul would willingly provide.

The sun had fully disappeared behind the mountains by the time he heard their camp. A chilly breeze wound through the trees, carrying laughter and song. Anger tightened his throat, but Paul held onto it with a tight fist.

"Azizi, *albaqa'*," Paul ordered, sinking his fingers into Azizi's back to keep her there.

He needed to regain his breath and plan a semblance of an attack. Over the sound of laughter, he couldn't hear anything else, and he feared moving closer would only encourage Azizi to attack.

"Stay here," Paul ordered. "I'll whistle when it's time."

Azizi did not listen. She crept closer, teeth bared and snarling, which didn't surprise Paul.

All right, then. All or nothing.

Straightening his shoulders, one knife gripped in his dominant hand, he strode forward. It took the group several long moments to realize he stood here, but their conversation and laughter eventually died. Paul counted nine at first glance and waited for the supposed leader to step forward.

They always did.

"I believe you took my wife."

A tall man, who looked far worse for wear, limped around the fire. He held a bottle of wine in one hand and a knife in the other. One side of his face had started to bruise. Good. He smiled, and Paul wanted to leap the remaining feet and punch that smile off his face.

"You're the woman's man?" He laughed again. "Quite the screamer she is."

Shoulders bunched, he held himself in check. He was going to slice open this man inch by inch.

"Sobbed her little heart out, crying for you as I slit her throat."

Liar.

Paul stilled, a slow smile spreading across his face. He glanced at the rest of the group, but they hadn't moved. They looked as if they'd spent the night drinking; several were clearly in no shape to be a bother. A few eyed the tall man, but each one of them remained silent.

"Azizi," Paul commanded in a clear, confident voice. "*Al-athour ola* Kaya."

Even if none of them understood Egyptian, they understood a snarling half wolf and scrambled backward. Azizi disappeared into the woods. Satisfied she'd find Kaya—alive—Paul returned his attention to the gang.

"You killed the Ferraris." It was a statement, but the leader nodded. "Why?"

"They didn't pay." He spat into the fire, and Paul actually wondered how Kaya hadn't taken him down, given his lack of manners. "You don't pay, you don't receive the protection we provide."

"Ah, yes, of course. How remiss of me." Paul laughed and advanced. He listened for Azizi, Kaya, anyone who might sneak up on him. "Send a message, right?" He nodded again, his gaze steady on the leader's.

"You think you can take us?" The man laughed again, the foul sound brittle in the night. Paul really wanted to punch him. "There are eleven of us."

"I count nine," he said conversationally, and he instantly knew where Kaya was. He grinned and nearly laughed. "I'm afraid the odds are not in your favor."

The man frowned and looked at his group, clearly confused as to what had happened to their tenth and eleventh member. "Nine against one is still better odds." He dropped his wine, which bled from the bottle and seeped into the ground.

Paul shrugged. "It's your funeral."

The leader attacked. He was sloppy, which didn't surprise Paul, given the bottle of wine he'd previously clutched. However, the man did know how to use a knife, and he wielded it with at least some skill. It wasn't enough. Even if he'd been a master in the subject, it'd never be enough.

This man had taken Kaya.

Paul's fury exploded.

He slipped his second knife from its hiding spot and advanced. No one else moved. Paul wondered about that, but he chalked it up to this leader wanting all the glory. Men like him were usually highly offended when anyone helped. They thought it made them look weak.

Still, Paul didn't take the man's drunkenness for granted. He ducked the long arcs and watched for his opening. They didn't have much room to maneuver; the fire only illuminated a small circle, and Paul had already raced through these woods. He had the scratches and sore ankle to prove it.

Somewhere in the nearby darkness, Paul heard Azizi howl. He didn't know if that meant she'd found Kaya or that she was finished playing by the rules her humans had laid out for her.

Either way, it had the desired effect. The group scrambled to their feet. Paul didn't look away to see them, but he heard motion in the dirt and knew they panicked. Good.

Paul deflected a swing and saw his opening. A quick jab to his left side stumbled the man backward. Another swing caught him directly in the chin, and he crashed to his knees. Flipping his knife, Paul held it against the man's throat.

"Your little operation is finished." He tugged on the man's hair, stretching his thin throat taut. "And your band of followers has deserted you."

The man tried to spit out some words, but Paul didn't release his hold.

"Kaya!" he called, certain she was within earshot.

"*Ya rouhi.*"

Paul did look up then, and he found her on the edge of the firelight. Beautiful in the flickering shadows, her hijab still covering her, she looked unharmed. She held her khanjar, Azizi at her side. Six men stood in front of her, stock still and clearly terrified. Two lay on the ground, moaning in pain as they held their hands against their chests.

"I'm all right," she promised, but she didn't take her gaze from the men in front of her. "Paolo here lost me in the woods."

Relief burned his throat, and Paul took a moment to swallow around the emotion. He pulled on Paolo's hair until the other man grunted in pain. It wasn't nearly enough. "He lost you?" He snorted and shook his head. "I'm not surprised."

"You. Sit. Now."

To Paul's complete lack of surprise, the men obeyed. He didn't know what she'd done to terrify them so—but then Azizi did stand there with her constant snarling growl. Paul would obey, too, faced with that.

"He killed the Ferraris, intimidated the staff, and tried to use me as some sort of ransom." She scowled at Paolo. "Then he tried to take my khanjar."

"A mortal sin if ever I heard one." Paul didn't know how else to respond. His knife didn't waver from Paolo's throat, but he wanted to shove the man to the ground and let Azizi take over. He felt his fingers cramp in Paolo's hair and forcibly relaxed them. The last thing he needed was to fall apart here.

"He's lucky all I did was punch him," Kaya admitted. He heard the thread of relief in her voice and desperately wanted to hold her close.

Paul pressed his knife harder into Paolo's throat. "He's lucky I don't slit his throat right here."

Kaya didn't immediately answer, and he met her gaze across the campsite. She didn't look as if she wanted to stop him, but she also didn't encourage him. He understood that all too well. Killing Paolo now, in cold blood, would do no one any good. It might even land them both in the prison he'd so recently retrieved Hannah from.

Paul started to speak, then stopped and switched to English. He wasn't confident in his Egyptian just now. He wasn't confident his voice wouldn't crack. "Have you rope?" He nodded to the cowering men. "Not that Azizi will let any of them out of her sight."

"No, and this is a very sparse camp. Wine, a few crates that look to be from neighboring inns and shops, nothing more."

"Probably more protection bribes." Paul kicked Paolo in the small of his back. "Scum bleeding off the hard work of others."

"What protection do they offer?" One of the men coughed, and Kaya paused, arching her khanjar in his direction. "I thought I told you not to move." The man stilled and nodded, hands held out to his side. "I don't understand. How does taking money from these properties protect them?"

Paul gave a short, hard laugh. "It protects them from these men. You pay the bribe, or you die."

"Like the Ferraris," Kaya said quietly. She glared at the men before her and snarled. "You are scum," she told them.

They said nothing in the silence, and Paul waited. He wasn't certain what to do next. Burning through these men and leaving them gasping for breath sounded like a fantastic idea, but he wouldn't put Kaya through that. So they stood in the cooling night, the fire slowly dying, the silence stretching between them.

"Signore Conrad!"

Frowning, Paul tightened his hold on Paolo's hair. He knew that voice. The roaring in his ears had lessened once he spotted Kaya, but it still took Paul a moment to recognize the man. The condottieri?

"Signore Esposito?"

"Nestor!" Kaya's surprised voice cleared some of the rage from his gaze, and Paul looked around. "What are you doing here?"

"He took one of the horses," Signore Esposito admitted as he stepped into the firelight. "Raced into town, found me, then led me here."

Nestor must have left immediately after Paul, raced to town, then back here. Paul blinked at the lad, truly impressed with his speed and skill. And his dedication—he hadn't needed to bring the condottiero here.

Paul wouldn't have blamed him if he had done nothing. Long after he and Kaya left, Nestor would need to live here. He knew these people, or some of them, no doubt. But what had he said about being proud that Signore Ferrari hadn't paid the protection money?

"Signore Esposito, have you a rope or something to hold these men?"

"I ordered my men to follow me with the prison wagon. But this is rough terrain, and it'll take some time."

"You walked?" Kaya asked, that cautious note back in her voice.

Esposito laughed, breathless. "I'm afraid we ran. Young Nestor here insisted on hurrying."

Paul accepted that explanation. He hadn't felt anything was off about the condottiero—thought him ineffectual, perhaps, but not a criminal. Still, it was best to be cautious. Paul wasn't familiar with any of the rules here, spoken or unspoken. Given the prevalence of these protection payments, it was best not to trust anyone.

"Then I suppose we wait." Paul met Kaya's gaze, and she nodded.

She slowly stepped around the men, ordering Azizi to stay—not that the dog might move, given these men had threatened her mistress.

Holding his gaze, Kaya walked across the camp and to his side. "Let him go, Paul," she whispered, her fingers brushing his cheek.

"What happened to the other men?" he asked, forcing his hands to obey her. He didn't want to, wanted to gut each and every one of these people who'd dared try and harm her. Wanted to burn the camp to the ground without caring what that fire might engulf.

"They wandered from camp, and it was a simple matter to incapacitate them." She shrugged but didn't look away from him.

Her fingers continued to dance over his cheek like a butterfly's wings. "The two on the ground tried to push past me."

"Always underestimating you." His own fingers opened, an excruciatingly slow movement, until Paolo fell to the ground, gasping for breath. The moment he no longer held Paolo at knifepoint, Paul turned to Kaya and pulled her into his arms. "I'm never letting you go."

"I know." Her arms tightened around him and squeezed, her face buried in his chest. "Do you trust the condottiero?"

"I don't care right now," Paul admitted, pulling back just enough to cup her face. "Are you unharmed?"

"Completely. Paolo didn't expect me to fight back." She scowled at the man now moaning on his side. "Coward that he is." She dismissed him with another scowl. "And you? What of you?"

"I'm fine now that you're here." He kissed her, uncaring who might be watching. "You terrified me when you weren't at the inn when I returned."

"It was me or Bea, and I was afraid what they'd do to her."

"I know." He brushed his fingers through her hair, kissing her forehead. "I know."

"What did you discover at the prison?"

"Just—just a moment. I need a moment to hold you, sweetheart."

A moment, a lifetime. He let the shaking overcome him and buried his face in her shoulder. He needed this time to compose himself, then he'd deal with everything else.

Twenty

By the time Kaya and Paul returned to the inn, the moon was high in the sky. She shivered in the cold night air—she'd left the inn without a shawl, too concerned with saving Bea to worry about how cold it might get once the sun set.

Or maybe she wasn't just shivering from the cold.

Signore Esposito's men had arrived eventually, and they set about arresting the gang. Kaya hadn't asked, but she had a feeling they'd either be out of prison by the end of the week or dead. She couldn't reasonably explain that last feeling; however, she wouldn't rule it out.

"Are you hungry?" Paul asked as the inn came into view.

"Yes. I left before luncheon. and Paolo and his ilk showed few manners. They didn't offer me a scrap of food." She'd hoped that might elicit a smile at the very least, but Paul merely tightened his grip on her hand. Not that she'd given those men a chance to offer her anything; she'd surprised Paolo, knocked him to his knees with her punch, and disappeared into the trees before he had time to recover.

"Azizi, go on, go hunt."

She'd been saying that since Esposito's men arrived, but Azizi refused to leave her. Kaya dropped her hand to the dog's head and scratched behind her ears. Such a good girl. Azizi's presence warmed Kaya, and as much as she worried for the dog, she appreciated her constant guard.

"I forgot." Paul stopped and turned just inside the tree line. In the shadows, Kaya couldn't see his expression, but his voice sounded stilted. "Hannah. Esposito released her from prison. With Ferrari's death, he hadn't much evidence to keep her." He shook his head. "I wanted to surprise you."

"I am surprised." She leaned up and kissed him gently, afraid he might break.

She'd seen him furiously angry; the rage over what Appleby and Rogerson concocted had infuriated him. She'd seen him worried; even in those early days, with the slavers in the desert, she understood his concern for her. In the souk when those men had tried to kidnap her.

This, this almost fragile disquiet had her at a complete loss. She had no idea what to say to make any of it better. Worse, she felt the same. For a brief, horrible moment, Kaya hadn't been certain she'd ever see him again. The thought had stayed with her until she heard his voice taunting Paolo in the camp.

"Thank you."

"For what?" he asked. "I didn't release her."

"You tried. You cared." She cupped the back of his head and urged him down so she could kiss him again. "You did all you could, and then you did more."

Paul shuddered in her arms. "I thought I lost you," he admitted.

"Never." Kaya wrapped her arms around him and held. She might never let him go. "I'm afraid you're quite stuck with me, my dear."

He let out a strangled laugh and a shaky breath. "Wouldn't have it any other way, sweetheart."

They stood like that for several more minutes, the wind a constant presence around them, Azizi leaning against Kaya and sharing her warmth.

"I love you," Kaya eventually whispered. "More than anything."

"I would have killed them all," Paul admitted. "If they had harmed you, I'd have killed them all."

"I know." Kaya kissed his temple but didn't release him. She couldn't, afraid she might not be able to stand upright without him. "I know. But it'll take more than a band of sloppy bandits to harm me."

He snorted a laugh. "When Paolo claimed you cried, I knew you were all right."

"Oh." She frowned. "I'm not sure how to take that."

"No." He chuckled again, a more normal sound than the shakiness of earlier. "Not that you wouldn't cry. But he said you sobbed as he slit your throat. Someone like that?" He gave an abbreviated shake of his head, which was still resting on her shoulder. "No chance he overpowered you. Even if he had somehow gotten lucky, you wouldn't have given him the satisfaction."

"Well, thank you." She tugged his hair to see him better. "I was afraid I'd never see you again. I didn't know if he sent his men to kill Bea and the others. I didn't know if anyone else was involved." He rested his forehead against hers, and Kaya swallowed her fears. "I didn't even know if Azizi understood me, if she'd wait for you."

"Oh, she did." He pulled back and looked at the dog, who was patiently sitting so close to Kaya it was a wonder she didn't merge with her. "Good girl that you are, yes." Paul scratched her head. He stared down at Azizi for a long moment. "I knew something was wrong when she stood in the middle of the road, snarling. Terrified me."

"I'm sorry for that," Kaya admitted. "I didn't know what else to do, and I was afraid that if Paolo took Bea, he'd abuse her."

Paul nodded and retook her hand. "Let's get inside. You're shivering."

Kaya had forgotten that until he pointed it out. With the walk and the hiding in the woods and the fighting, the night had become chilly. The circle of torches remained lit despite the late hour, and no sooner had they stepped into the light than Rosa called out.

"They're back!"

Before Kaya registered the greeting, they were surrounded. Hannah hugged her tight, Charlotte next. Bea, Ginevra, Rosa, and Tino came after, each expressing their pleasure in seeing her again.

"Nestor, he ran right after Paul," Hannah was saying. "He raced to the barn, took one of the horses, and disappeared into town at a gallop. Is he all right?"

"Should be right behind us," Paul assured her. "He brought the condottiero to the clearing." He paused and looked to the staff. "How much do you trust Signore Esposito?"

Rosa shrugged. "As much as anyone is trustworthy."

"Signore Ferrari tried speaking with him," Tino admitted in a soft voice. "But when the signora was...Ferrari had to blame someone. Sorry, Contessa, we couldn't say anything."

Hannah nodded and smiled gently at the boy. "I understand. I wish never to have seen the inside of that prison, but I understand."

"We all must do what's best for ourselves and our families," Kaya added quietly. However, she had a feeling Rosa knew something about the condottiero. Perhaps they all did but feared retaliation. Or perhaps Kaya was reading too far into their reactions. They were all scared.

Their happiness now seemed genuine enough. And it'd been such a long day.

"Come inside," Hannah said, guiding them toward the doors. "Do you want dinner?"

"Don't go to any trouble," Kaya insisted, looking to Bea. Her feet dragged, and she honestly debated food or bed.

"We'll dine in the kitchens," Paul agreed. "Warmer there, too."

Once settled at the long, wooden table, Bea served them

steaming stew and hot coffee. Kaya wrapped her fingers around the wooden bowl and let the warmth seep into her. Hannah and Charlotte sat opposite them, looking uncomfortable at the informal location but eager to hear what happened.

"However did Paul find you?" Hannah eventually asked.

"Azizi," he said, eyes closed. "She followed Kaya's scent and ran straight for her. For the camp, at least."

Before either of them could elaborate, Nestor appeared. He looked ragged and cold, but pleased with the attention. Paul motioned for him to join them, and though there was plenty of room at the table, Kaya slid closer to him.

"Nestor, good lad." Paul raised his coffee cup in salute. "How did you find us?"

Nestor blushed and looked down at his own bowl of stew. "I knew they camped north of the inn. The closer we came to their camp, the easier it was to hear you. Followed the sound."

Kaya desperately wanted to ask if Nestor knew where the camp was located because he'd been there. Or knew someone in that gang. But what if he had been there? What if he did know someone? She and Paul planned on leaving, especially now that Hannah had been released. What did knowing what Nestor did or did not know about the extortion bandits offer any of them?

Even if she and Paul bought the inn, which she'd been debating in Ferrari's office before Bea returned at knifepoint. Even if they bought the inn, she still didn't wish to stay here, and she knew Paul didn't, either.

"Did the rest of the shipments arrive?" she asked instead.

"No, signora." Bea shook her head. "More stew? I made plenty."

"Thank you, Bea." Kaya wasn't hungry anymore, but the warmth of the tuna, olive oil, and pine nuts made her feel slightly less exhausted, though Bea looked anxious still.

"When do you expect them?" she asked, returning the conversation to the shipments.

"Tomorrow, probably." Bea shrugged. "I don't know. Signore

Ferrari, he was in charge of them." She quickly crossed herself and looked to Rosa and Ginevra. "Who will run the inn now?"

"I don't know," Kaya admitted.

"I did ask Signore Esposito about possible heirs, but he didn't know of any." Paul looked into his refilled bowl and sighed. "Given both Signore and Signora Ferrari are dead, I don't know the procedures to take over the place."

"What are we to do in the meantime?" Ginevra asked. Kaya thought she looked steadier tonight than she had when they spoke —was it yesterday? She couldn't remember. "The summer guests are expected to arrive next week, and you promised we'd remain open."

"I did," Kaya agreed, her tone calm and even. She was far too drained for anything else. "However, with Signore Ferrari now also gone, we need to figure out the inheritance laws."

She nudged Paul, who sighed but nodded. "In the morning, we'll return to town, and I'll speak with Signore Esposito about it. We have friends in Villa San Giovanni; they might be able to help."

Yes, she'd thought of Roberto Spanó, too. By now, Marta had to have arrived and settled in. Kaya thought it would be good to write and see how she fared with the new babe. And Olivia; Kaya missed her as well.

She wanted to tell them all where she and Paul planned to travel to next, should any of them wish to write. But at the moment, Kaya wasn't sure where they were headed. She'd have to speak with Hannah about traveling north to Prussia and Paul about what their next step might be.

Kaya hadn't the energy to follow the conversation as it flowed around them. She leaned against Paul and fed Azizi a bite of tuna.

"Ready for bed?" Paul asked quietly.

"More than," she agreed.

He helped her stand from the bench, and she nodded to the group, silently promising them all she'd speak with them in the morning. Then Kaya allowed Paul to lead her from the kitchens.

Azizi slipped out one of the doors, and Kaya paused, leaning against the wall.

"She's a good dog," Paul said, winding an arm around Kaya's waist. "I think she understands far more than we give her credit for."

"I do not believe I can imagine our lives without her," Kaya admitted. Then she turned and smiled at him. "Even if dogs are not meant to be pets."

He laughed, a strong, confident sound that warmed her. "Pet or not, I think she makes the finest of guard wolves."

She sniffed. "Azizi is a *dog*."

He kissed her temple and rested his forehead against it. "She's worth whatever we have to pay to keep her with us," he admitted. "She's the only reason I found you as quickly as I did."

Kaya let the silence settle over them, comfortable and cozy despite all that had happened that day. Eventually, she asked, "Do you really think we'll be able to keep the inn open?"

"I've no idea. But with enough money, anything is possible."

"We'll write Roberto. Even if we purchase it, I wish to stay here even less now than I did two days ago."

Paul chuckled, a tired huff of a sound. "Worst case scenario, he can take over the everyday running of the inn. Perhaps move the family from Villa San Giovanni. It's not secure there, what with the earthquakes."

"As a port city, it's as prone to attack as Riccione. I'm not certain it's any safer."

"Perhaps not, but it's far from the dens young Marco visited, and getting away from that temptation has to be a good move." He sighed. "And, yes, I'm certain there are opium dens here. But he won't know where they are; he'll have no contacts."

"We'll write in the morning," Kaya agreed. "After we speak with Signore Esposito."

Azizi finally returned, shaking herself as she reentered the back door. Nodding to no one in particular, Kaya walked up the stairs and into their room. Drained as she was, she completed her rituals before falling into bed. Paul didn't disturb her—he never did—but rather knelt silently beside her, eyes closed.

"I'm not moving for three days," he said as he pulled the blanket over them.

Azizi, ignoring Kaya's rules, rested her large head on the bed and stared at them. Kaya placed her hand on her head and smiled. Paul hadn't yet snuffed out the candle, and in the faint light, Azizi looked truly pathetic.

"You're far too large for the bed, Azizi. The three of us will never fit."

Azizi whined, and Kaya understood. Today had terrified Azizi, too, and she needed as much comfort as Kaya and Paul. Behind her, Paul sighed.

"All right, come on. We'll sleep on the floor and not our soft, comfortable bed." He threw back the blankets and sat up. "But she's not getting our blankets."

Several minutes later, they settled on the floor. Kaya once more curled in Paul's arms, with Azizi at her back. She snuggled into Paul's embrace, head resting on his chest.

"I'm glad you're safe," she whispered into the darkness. "I don't know what I'd have done if anything happened to you."

Paul had said he'd burn the camp to the ground, and Kaya had a feeling she'd have done the same if anything happened to him.

"I am truly never letting you out of my sight again," he growled. "It doesn't matter what the situation is—never."

"I'm not arguing." Kaya had a feeling he meant that, too. Paul never promised her anything he didn't intend to see through. Even something like this, which might be difficult.

"Good night, sweetheart." He kissed the top of her head.

"Good night, Paul." Kaya closed her eyes and let the warmth of him chase away the lingering fear of the day.

Twenty-One

Kaya made her rounds in the inn, followed by an eager Azizi, ever hopeful for a morsel of food, and a stoic Paul. They planned to meet Hannah and Charlotte for breakfast in an hour or so, but first she wanted to ensure the staff needed nothing to keep the inn functional.

"What do you plan if Esposito closes it down?" Paul held open the door and ushered her outside toward the stables.

"You mean if we can't purchase it?" Kaya took his arm and slowed their step. The last few days had been rushed, and she needed this time to reclaim their own pace, the one they'd only just reclaimed before meeting Hannah. "See they're all adequately taken care of, find someone we can trust who writes the language"—Paul snorted, and she chuckled—"and ensure they all have proper references."

"I'll work on finding someone to write the letter." He growled something here she couldn't make out. "We'll have to venture into town; I don't want to leave you alone here."

"I know." She rested her head against his shoulder. "I think that's for the best. I don't want you alone in town, either. I'm not certain everyone involved in that little scheme was arrested."

"They rarely are."

They slowed as they reached the stables. Even Azizi, who normally bounded ahead in greeting, stayed beside them. Kaya didn't blame her. She didn't know how much dogs, even half wolves, understood about the human world, but Azizi was smart enough to sense danger.

Whatever she sensed, Kaya knew she had been troubled by the events of yesterday.

"I'm still not convinced Esposito isn't involved." Paul sighed and stopped just out of earshot of the stables. "And, much like the opium, there's no stopping this sort of extortion. I've seen it everywhere. England, Bombay—I suspected it in Sicily, but we never stayed in one place long enough."

Kaya offered a small smile and sighed her agreement. "I'm afraid you're right. Even if we stayed, we couldn't stop it, not completely. I believe in taking a stand, in doing what's right, in helping and protecting others. However, I've no desire to find you stabbed to death in the hallway."

He shuddered and jerked her close, his hands resting on her hips. "No."

She blinked that all too vivid image away and focused on the here and now. All her life, she'd looked forward to a future where she might make her own choices. Experience what *she* wanted to experience, see what interested her, travel and explore and enjoy life. With each passing day, Kaya realized how different reality and dream truly were.

"Let's check in on Nestor and Tino." Paul kissed her softly. "I'm keen to leave sooner rather than later."

"All right." She turned to Azizi and nudged her forward. "Tino! Nestor!"

The boys came running out, greeting Azizi enthusiastically. "Signora." They bowed to Kaya in rigid formality. "Signore." Then they bowed to Paul with that same formality, and Kaya tried not to laugh.

"Do you require anything before the guests arrive next week?" Paul asked.

Kaya once more hid her smile as they tried to focus on their duties and not playing with Azizi. She tuned out their responses; they seemed well-equipped for the yearly influx of visitors. Closing her eyes and lifting her face to the sun, she let the warming day chase away her nightmares.

She hadn't told Paul about them—no sense worrying him more than he already was. She'd dreamt in jumbled images—Paul in the darkened streets of Cairo, which she'd seen only that once, fighting slavers, opium dealers, and mountain bandits, the line stretching across the city. Never-ending, always coming, even as he grew weaker. As more knives dug deep into his flesh.

Shivering, Kaya opened her eyes and curled her hands into tight fists, nails digging into her palms. The here and now—she needed to remember that.

"Nestor," Paul called as the boys started for the stables. "Who do the other horses belong to?"

"Oh, Signore Ferrari bought them. He wanted to look fancier than the other inns and offer the *latifondista* a nicer drive."

"On these roads?" Paul muttered. "Donkeys would be better."

Nestor shrugged and disappeared inside the stables. Paul whistled for Azizi but didn't let go of his scrutiny.

"When Hannah was first arrested, Bea said Ferrari was a spendthrift. I guess this was one of his poorer ideas."

"Where did he get the money?" Paul asked, finally turning. "And where's the carriage for the horses?"

"Perhaps it's one of the shipments the inn is expecting." Kaya swallowed and forced open her fists, stretching her fingers and massaging her palms.

"What's wrong?" Paul set his hand on the small of her back and guided her toward the inn.

"Nothing." She paused and remembered her own admonishment to speak the truth. If she wanted him to do so, she'd need to offer the same. "Thinking about possibilities. What might happen. What might *have* happened."

"Never a good idea," he agreed. "Worrying about the future paralyzes you."

"Is that why you lived in the moment?" Kaya asked as they reached the kitchen doors. "Because you didn't want to worry about the future?"

"I've never thought about it like that." He paused and glanced around the yard, squinting into the tree line. "It wasn't always like that. When I met Tahir, I still thought joining the Company was the right choice. A way to dig myself out of the poverty of my youth and make something of myself. Become respectable. It's because I saved him that I earned a promotion to the officer ranks."

"What happened?" she asked quietly, carefully. He rarely spoke of his time with the East India Company, and he even more rarely anything positive.

In fact, from what little he'd said, one of the only positive things to happen during his time there was meeting Tahir. Because Paul had saved her grandfather from a horse that suddenly went wild, Gidd had written him, years later, to contract their marriage.

The world was a strange place.

"I—" He tilted his head in thought. "I'm not sure. I can't pinpoint where it all spiraled downward, but I'm sure it was small things at first. Harry offering me a bit of opium. Drinking too much with Oliver and John. Gambling with Basu."

He stumbled to a stop and scrubbed a hand down his face. Shaking his head like Azizi after a rainstorm, he looked skyward. "I don't want to talk about it. Not now."

"All right," she said easily enough. Stepping into the kitchens, she nodded to Bea, who had enlisted her sister to help with the preparations. "We'll need to return to town this afternoon," she told both women. "What about the shipments?"

Bea shrugged and waved a hand. "They may come today or tomorrow. All I know is what Signora Ferrari told me, may she rest in peace. She said they were expecting items for the summer season."

Kaya grimaced but nodded. "All right. They'll..." She glanced at Paul, who looked at her with a fiercely set look. "If they arrive while we're in town, they'll have to wait, I'm afraid."

Bea looked concerned, her eyes flicking from Kaya to her sister and back. "We...will you be gone long?"

They had to find someone Paul trusted enough, or who would be discreet enough after proper payment, to write several letters. Then they needed a courier to take the letter to Roberto in Villa San Giovanni as well as send the inquiries into who now owned the inn—it was going to take all day.

"We'll return by dinner," she promised. "See if they can stay until then. Promise them food, anything to keep them here until we return."

Paul stepped beside Kaya. "If you know anyone who is good with a knife, someone you trust, hire them. Don't worry about cost; just find protection." The two guards Ferrari hired had mysteriously disappeared once the man had been found murdered. "You'll need the protection."

Bea looked relieved and nodded. "*Grazie*, signore."

As they walked from the kitchens to the dining room, Kaya looked at him in a new light. "That wasn't about being paranoid, was it?"

"They're scared. The guards disappeared after Ferrari's death, and they have no protector. There's no guarantee they'll survive the day, let alone have a job at the end of the week."

Kaya leaned up and kissed him. "You're a good man, Paul Conrad."

He snorted. "Because I see danger in every corner?"

"Because you care enough to step up and help."

As much as Paul did not want to leave Kaya alone, he also didn't want to bring her to the less-than-respectable establishments in Riccione where he'd seek out the forgers he needed. Signore Esposito hadn't been aware of any heirs to the Ferrari inn, and Paul had no real idea what their next step might be.

With no one to run the inn, and a very slim chance of producing a will, the future of the place looked to be in limbo.

"I don't mind coming with you," Kaya assured him, one hand on his arm, the other resting on Azizi's head. "I've never met a forger."

"I don't want you exposed to such places," he growled. "I also don't want to leave you alone." He held up a hand. "I know you can take care of yourself. But after the last week, I don't like it."

"I have Azizi." She sighed and nodded. "I think it's best we stay together. Far too many people know about what happened now; I doubt Signore Esposito was discreet."

Paul doubted the man was discreet at all, but then he doubted most people. "All right. We'll be fast."

What he meant was he'd find the darkest alley in Riccione, the grimiest corner, and hire the first man he saw who didn't look at Kaya like she was his gift from Heaven. But that took far longer than Paul wanted, and he had been forced to ask far too many people.

Eventually, Rossi, no first name, eyed Paul over a heavy magnifying glass. The room was illuminated by only a single candle set beside Rossi's work.

"*Che cosa?*" Rossi spat.

"I'm in need of several letters." Paul cast a quick glance around the dark room. "By week's end."

"It'll cost you," Rossi said in a dismissive tone. "I don't work for free."

"No one does," Paul agreed. "Five letters of reference, one more to be sent south."

"Why?"

Paul paused. "Why do I want the letters? Or why have I come to you?"

"Either." Rossi shrugged. "Both. You're the couple who stopped them in the mountains."

Paul had been afraid of this, and he remained silent. He felt Kaya move, a slight twitch of her hand as she unsheathed her khanjar. Azizi, who remained constantly on guard since Kaya's kidnapping, tensed.

"They kidnapped my wife," Paul growled.

"They killed my son," Rossi said in a quiet voice as dark as the room. "What do you need?"

Paul repeated his request, outlining the letters of reference from the Ferraris and the more detailed one to Roberto Spanó, asking for help in securing the inn.

"Signore Rossi," Kaya said after Paul handed him half the required payment. "Do you know anything about inheritance laws here? What happens to the inn now?"

"I'll ask around. Why?" He eyed her. "You want it?"

"Yes."

Paul did not sigh. But he did roll his eyes.

"I'll make it happen."

"*Grazie.*"

"I'll be back in two hours," Paul warned.

"*Sì, sì.*" Rossi waved him away.

Outside, in the alleyway littered with rubbish and sewage, Paul steered Kaya toward the beach as quickly as possible. He did not want to be seen, but, given Rossi had recognized them, he figured obscurity was impossible.

"Word travels quickly here," she said as they crossed town. "I had not expected so many to know about what happened."

"Want to walk the beach while we wait?" Paul kept an eye out for onlookers and an ear out for eavesdroppers. Or thieves.

"Oh!" She smiled at him. "Yes, that sounds lovely."

Once on the beach, she stood at the edge of the water. Face

tilted to the sun, eyes closed, hands spread out at her side, she utterly entranced him.

"We should find a private beach," he said, watching her enjoy the day. The sun shone high in the sky—just past luncheon, he estimated.

Boats still dotted the sea, fishermen working the catch. Or perhaps some rowed holiday crowds onto the tranquil water. Kaya held out a hand and silently beckoned him. Azizi sniffed the waves, snorting when one broke over her nose.

Shoulders bunched, Paul followed her along the waterline. He didn't like this openness, nor the sheer number of people.

The constant sea breeze stung his cheeks, threatening to take his hat. Then Kaya laughed and turned her face into the wind, eyes closed. She stole his breath, and for the first time in days, Paul felt some of that constant tension unwind.

She laughed and spun in a circle, rushing into his arms and splashing water onto them.

"Kaya." Her eyes snapped open. Light with happiness, but heavy with passion, she grinned at him. "I love you." Another layer of tension evaporated, and he brushed his fingers against her cheek. "I only want you safe."

He hadn't meant to say that, but the words had tightened his throat since he'd discovered her gone from the inn.

"Life isn't always safe," she whispered. "But I'd rather see the world with you than stay locked in my house.

Paul's lips twitched in understanding. He knew she had long wanted to see the world. "You said you liked the beach. Let's enjoy the day before returning to our duties."

"It's quiet," she admitted. He had to agree; even with the number of people there, the beach was quieter than he'd expected. "But I do enjoy walking in the sand. It's relaxing and refreshing."

"Is it?" Paul looked along the coastline, but all he saw were threats. "I've never taken the time to discover it."

She paused for only a heartbeat. Then, gathering her skirts into one hand, she held out her other. He immediately took it, smiling down at her, and another small bit of tension loosened in his shoulders. A gull called out over the sea, and Azizi bounded farther into the water.

Paul grinned in the brightening day and fell into step beside his wife. For one beautiful moment, his world was perfect. "What do you see out there?"

"The sea. The fishermen. Birds." She sighed wistfully. "I'd like to draw here; the sea is a rich shade of blue, and the boats dot it like birds in the sky. But I still don't wish to stay any longer than we have to."

"Yes, I know." They walked in silence for a few moments, enjoying the warm day, Azizi running in the water, splashing them. "Do you still wish to travel to Prussia with Hannah?"

"Yes," she admitted. "But—"

"But what?" he prodded when she said no more.

"I'm afraid if we do, something will happen."

Paul laughed. He laughed so long, he felt Kaya's concerned gaze on him. When he looked at her, however, he saw her answering smile.

"Because we always do? Because we haven't been able to spend more than two days without encountering thieves, slavers, opium smugglers, protection scams, or forgers?"

"Yes." Kaya grinned wider. "I'd like a week, at minimum, to simply enjoy life with you and not worry."

"Kaya, sweetheart, I'm not sure that's possible." Still smiling, he shook his head and started back along the water's edge. "If nothing else, life together is never boring."

"You do take me to the nicest places."

"Hey, you *wanted* to see the—well, the grime." He sighed. That wasn't strictly true, but he was absolutely not ever letting her out of his sight again.

"Oh, that wasn't a complaint," she insisted. "I've never been inside a forger's...den? Room? Office?" She tilted her head. "What does one call such a location?"

"That one?" Paul jerked his head in the general direction of Riccione. "A hovel."

She snorted. "Still hadn't ever been to one."

"Cross it off your list of places to see and enjoy." He sighed again. "But I'm certain we'll be visiting hovels more often than I'd like—especially if you plan on purchasing a string of inns from here to Brandenburg."

She brightened, and he cursed. "I hadn't thought of that, but I like it."

"No." He stopped and turned her around, back the way they came. "Let's see what trouble this one gives us first."

"I make no promises."

Twenty-Two

Paul studied Kaya from the open office doors. For a woman who hadn't spoken with more than three people most of her life, she fit in seamlessly here. The staff obeyed her without a single hesitation, and the deliveries had gone smoothly—for the most part.

He attributed that to her fearsome reputation. Word had spread like wildfire about how she'd let herself be taken rather than Bea. How she'd fought the hapless Paolo, who even now remained in prison, and brandished her dagger like a true warrior.

Or perhaps it was Azizi's constant presence.

He snorted at that, but both were true. Nestor had seen that everyone within hearing distance knew of Kaya's prowess with her dagger and how amazing Azizi had defended her.

Also, for someone who didn't read the language, she seemed to balance the books exceptionally well.

"They're numbers," she'd told him. "They're the same in every language."

He'd never thought of it, but then, until Kaya, he hadn't thought about many things. She certainly had a way of expanding his perception.

Azizi curled beneath the desk, an impressive construct

Signore Ferrari had to have spent a pretty penny on. Paul wondered how much it'd fetch on the black market. Enough to keep this inn open and running until they heard back from Roberto?

True to his word, Rossi had managed to convince both Signore Esposito and the local populace that Kaya and Paul were the rightful owners. Paul didn't ask, Rossi didn't tell, and no one seemed to care.

Kaya stretched and rolled her head from side to side. She looked beneath the desk with a fond smile. Paul wondered if that was because Azizi was too large to fit, or if the dog had done something that made Kaya laugh.

"You look relaxed." He entered the office, his own wide smile feeling natural as he crossed to his wife. He set his hand on her shoulder and didn't feel the tension of the last months despite the long hours she'd sat here. "I'm going to regret saying this, but proprietorship looks good on you."

"The books were easy enough." Kaya reached up to rest her hand on his. "And I found his lockbox. Not a lot of coin there, but enough to cover the shipments that finally arrived."

"The shipping business isn't exact," he agreed. Leaning against the desk, he stroked a finger down her cheek. "The carriage looks to be in decent shape, very fancy."

She raised an eyebrow. "Fancy enough to impress the rich landowners set to arrive in the coming days?"

"Definitely. Lots of gilt—even the seats were cushioned." She frowned at that, and Paul laughed. "One day, my love, we'll take nothing but the nicest carriages with the finest horses."

"As I know nothing about either, I'm sure that won't be difficult." But she grinned and stood, stepping close. Hands flat over his chest, she leaned up and kissed him. "Are you going to stay out there all afternoon?"

"Kaya, it's been two days since you were kidnapped."

She scoffed, but her smile remained soft and understanding. "I was most certainly *not* kidnapped! I willingly accompanied that odious man so he wouldn't slit Bea's throat." She shivered, and her eyed darkened. "Or worse."

His hands tightened on her hips. "That is not the way to persuade me to leave you alone."

"I didn't say I wanted to be left alone." She rested her head on his chest and hugged him close. "I asked what else you planned for today—other than watching me balance accounts."

"I need to speak with Rossi again. He seems to have settled the inheritance issue, but if Roberto accepts our offer, I want no questions." He sighed, then admitted, "He's the most trustworthy person we've met in months."

"He's angry," Kaya said. "That gang killed his son, and he wants revenge. They're still in prison, and I'm sure Signore Esposito will keep them there at least until we depart."

"I half expect Rossi to plant a firebomb in the prison."

She jerked back in surprise. "I had not expected that." She sighed and leaned back against his chest. "Then I suppose we should provide him with another outlet for his anger. Not that I blame him. I've tried imagining what I'd do, how I'd react, if someone killed Olivia."

"Aren't you the one who tells me not to dwell on what-ifs?" Paul shook his head but couldn't quite banish the image of Olivia's dead body. "I'll talk to him." Not that Paul knew what Rossi planned, or even wanted from the rest of his life. "Out for revenge is no way to live."

"How much longer should we stay?"

Her question surprised him, and Paul peered down at her. She fit in here so well, keeping the inn running, hiring more staff, listening as they asked questions and offered improvements. Despite having no clear idea about how to run an inn, Kaya operated with efficient speed.

Now, as he studied her, he saw what she meant.

"Still not the place for us to settle?" He nodded. "I understand that." Azizi nudged him from behind, and he stepped away from the desk so the dog could exit. "I think she's ready to leave as well."

"I like the people here," Kaya admitted. "However, this is not the right place for us."

"Agreed." He kissed her forehead. "Another week, probably. I've no idea how long it takes a courier to make it to Villa San Giovanni and back, but I imagine longer than a day." Paul ran his hand up her back and down her arms. "A week via ship, a month walking?" He shrugged. "What will you do if Roberto wants no part in running an inn?"

"Would Rossi?"

"We'll ask," he promised. "If it comes to that, we'll ask. Now, it's past luncheon; are you hungry?"

<hr>

Kaya sat on the terrace with Hannah and Charlotte, enjoying the afternoon sun. The air around Riccione had changed now: louder, busier. As if readying for the influx of summer guests. Even the air around the inn had shifted, no longer oppressed and heavy.

"Now that you've managed to keep this inn open, what next?" Hannah shifted in her chair and watched Kaya intently. "Do you still wish to travel with us to Brandenburg?" She offered a small laugh and shook her head. "After all this, I wouldn't blame you if you didn't."

"We've talked about it," Kaya admitted. "And right now, we think it best to leave here." She tilted her head, her eyes on Paul and Azizi at the far end of the terrace.

Paul was trying to teach Azizi how to fetch, but Azizi had no concept of it. She'd race after the stick fast enough, but rather than return it, as was the custom, apparently, she played tug-of-war instead. Kaya grinned as Charlotte stifled a laugh.

"I'm not certain Azizi understands the game," Charlotte said, sipping her lemon juice. "Or perhaps Herr Paul does not."

"Possibly both," Kaya admitted. Turning back to Hannah, she smiled. "We need to wait until we hear back from our friends in Villa San Giovanni; I don't want to leave the staff uncertain about their future."

"I applaud your dedication," Hannah said quietly. "I don't believe I've ever met another like you."

Paul told her that often, but this was all Kaya knew. Derya and Gidd had imparted it on her from an early age, even from before Gidd taught her to defend herself. Helping others where you could was more important than boasting of your strength or wealth. Growing up, Kaya believed everyone thought that.

"If you don't wish to wait..." Kaya began, uncertain what Hannah's plans were.

But Hannah laughed. "Now that I'm no longer in that prison with a hangman's rope threatening me from above, I find myself in no rush. Though I do wish to see home again."

"It's been a very long time," Charlotte agreed. "We had originally planned on touring the coast. Ravenna is not far north and boasts a splendid history of the Romans. I particularly wanted to see the Mausoleum of Theodoric." She frowned but still looked pleased to impart her knowledge. "Not exactly Roman, but fascinating nonetheless."

"I should like to see this mausoleum," Kaya agreed, one eye on Azizi, whose large paws seemed ill-equipped for the stone flooring. Better suited for mountain terrain, definitely. This inn? Not so much. "Have you booked passage?" she asked carefully, sipping her lemon juice and trying not to look obvious.

"Not yet," Hannah admitted. "We wished to see the coast, but, well." She shrugged and shivered in the warm afternoon. "Our plans had other ideas."

Kaya laughed and patted Hannah's hand. "Paul will see to the ship. He's most peculiar about our passage, and with Azizi, it's best the captains know beforehand."

"She is rather large," Charlotte agreed. "Are you sure she's a Calabrese Shepherd?"

"That's what I've been told," Kaya hedged.

"Signora Conrad," Rosa said apologetically as she appeared beside them. "Another delivery is here, the wine. The driver refuses to unload it without additional payment."

"Signore Ferrari already paid." Kaya narrowed her eyes and stood. "Has word spread about the Ferraris' deaths?"

"*Sì.*" Rosa held her head high and motioned toward where the driver waited. "We, the rest of us, we feel they take advantage of you."

"I'm sure they do. Paul!" Kaya smiled and gestured for him. He sidestepped Azizi and teased her with the stick but closed the distance in rapid strides. "I need to handle the wine delivery."

"I take it by 'handle' you mean this won't be as simple as accepting the caskets?" He sighed without waiting for an answer and whistled for Azizi.

Taking his arm, Kaya led him toward the courtyard. The halls sparkled in the open air. All the doors and windows were open to the bright day. The scent of lemon oil wafted from the banisters and banished whatever lingering scent the inn held. No longer did it smell of decline. Now, it smelled of hope.

Kaya grinned and took Paul's hand. They'd done this together, and she liked that knowledge.

Stepping into the courtyard, she eyed the mustachioed man, who had a practical donkey hitched to the cart. The sun shone brightly here, as welcoming as the inside of the inn. A pair of guards—handpicked by Paul on Rossi's recommendation—stood on either side of the door. They didn't exactly barricade the man's entrance, but they stood on guard well enough that he eyed them suspiciously.

"Signore."

The man turned and frowned. He dismissed her and spoke to Paul. "Ferrari, he did not pay me the agreed-upon amount."

Paul snorted and crossed his arms over his chest. "Signore, you either speak with my wife about this, or you don't get paid at all."

He didn't look pleased, but he reluctantly turned to Kaya.

Beside her, Rosa snickered and seemed all too delighted. Kaya had a feeling she was listening carefully so she could tell all the others exactly what happened.

"I've looked over his accounting, signore, and I assure you he paid well in advance." Kaya wasn't exactly certain this was true, given Ferrari's spendthrift ways; however, a payment for this year's delivery had been recorded. "This is how you have always conducted business, yes?"

"Bah! Half he paid. Half then, half now." The man glowered and folded his arms over his chest.

Kaya sighed but settled in for negotiations. She may have never bartered before, but she was not unfamiliar with the concept. She had no idea what Gidd and Derya had planned for her future, or if Gidd even had a plan beyond keeping her safe and alive, but Derya had taught her everything she'd ever need to know when interacting with local merchants.

Kaya was thrilled to finally use that knowledge.

The sun had shifted over the courtyard. Azizi grew bored with the proceedings and wandered off. Rosa stayed to listen, wide-eyed and fascinated. Paul smothered his laughter but hadn't left her side. Eventually, Signore Ricci was satisfied with his additional payment and unloaded the wine caskets.

"Amazing, signora!" Rosa laughed. "I can't wait to tell everyone else."

She raced away, oddly delighted. Kaya didn't understand, but exhilaration danced in her veins.

"You were amazing." Paul lifted her hand. "I've never seen you barter; perhaps I should let you do all the negotiating from now on."

"It was my first time." But she grinned, happy with the outcome and not at all annoyed with the extra coin. "Derya trained me," she laughed. "However, I've never had the chance to use those skills. I'm not sure how I feel about owning an inn, but I like knowing I've helped."

"I'm still not certain I want a string of inns between here and

Brandenburg." Paul tugged her close and kissed her softly. "But if it means watching you like this, I'll buy all the property."

"Let's settle this one first."

"Eager to travel again?" Paul took her hand and led her along the edge of the sunlight, whistling for Azizi.

"I want to see what's out there, yes." She rested her head on his shoulder. "And I want to explore with you. Riccione, Brandenburg, wherever. It doesn't matter."

"With you?" Paul grinned down at her. "Sounds perfect."

"Right now, what sounds perfect is sneaking upstairs with you."

"My love, I do love the way you think."

Their room was freshly cleaned, the balcony open to the breeze, the scent of lemon clean in the air. Paul hastily performed his usual security measures, and Azizi curled up in her corner, nose tucked into her tail.

Kaya lost herself in his kiss, winding her arms around his neck and arching her body against his. Paul's hands settled on her hips and pulled her even closer, backing her to the bed. One hand pressed to the small of her back, the other tangling in her hair.

It was such an innocent move, the gentle touch, the press of fingers through her clothing. Arousal rushed through her, making her moan against his mouth.

Kaya always wanted him, loved kissing him, touching him. Paul urged her onto the bed and knelt before her, dancing his fingers up her legs. He untied her stockings and kissed her bare skin, leaving goosebumps in his wake. His fingers teased closer, and he nipped the sensitive skin on her inner thigh.

Kaya shivered, and his tongue darted out, caressing the light bite. Hand curling into the bedding, she opened her legs and urged him closer. She shivered again and gripped his shoulders, holding him tight as his mouth found her, his fingers teasing her.

She whimpered, a low sound in the back of her throat.

"That's it, Kaya." He slipped a finger into her, kissing along her thigh. "Let go for me."

He teased her. The pace was slow and playful, yet every touch wound through her until she thought she'd scream.

"Yes," he said, as if he read her mind. "Scream, go on."

He pressed hard to her nub, circling it as his fingers thrust into her. Her orgasm crashed against her, surprising in its ferocity, and she let go, wordlessly crying out.

Paul didn't say a word—he didn't have to. He kissed her gently, then leaned up and kissed her chin, her cheek. Kaya opened her eyes and met his, her breath still panting through her. She nipped his throat and drew him closer until he settled between her thighs, hard and hot for her.

His nose nudged along her throat, pressing soft kisses along her skin. She sighed and stretched, words abandoning her with his every touch. His fingers brushed her core again, easily slipping in, and he teased her once more, slowly moving his fingers, his thumb brushing her clit.

With her breath trapped in her throat, she arched against his touch. Her fingers dug into his shoulders, and she kissed him hard, nipping his bottom lip with a hint of desperation. His fingers slipped out of her, and she moaned at the loss, even as she tugged his shirt over his head and unbuttoned his trousers.

Her fingers danced down his chest, teasing just above his cock. His breath caught in a growl, and Kaya smiled, caressing the tip of him. She ran her fingers over the head of his cock, then scraped her nails down to his balls.

Paul shuddered against her, breathing deeply into the crook of her neck. Kaya gasped and tilted her hips against his touch. Trailing her nails along his hip, she raked them across the small of his back, reveling in his shudder, the near snap of his control. He settled between her legs once more, the tip of his cock teasing her. Kaya reached down and guided him in. She tilted her hips and sighed when he slid deeper into her.

Her head fell to the bedding, and her breath caught. Oh—oh, this was *perfection*.

He ran his thumb over her clit, and when she opened her eyes,

Kaya already knew he would be watching her. Her lips parted, and she breathed his name, her hips meeting his with every thrust.

Paul groaned something she didn't hear and moved faster, thrusting harder into her. Kaya welcomed him with every pounding movement. His teeth nipped her throat, found her lips again and kissed her hard.

Her nails dug into his back, hips meeting his. She slid one hand between them and chased her own pleasure. Her orgasm crashed through her, and she cried out, eyes closed, his name falling from her lips. Only then did his control snap.

Paul kissed her, a sloppy, bruising kiss, and pounded into her. It wouldn't be long—he was already on the edge—and he fell, shattered, pulling out and shuddering in her arms.

Kaya caught him and held him tight. She always did.

Twenty-Three

"See? Your stomach is getting better."

Kaya glared at Paul, but he looked undeterred as he gently guided her off the ship. A lovely spring breeze carried the freshness of the sea and reminded her of those early days in Sicily. Just the two of them and an entire world spread out before them. Above, the gulls called to each other and swooped toward the fishing ships.

The sun barely dented the dawn, but ships, she had learned, cared not for time. Only for the tides.

"Where's Azizi?" She swallowed, refusing to let the seasickness overcome her. A test of wills, a battle between her fierce desire to not be sick and her stomach's contrary notions.

"I brought her down already." Paul steered her off the gangplank and onto the dock. "Steady. There you are. She's waiting for us on the wharves, guarding our luggage."

"Good dog." Kaya wasn't sure she said that aloud and swallowed hard. They'd sailed from Riccione, bypassing Venice no matter how Kaya badly wished to see the canals abut the houses, and headed straight for Bibione.

"Perhaps we ought to have stopped in Venice." Paul peered at her, concern tightening his mouth. "Sweetheart, can you stand on your own?"

Not particularly. "I shall be fine." It was a small lie. "However, perhaps a seat might not be amiss." She sighed and instantly regretted it. "I loathe being incapacitated."

"I know." Paul kissed the side of her head. "I'll find an inn for the day, and we'll plan the next leg of the trip. Here." She looked down and saw their trunk and Azizi. "Sit while I speak with the agents."

"Thank you." She sank onto the trunk, willing her stomach to stop moving and her head to stop swimming. "Still not as rough as the Strait of Messina."

He snorted. "Nothing is as rough as that, and I sailed around the Cape of Good Hope." He shuddered. "I never want to be on a ship for that long ever again. I promise: No more ships for a while. Perhaps a nice rowboat on a lake, but nothing more."

She leaned against his leg and closed her eyes, secure in the knowledge he wouldn't leave while she remained so unsteady and unable to defend herself. Her hands shook slightly, but the sickness hadn't been as terrible as it was crossing the Mediterranean. She needed rest, but should be recovered by midday.

"Kaya, dear, how do you feel?"

Her new friends.

"I'll be all right shortly, Hannah," she promised and forced her eyes open. The sun slowly brightened the day, and the glare made her eyes ache. She shifted so her back remained to the horizon for as long as possible. "I need to find my land legs."

"Your what?" Hannah laughed and moved to block the sunlight. She peered down at Kaya, but the worried pinch around her eyes eased. Apparently, Kaya didn't look as terrible as she felt. "Do you need anything? Food, water, wine? Not wine—I apologize."

Kaya gave an aborted shake of her head.

"I'll find an inn," Paul promised. "With rest, she should be well come luncheon."

"Oh, I have an inn—but no, of course not." Hannah laughed again. It was the joyous sound of being unburdened. Since leaving Riccione, Hannah seemed lighter. Happier. That made Kaya happy, too. "I almost forgot. I'm so used to planning ahead, ensuring there's a room for us in a reputable location."

"I'll find something," Paul said again, but this time Kaya heard an easier tone. "You stay with Kaya. Azizi." He leaned over the dog. "*Al-baqaa ma* Kaya."

Azizi woofed and licked Paul's hand. He grimaced and rubbed his palm on his trousers. "I'm sure that's her way of agreeing, but I could do without."

"Be safe," Kaya told him, using a moment's strength to glare. "Come back to me."

He traced her cheek and kissed her forehead. "Always."

She watched him disappear into the crowd, blending in naturally, as if he always wandered these docks. Kaya easily tracked him until he turned the corner and vanished from her sight.

"We're not going to stay in a reputable location, are we?" Hannah sighed and grimaced. "I suppose I shouldn't complain, given I know he wants what's safe, but I do hope it's clean." She made a face, wrinkling her nose. "I so dislike bedbugs."

Kaya laughed and felt herself steady. Resting her hand on Azizi's head, she peered around the area. "Where's Charlotte?"

"Overseeing the last of our trunks. She's a bit untrusting, given all that's happened, and without Fritz here." Hannah shook her head, then straightened and smiled, banishing the bleak thoughts. "How are you, truly?"

This wasn't the first time Kaya had experienced such seasickness, and now that they were on dry—and, more importantly, solid—land, she already felt her stomach steady. Her khanjar sat in her lap, her fingers curling around the hilt, but she sensed no danger. More notably, Azizi did not either, despite her lack of love for such crowded areas.

"Better," Kaya reassured her friend. "Are you upset we didn't see Venice?"

"I'm not, but I'm wondering if we should've stopped there so you might rest."

Laughing, Kaya shook her head, then stopped. No, no movement yet. "Paul said the same thing."

"We worry about you." Hannah rested her hand on Kaya's arm. "I've never seen a more devoted husband. How did you meet?"

Kaya frowned and watched Charlotte direct one of the sailors, who carried a heavy looking trunk, in their direction. Had she not told Hannah? Clearly not.

"My grandfather contracted me to marry him. I met him the night of our wedding."

"Ah, yes, when he broke in, was it?" Hannah laughed, and the clear sound made Kaya smile in return. "I had thought that a bit of humor, but it's true?" She shook her head. "Perhaps one day you'll tell me the entire story."

One day. Yes. "I'd like that."

"Frau Kaya, I brought the remainder of the tea the cook prepared for you. Angioletto wished you to have it." Charlotte shook her head. "I'm not sure he believes you'll be cured once on land."

Kaya accepted the stone cup and sipped the cold tea. "Most sailors don't understand," she conceded. "On our initial journey, the cook tried everything, Paul says. He insisted his grandmother's recipe would work." She sighed and let the cold ginger tea settle through her. "I'm afraid it did not. He was most disappointed."

"How long until Paul returns?" Hannah shifted on the trunk beside her as the sun rose higher in the sky.

"Not long," Kaya promised, eyes closed. She listened to the crowds but heard only the unfamiliar calls of sailors and dock-workers. Paul didn't leave her alone for long these days. Not since the incident at the inn. Kaya didn't blame him and preferred him close by. "We find enough trouble without looking for it," she told the women. "It's better when we're together. Less chance of a fight."

"I've seen the trouble the pair of you don't look for." Hannah's voice carried that slight mockery it always did when they discussed their lack of desire to find trouble.

"It's worse when we're apart," she assured her friend.

"I find that difficult to believe."

Kaya grinned and sipped the tea again, feeling better with every breath. Perhaps not solely the tea's doing. "How did you plan to travel to Brandenburg? It's quite the journey, yes?"

"Several hundred miles," Charlotte agreed. "Do you want more? Or shall I return the pot to Angioletto?"

"Please tell him I'm grateful, and thank him for the care he's shown." Kaya handed the cup back to Charlotte.

As she disappeared toward the ship, Kaya turned to look for Paul. He hadn't been gone long, but it was long enough that she wondered. Not worried—that was a long way off. But yes, wondered.

"I had planned on sailing at least part of the way." Hannah gave her a significant look. "I confess, when you told me of your seasickness, I didn't believe it was this bad."

"No one does," Kaya agreed. "I don't think I can handle any more sea travel, even river travel."

"Coach it is."

Before Hannah could say more about their altered plans, Azizi perked up. She gave a great bark, which terrified several people in their general vicinity, but Kaya knew what it meant: Paul had returned. She followed Azizi's eyes.

"There you are." Kaya held out a hand, and he helped her stand. "Have you found someplace safe enough for you and clean enough for Hannah?"

He glanced at the other woman and offered a brief nod. "Yes, and without even a moment's trouble."

"I don't believe you." Kaya peered up at him. "A truly momentous occasion, to be sure."

"Where's Charlotte?" Paul looked around, then gestured for someone off to the side. "I even hired help."

"You did?" Kaya paused, at a loss. "From where? Who?"

"Antony here works at the inn and agreed to transport our luggage."

She frowned. That certainly didn't sound like Paul. "And you trust him?"

"No, but I paid him enough he'll be easy to track if anything happens to our trunks."

Now that sounded like Paul.

Laughing, Kaya tried to help Hannah stand.

"No, no, you sit, dear." Hannah waved her back down. "I'll see to Antony and our trunks. Where have you decided we're staying?"

"Locanda di Piccola Cosa." Paul stepped closer and lowered his voice. "Be careful. I trust Antony as far as our money goes, but we're still strangers here."

"Believe me," Hannah whispered back. "I'm far more alert to such things than I once was." She nodded to Kaya, who had taken their time in Riccione to begin both her and Charlotte's training. The other women, too. Whoever wished to learn, she and Paul trained.

Kaya watched her walk to the boy, who was no older than fifteen, and smile brightly at him. Resting her head on Paul's arm, she sighed.

"I'm glad we decided to travel with them," she admitted. "I enjoy our time wandering the mountains, but it's nice to have someone else to talk with."

"Especially now that you know Marta and Olivia are well cared for?"

"Yes, especially now," she whispered, adding a silent prayer for their continued well-being. "Thank you for waiting until we heard from Roberto."

"It wasn't long, a month." Paul brushed it aside, as he had for weeks. "Waiting for word from them seemed a small price to pay for peace of mind."

"Nonetheless, I know you wanted to leave."

"It's good we left when we did," he admitted. "As much as I'm glad we helped the inn stay open and the staff retain their pay, too many knew who we were." He scowled and tightened his hold on her, as if one of the gangs threatened them even now. "Even Rossi, the forger, had recognized us."

True, but Kaya still maintained that was because he wanted revenge on the gang. They'd killed his son for standing up to them, and Rossi lived for the promise of reprisal.

"Do you think they'll be all right?"

Paul steered her around a corner, and it took Kaya only a moment before she saw the wharves again. Always taking the long way, her Paul. She understood why, of course. Better to lose any purse thief than lead them to their lodgings.

"I think Marta knows how to run an inn better than any of us—all of us combined. And I think it'll be good for Teresa to be away from that town."

"I'm still sorry about Marco," she whispered, feeling her strength return with every step. "I had hoped—"

"I know." He kissed her temple and pulled her tight against his side. "I know. I had as well. I'm afraid the opium took too much a toll on his body."

"Perhaps the change will do all of them good—Antionette and Roberto as well." Kaya had wished to see them again, but Paul had grown restless.

He prowled the inn day and night, ensuring everyone's safety, making sure the guards were stationed where they were supposed to be. With each passing day and interminable night, he grew more anxious to be away from yet another place that held dubious memories.

"One day," she promised. "One day, wherever we live will have lovely memories."

"One day," he agreed. "At least now we know where to write Marta and Olivia. I think they'll be happy there."

And the new babe, Marco. Kaya smiled as Paul slowed near another corner. Marta had been grateful to the Spanós for their hospitality, and she named her child after their son. Kaya hoped they'd all find their way in their new town. Perhaps not away from the memories—those followed like a storm. But together.

Kaya and Paul hadn't waited for them to arrive, but they had entrusted the staff to give them a proper welcome. It'd be another month, at the very least, before they arrived, and neither she nor Paul wished to stay in Riccione any longer.

"This is the inn you chose?" She looked around the area. Clean, crowded, close to a busy market. "A far cry from the *El Reyah*."

The inn they'd stayed at in Damietta was a small, dubious establishment. It had been far from the wharves, the souk, and anything remotely resembling respectable.

"I decided to try a new approach," he confided. "A place in the center of town, not too fancy, and see what happens."

"Who are you, and what have you done with my Paul?" Kaya shook her head, stopped, and suddenly didn't care where the inn was. She needed a bed and rest.

"They were the only ones willing to accept Azizi," he admitted. Shrugging, he offered a sheepish smile. "Only cost me twice as much."

"She's worth it," Kaya insisted.

"You're worth it," Paul countered. "Always."

"I love you," she whispered as they stood just outside the inn's door, people bustling past them. "Perhaps it was not the most auspicious beginning to a marriage, but I'm glad Gidd chose you."

He lifted her hand and kissed her wrist just past her glove. "I once told you that words were inadequate to convey all I feel for you. But I'll protect you with my last breath, and I'll love you in this life and whatever comes after."

Uncaring about the people, the openness, the scandal, Kaya raised onto her tiptoes and kissed him gently. "*Ya rouhi.*"

Thank you for reading!

If you enjoyed this book, I'd really appreciate it if you helped others enjoy it, too. Reviews are precious and help persuade other readers to give my romances a try.

Sign up to my VIP list for a short story, *One Day with You*. This story, along with more short stories about Louise and Malcolm, are only available to my list. https://bit.ly/ 3kSzMjI

I send weekly newsletters with things like new releases, special offers, pictures of my dog, recipes, and other exciting news about my stories, research, and travel that I hope you'll enjoy as much as I do.

Coming March 2023

The Lady's Marquess, Book 1 in The Conrad Legacy

Miss Esme Conrad is tracking down the person responsible for disrupting several of her family's cargo shipments.

Landon, The Most Honorable Marquess of Strathan, is searching for a French spy. The year is 1806, the ship is the *Brittiana*, he's a titled gentleman and she's the daughter of—horrors—*a merchant.*

They have 35 days between Portsmouth and Halifax. What could possibly happen?

Stay Connected

ckmackenzie.com

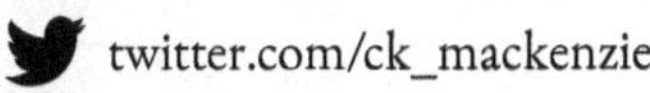 twitter.com/ck_mackenzie
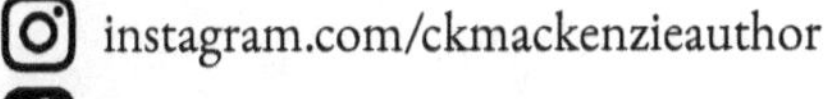 instagram.com/ckmackenzieauthor
tiktok.com/@ckmackenzieauthor

Also by C.K. Mackenzie:

Kaya and Paul: The Conrad Chronicles

Husband of Convenience

Sins of a Rogue

A Lover's Promise

Nadia and James: Part of the Conrad Chronicles:

Smuggler's Captain

Her Captain's Honor

www.ingramcontent.com/pod-product-compliance
Lightning Source LLC
Chambersburg PA
CBHW051152130726
47988CB00005B/2096